THE

LIGHT

FANTASTIC

THE LIGHT FANTASTIC

Sarah Combs

CANDLEWICK PRESS

First edition 2016

Library of Congress Catalog Card Number pending
ISBN 978-0-7636-7851-7

BVG 21 20 19 18 17 16
10 9 8 7 6 5 4 3 2 1

Printed in Berryville, VA, U.S.A.

This book was typeset in Adobe Garamond Pro and Univers.

Candlewick Press
99 Dover Street
Somerville, Massachusetts 02144

visit us at www.candlewick.com

FOR **KARY,** SISTER WHO SHINES

Nowadays the world is lit by lightning!

—TENNESSEE WILLIAMS, *THE GLASS MENAGERIE*

We've got to live,

no matter how many skies have fallen.

—D. H. LAWRENCE, BORN SEPTEMBER 11, 1885

APRIL IN DELAWARE

(9:43 AM EDT)

I was born on April 19, 1995, at 10:07 in the morning eastern daylight time. Minutes before, one time zone to the west, a man named Timothy McVeigh was busy sending a bomb through the Alfred P. Murrah Federal Building in Oklahoma City, Oklahoma, a metropolis long known for its livestock and vibrant arts community, but now forever haunted by the events of my birthday morning. What was I doing that morning, over on the East Coast? Howling, probably. Opening the slits of my newborn eyes to the startling brilliance of the NICU lights angled over my bassinet. I had arrived early, was impossibly tiny; my lungs were weak and underdeveloped, and it was feared that I wouldn't survive.

I did, though. Survive.

» » »

My mother likes to say I was a miracle; that my birth and survival were proof of hope and light on an otherwise dark day for America. I was born in the exact middle of what she called a "flashbulb moment"—that is, people remember where they were or what they were doing when they first heard about what was happening in Oklahoma City: how 168 innocent people had died. Nineteen of those people were infants and young children. Three of them were women pregnant with babies who might have grown into graduates of the class of 2013.

You have a flashbulb moment like that, right? We all do. Chasing Lincoln Evans on the playground, Lincoln Evans with Pokémon on his shirt, racing him to the biggest swing, reaching it first, sailing to the tops of the trees, purple sneakers almost brushing the leaves, then leaping to the ground before the swing stops all the way, caught like that in midair, *flash,* and there's the moment: the sky a perfect blue, only something must be wrong wrong wrong because the first-grade teacher is suddenly crying.

On that Tuesday, September 11, 2001: Miss Rosen's cry lifted up to that dream-blue sky just as Lincoln Evans, a week away from turning seven, my next-door-but-one neighbor for all of my days since that first one under the heat lamps in the NICU, grabbed my hand, sweaty and still burning with swing-set rust, and kissed me, not on my mouth but, weirdly, on my closed eye. My very first kiss: less like a kiss than an accident of awkwardness and proximity. I wasn't sure it had really happened, just like later—huddled on the couch with my sister in front of the TV, the towers collapsing like stacks of cards over and over again, a replay we couldn't bear to watch but strangely couldn't get enough of—I wasn't really sure any of that day had happened, either.

But it had.

Two days later, I learned that Lincoln Evans's father—in New York on business, a flukish, freakish accident of fate—had been on the ninety-eighth floor of Tower One when it was hit.

Two months later, Lincoln Evans moved away.

Just before he left, Lincoln showed up at my house with his U.S. quarter collection. The quarters were in a glass jar, and Lincoln gave it a musical shake as he explained that he had been collecting the quarters with his dad, that it was something they did together. Lincoln thought it was cool that the Delaware quarter came first, just how our state was the first to join the Union.

"Here," he said, thrusting the jar at me. He seemed in a big rush, like if he didn't hurry up, he might change his mind. "You keep it. It should stay in Delaware."

I stared at the quarters. *Thank you* seemed the wrong thing to say, but I said it anyway.

"I've got Kentucky now, so that makes all fifteen," Lincoln said. "Look for Tennessee in January, okay?"

Then he smiled at me, ran back to the Ryder van packed

full of his whole life, climbed in, and left for wherever it was his mom's parents lived, wherever their new beginning would begin.

Wednesday's child is full of woe.

I was my mother's flashbulb moment on that Wednesday morning in April of 1995. It's how I got my name: April Hope Donovan. My lungs turned out fine, just like the rest of this body, a body that maybe isn't perfect but can get the job done—I have swimming medals to prove it. I have a blush-worthy story about the back of Drew Bennett's car, and my weirdly limber body (Where'd I get it? Nobody knows) plays a starring role. Somehow I managed to escape all the things my parents worried about when I was born—cystic fibrosis, asthma, brain damage, and worse—but it wouldn't have occurred to any parent to worry about the weird thing I do have. My—what, exactly? condition? phenomenon?—isn't going to kill me. Some people might even call it a blessing, but I'm here to tell you: remembering all the days of your life—or most of them, anyway, starting with purple shoes against a blue sky, a first-ever kiss on the eye—with flashbulb-moment clarity isn't always a blessing.

Sometimes (lots of times) it's a curse.

Take now, for instance. Today. It's April again, a Friday, and my country is still reeling from the bombings that happened at the Boston Marathon four days ago—on Patriots' Day, a holiday, freedom and justice for all. But how's that old saying go? You can count on only two things in this world: death and taxes. Benjamin Franklin said that. Boston-born

Ben Franklin, that's who. On Monday—April 15—that was hellishly true.

It feels wrong that we should even be in school today, while the world is holding its breath like this. Beautiful Boston has been robbed of her heart, and the thief is still on the loose, and there's a manhunt raging across a city now closed for business, effective immediately, out like a light, the end. There's a dark piece of flashbulb history happening in our midst right this actual second, but here we are. Never mind that thing that happened four days ago, class! Business as usual, so let's turn our attention to something that happened in 19-freaking-36.

It's my eighteenth birthday.

It's also really, unbearably hot in Ms. Standish's American history class. There's a test on Roosevelt's New Deal, and if you think for one second that my brilliant memory can dredge up any of the names and dates and acts and coalitions I tried to cram into my head before school this morning, then you're wrong. Way. Rote memorization has nothing to do with how my whacked-out mind works. It works more like a bizarre game of connect-the-dots, where the dots are landmarks in my personal autobiography, and the lines are threads made of . . . what? Coincidences. Mysteries. I don't even know. I just know it's weird to have a brain that plays dot-to-dot with Boston and Ben Franklin and April 15 and taxes and killing people.

The stuff on Ms. Standish's test—I don't know it, because I didn't study, which means I didn't take the time to ingest the reading and to connect the lines and dots as they surface, unbidden, on the page. I've got nothing, so I'm as likely to fail as the next regular person who spent last night watching the news out of Boston instead of preparing in whatever way regular people prepare for exams. This is the kind of thing that frustrates my parents: Why can't I apply myself? Make this memory thing work in my academic favor? By which they mean: You've got a photographic memory, right, so what's with all the C-minuses in math and physics? You see the material once and it's there in your brain forever, right? To which—ugh—I just want to scream. But I try (and fail every time) to explain: No, no, photographic memory is a different thing altogether, that's not how it works—"it" being *hyperthymesia,* a word that makes it sound like there's something wrong with my glands. My glands are fine. My capacity for personal memory, on the other hand, is accidentally on steroids. Sorry, Roosevelt and your New Deal: Even if I had conjured my lines and my dots, I wouldn't be able to recall all your details at the moment, because at the moment I'm in the middle of my usual split-screen life, which looks something like this:

Left Side of the Screen: The Present
- Ms. Standish is absentmindedly scratching her scalp with the capped end of her pen. Her glasses are hanging around her neck on a beaded chain.
- Ben Higgins's left leg is jiggling nonstop; it's his typical test-taking MO.

- Izzy Goff just finished her test, first as always. She exhales laboriously and flips her blue book over with a noisy slap, daring us all to catch up with her, to even *try* to mar her perfect grade point average and her inevitable role as valedictorian. She has been doing this for twelve years, and the only person likely to catch her is Pal Gakhar. Where is Pal? He needs to get in here and school Izzy Goff.
- Drew Bennett, he of the Backseat Incident, is also notably absent, but so is a fourth of the class; it is, after all, Senior Skip Day. Ms. Standish knows this, of course. Hence the test on the New Deal.

Right Side of the Screen: The Past, or Random Dot-to-Dots Associated with It

It's high April, so I'm checking everybody out, making sure nobody in American History looks in the mood to lose it and open fire in the cafeteria. I get wary of this sort of thing during the month of April, because my involuntary little *condition* makes sure it is not lost on me that life is a series of checks and balances, and the following things happened on the following days:

- April 14, 1865 (Good Friday, also not lost on me): Abraham Lincoln is assassinated at Ford's Theatre, Washington, D.C. Just before he shot the president, John Wilkes Booth was heard to cry *sic semper tyrannis* ("thus always to tyrants"—but dude, who is the tyrant here?), which, in addition to being the motto of the Commonwealth of Virginia, is the exact thing that the tyrant Brutus is said to have shouted before assassinating Julius Caesar on the Ides of March, 44 BCE.

- April 4, 1968: Martin Luther King Jr. is assassinated in Memphis, Tennessee.
- April 19, 1993: FBI sets fire to cult leader David Koresh's ranch in Waco, Texas; Timothy McVeigh's attack in Oklahoma City on the day of my birth two years later was apparently designed as a nod to this freak show. And while we're connecting dots: on that day, McVeigh was wearing a shirt emblazoned with the words SIC SEMPER TYRANNIS.
- April 20, 1999: Columbine High School massacre, Littleton, Colorado. I was four years and one day old. It happened fourteen years ago tomorrow but seems, somehow, in the back of my mind, always to be happening still.
- April 16, 2007: shooting rampage at Virginia Tech University, Blacksburg, Commonwealth of Virginia, home of (*connect the dots, connect the dots*) a state motto that has proved itself to be completely devoid of good karma and needs to be changed, like, yesterday. Or fourteen years ago. Or eighteen. Or way back in 1865, as soon as it escaped the twisted lips of John Wilkes Booth.

And so on and so forth. Do you even want me to go on? I could go on for days but won't, because I'm sure you've seen pictures of what Boston looks like today: it is silent and still as a graveyard, and I'm not going to think about it. I can't think about it for another second, or I'll break apart and cry. April Is the Cruelest Month, April Is the Weirdest Girl. Welcome to my world! Just be sure not to do anything embarrassing or regrettable in my presence, because chances are I will remember it. I will connect that dot with you and with this ordinary day for the rest of *ever*, whether I want to remember it or not. Your embarrassing incident and the details associated with it will occupy space in my brain that should be reserved for things like the locker combination I can't remember to save my life, or the quadratic formula, or where I might have put my stupid keys, lost for the thousandth time this week.

Blessing, you say?

Ha.

Ask me about my own regrettable moments. The way things from years ago simmer daily at the edges of my consciousness. It's like being haunted, and here is what the ghosts like to whisper in my ear: *Checks and balances, April Donovan. Checks and balances, checks and balances, checks and balances.* Sometime when you've got a couple of spare hours or days, you should pull up a chair and ask me about that.

Meanwhile: back to Lincoln Evans, he of the September 11 Pokémon shirt and inexplicable eye kiss, and then the state quarters and the Ryder moving van, circa the most heartbreaking day of November 2001. In my memory, the van carrying Lincoln away is yellow. It was first grade, the year the written word exploded for me and everywhere there were words I could suddenly read: R-y-d-e-r spelled out on what my memory insists was a yellow van—but that can't be, because (*Fun fact! Connect the dots!*) Ryder vans stopped being yellow after Timothy McVeigh used one to bomb the Alfred P. Murrah Federal Building in 1995. After that, Ryder vans were red and white.

How do I know these things? Which parts do I actually know? What color is the truth? It is so hard to say.

What I can say is that I haven't seen Lincoln Evans since that Black Friday when he moved away, but for years after he left, I thought of him often—or at least every time I found a new quarter to add to his collection. I got kind of obsessed with collecting the quarters, and at some point my mother bought me a display—this stiff cardboard map of the United States, complete with little circular cutouts where you stick the quarters in. Just like Lincoln promised, Tennessee came next, then Ohio and Louisiana. The Hawaii quarter came very last, and by that time I was in eighth grade and so excited about completing Lincoln's collection that I walked to the bank on the day of the quarter's release: Monday, November 3, 2008. The following day, Hawaiian-born Barack Obama was elected president of the United States. The election felt huge and important and unforgettable, and some part of me felt moved to look up Lincoln Evans, to find him and say, hey, I've got all the quarters, and, hey, look at this world we're living in now, this new president, all this hope. What does life look like for you, Lincoln Evans?

I didn't look him up, though. The urge to find him came and went, and after all fifty quarters were pressed into my cardboard map, I didn't think much about Lincoln Evans at all. The map is in our attic now, and I haven't thought of Lincoln in forever. Which is why it's strange and a little unsettling that he showed up in my dream last night.

Dreaming. It's my absolute favorite activity, hands down. When I'm asleep, dream-events unfold in beautiful, linear, start-to-finish fashion. My dreams get straight to the point; there are no dots to connect, none of that infuriating split-screen craziness that plagues my waking life. When I'm dreaming, I'm wholly, vividly there. Last night, *there* was up in the boughs of some huge tree, which I had climbed all the way to the top, where Lincoln Evans was waiting for me in this shoddily fashioned wooden tree house that looked to be the handiwork of somebody's well-meaning dad.

Dream-Lincoln wasn't seven, how my waking self remembers him. He looked eighteen like me, and he was grinning this sneaky, delicious, I-have-a-secret grin, and I recognized him right away. It was like he'd been in that tree waiting for me forever.

"What took you so long?" dream-Lincoln inquired,

grinning. He flipped a shiny quarter in the air and slapped it on the back of his palm: hedging some bet, revealing some secret fortune.

Dream-me was too happy and surprised to see him to say or do anything else, so dream-me just smiled and shrugged.

LINCOLN, NEBRASKA

(8:43 AM CDT)

"Mr. Evans, are you with us?"

Ms. Heslip looks at me pointedly. A little desperately, actually, which makes me feel bad. I've had a lot of teachers but never one like this. Ms. Heslip knows her stuff, for one thing. For another thing, she reminds me of . . . I don't know. Somebody's mom, or something.

"Sure," I say. Has Ms. Heslip asked me a question? If she has, I've already forgotten what it is. Under her accusatory gaze (not mad but disappointed, which is worse — did she learn that stare from *my* mom?), I can feel the tips of my ears going warm. I shift my arm to cover my notebook, on which I've just sketched a not-bad rendering of the back of Laura Echols's head. Laura's got this great hair: thick, long, smells like apples. Today she's got it braided so it looks like a fish bone winding down her back. Adds to her mermaid

» » »

appeal. Laura's the kind of girl you can imagine banked on a rock in the middle of the ocean somewhere, dazzling woebegone sailors with her siren song.

Laura's out of my league, is what I'm saying, and she knows it.

She knows it as she turns in her seat and hooks me with her ice-blue stare. "Page ninety-one," she whispers.

I open my copy of *The Glass Menagerie* and flip to page ninety-one, where the words bob around meaninglessly on the page. I look to Laura for further direction, but she shrugs and turns back around.

Ms. Heslip crosses her arms across her chest. Really. She and my mom could be best friends. The I-am-disappointed-in-you twins, frowning and hoping and waiting.

"We're waiting." Ms. Heslip's words, her attitude, seem to mirror the line that rises to the surface of the page in front of me: *What is the matter with you, you silly thing?*

Good question. Who knows?

By now Ms. Heslip has registered that I'm not going to be able to answer whatever question she's asked, that I haven't done the reading, that I, like so many students before me, have failed her. At least I'm here, though. More than half the class is gone.

"Where *is* everyone?" Ms. Heslip asks, banging a piece of chalk into the little trough beneath the board. Ms. Heslip, man, still using the old-school chalk. She dusts her hands on her dark skirt; now it looks like she's been groped by a ghost. "Does anybody know?"

Laura acts like she's looking around the room, as if to take an inventory, but her eyes land on me for a second. Laura Echols, who because of the luck of the alphabet sits in front of me in English. Laura Echols, who because of her name got to read aloud the role of Laura Wingfield from the play. Laura Laura Laura.

"Um, it's Senior Skip Day?" someone ventures.

Ms. Heslip narrows her eyes and tilts her head to the side, like maybe she didn't quite catch that. "What?"

"Yeah, four-twenty," offers Bruce Franklin, who doesn't look up from the scab he's picking on his knee. Gross.

Ms. Heslip shakes her head, a quick snap of disbelief. "Isn't today the nineteenth?"

Bruce shrugs. "Guess you gotta observe on Friday if four-twenty's on the weekend, yo."

"Ah," she says. "*Guess* I didn't get that memo."

Ms. Heslip glares at us for what feels like a full minute. In that minute, I come close to saying something. What to say, though? *Stop looking at me like that. I'm sorry. I'm sorry. Even though I didn't do my paper for* The Odyssey, *I want you to know that I read the whole thing. I loved it, and I think about it all the time. Also there's chalk all over your skirt and it's embarrassing and makes me feel sad for you. You and my mom, the sad twins. Please just go be sad at someone else for just five minutes and leave me alone.*

Finally, Ms. Heslip sweeps an arm in the direction of the door. "Well. What are you waiting for? Let's not waste one another's time."

Bruce is the first to get up. He's got this apologetic grin on his face as he lopes to the door. One by one, caught somewhere between ashamed and thrilled, not really sure what just happened, we get up and start following Bruce.

"Mr. Evans," Ms. Heslip says, blocking my exit with her voice.

I turn around. *Who, me?*

"Let me remind you that if you want to graduate, you have to pass this class."

I smile and nod and turn again toward the door.

"And Mr. Evans?"

I can't even look at her. I've heard this one so many times over the past twelve years that I can guess at what will come next, always some variation on the same theme.

"You're way too smart to fail."

Laura Echols is in the hall, pretending not to wait for me. She's got her braid wrapped around her fist: expert mermaid nonchalance. Her siren song buzzes lightly in my ears as I walk past.

"Where are you going?" Laura calls. I'm almost to the door that leads out to the parking lot, and the chances that Vassar-bound Laura will follow me are slim to none.

"I'm going to the movies," I call over my shoulder. That much I remember from today's read-aloud in Ms. Heslip's class: Bruce Franklin as Tom Wingfield, sounding bored.

The sunlight seems cranked up, dazzled by its own self. It glints like something mean on the rows of cars in the student lot. So this is what the middle of the morning on a Friday looks like: white-bright, possibility-filled. I'm full of the urge to go somewhere, but don't know where to go. People are congregating in their cars, listening to music or sneaking a smoke before the vice principal or whoever comes out to round everybody up.

The luxury and ridiculousness of it kills me. If I had a car, I'd be halfway to California by now.

A few yards ahead of me, a white Lexus chirps and blinks, magically awake and unlocked. "Get in," Laura Echols says, brushing past. She is embarrassed of this car in the same way she's embarrassed of her beauty. It's a burden she didn't ask for, an extravagance she doesn't think she deserves.

I do what she says and get in.

Laura climbs in beside me and tosses her purse in my lap. She does a quick scan of the lot, places an arm across the back of my seat, cranes her swan-neck around, and backs out of the parking space. Then she spins the wheel in a graceful arc and gets us out of there, just like that.

When Laura Echols makes up her mind to do something, she doesn't mess around.

APRIL IN THE MORNING

(10:47 AM EDT: FIRST LUNCH)

Gina is waving at me from our table in the cafeteria. She's wearing a sparkly headband that says HAPPY NEW YEAR 2013. Sitting in front of her is a white bakery box with who-knows-what inside. Gina loves surprises almost as much as she loves other people's birthdays. I consider bolting to avoid imminent embarrassment, but I'm really happy to see Gina. One of the things I've loved best about her since practically birth is that she makes ordinary stuff—limp lunch in the cafeteria, the dull ride to school—seem novel and thrilling. As I approach our table, she's reaching out to me for a hug, launching into her trademark birthday serenade, à la the Sugarcubes.

"Love the headband," I say.

"I know, right? I couldn't decide between this and a graduation cap."

« « «

Gina likes to celebrate one occasion with random para-phernalia pertaining to another. It's this thing she does to make me and Gavin laugh, and it's never not hilarious.

"Where's Gavin?" I ask. Gina, April, and Gavin: we're a trifecta, semi-affectionately known around these parts as GAG, as in We Make Other People.

Gina sighs. "He skipped this morning, but *swore* he'd be here at lunch to help celebrate. Open your present!"

I hesitate. This innocuous-looking box could contain anything. The side of my mind devoted to bygones does a quick movie-reel shuffle of Scenes from Birthdays Past. Gina tries to outdo herself every year, which explains why last year on this date, Gavin and I were driving into Wilmington in search of treasure buried near the shore of Brandywine Creek. The treasure was supposed to be tickets to see the Sky Drops on the following Saturday, but Gina couldn't remember where she'd buried the tickets and all was lost.

"It's the thought that counts," Gina announces, mind reading. "Just *open* it."

Inside the box is a huge wad of tissue paper—"That's not the present," Gina cuts in—underneath which is another cardboard box. Gina's into the Russian-doll method of gift presentation, but then she gets all impatient if you don't open fast enough. The second cardboard box contains a single red-velvet cupcake—my favorite, slathered in a mountain of cream-cheese icing—with a little flag stuck in it. Printed on the flag in Gina's loopy script is a name I don't recognize and a phone number, complete with mystery area code.

"Who's Dr. Angel?" I ask. First I imagine someone with wings, smoking a pipe: Professor Plum in the Billiards Room of Heaven with the Lead Pipe. Or maybe it's code for the magician Gina's obsessed with. As soon as she turned eighteen, Gina wasted no time in getting a tattoo like his — a pair of wings with the word *believe* scrawled between them. Talk about Mindfreak: Gina's mom almost died. This all happened on January 21 of this year — a Monday, Martin Luther King Jr. Day, which means there was no school. It was also the president's second inauguration day. The First Lady held the Bible in her purple-gloved hands.

"This guy's a doctor," Gina explains. "Out in California. At some university? He studies people like you, like, with your freaky memory. April. Listen. There are only like twenty-one documented cases in the whole world. You could be number twenty-two! You could be famous and maybe even be on *Ellen*. I could be your wingwoman. The requisite wacky friend."

This is vintage Gina. She's always looking for a way to get famous, or famous-by-proxy. She was actually the one who started noticing that my memory seemed super-charged: *What'd I wear last Thursday?* she'd quiz me. *What's the name of that skinny kid who only went to first grade with us and then moved away after his dad died? Remember that kid?* She'd ask me stuff like that.

"There's a name for what you have," says Gina. "It's

a bunch of letters, only I forget what they stand for. Mindfreak memory, basically. It's an actual thing."

This information is, of course, not new to me. I first heard about HSAM (or Highly Superior Autobiographical Memory, which has apparently replaced the outdated, bad-gland-sounding hyperthymesia) on TV—an ordinary Thursday, suffering from post-swim-practice malaise, eating Oreos one after the other out of sheer boredom, too tired to start my homework or even think about it—flipping listlessly through channels when I caught a slice of this actress talking about how she could remember what every day of her life looked like, starting at age twelve. She described the split-screen feeling and everything. She talked about how, in her memories, she was always inside her own body, looking out. Hearing her put words to what happens daily in my head was scary; tiny threads of ice went pulling at my spine, and I actually looked around the room, eerily convinced I was being watched, or that a ghost had suddenly entered through the chimney. As I listened to the actress talk, realization accumulated in my stomach. Without even thinking, I started walking toward the television, as if the woman inside were my doppelganger, recently arrived from the moon and wearing all my secrets on her skin.

The thought of calling the doctor in California was scary: Obviously this wasn't just some adorable, isolated tic I had. What if there was something badly wrong with my brain?

Then again, maybe this Dr. Angel could swoop in, be

my eponymous guardian, and save me. Maybe he could turn the split-screen off, give me a prescription for some of that elusive Eternal Sunshine.

"Gina," I say. "Only you."

"You love me," Gina says. "You gotta call this guy."

I do.

And maybe I will.

LINCOLN, NAVIGATOR

(9:47 AM CDT)

The drive-in looks different in the daylight. At night, the place is mysterious, ghostly, haunted-feeling in the best possible way. By day, it just looks sad. Forgotten, which it is. The screen is ripped in places; behind it, planks of wooden backing reveal themselves like bones. A lone paper cup skitters across the dusty ground, where monitors rise from patches of weeds. They look like half-finished grave markers, which I guess they are: *Here Lies* Cool Hand Luke. *RIP,* North by Northwest.

"What are we watching?" Laura asks.

Laura Echols is a girl of many secrets. One is that, in the only-child household in which she grew up, TV (along with computers, cell phones, alcohol, and half of all things

» » »

normal in this world) was discouraged. So Laura came to movies late, and movies are how we accidentally became friends.

Back in the fall, when Ms. Heslip was introducing us to Keats and Shelley and Tennyson, she made us watch *Dead Poets Society* in class. We watched it in parts over the course of three days. On the third day, when it was over and Ms. Heslip flicked the lights back on (back to reality, always so hard for me), I noticed that Laura had sunk so low in her chair that she was close to sliding off. I couldn't see her face, but there was a tremor in her shoulders. Still caught in the spell of the movie, thinking stupidly *that could be me,* I reached out to touch her, but she was up and out the door before my fingers could dare. Moments later the bell rang, breaking what was left of the spell. Out in the hall — sea of people flowing around her in all directions — Laura stood tall and perfectly still, hugging her books to her chest, staring out at something I couldn't see. When I approached her, she didn't look at me until I spoke, and even then it was like her awareness of my voice — of anything in the actual world — was operating on some kind of delay. It was a feeling I understood.

"You mean you've never seen it before?" I asked her then. Laura shook her head no.

Well. Movies, man. They are my thing.

After that, I started coming to school with movies for Laura Echols. Every day a different DVD from my prized (epic, canonized, do not mess with it) collection. Laura would watch one every night and return it the day after, not saying a thing, just looking starved for the next. Exactly like a siren, all alone on her rock.

After the poets, that was when we did *The Odyssey*. Ms. Heslip might be the only teacher in all the schools, all the towns, who has ever taught me anything I've actually wanted — *needed,* feels like — to know.

Maybe I shouldn't have walked out of her class.

It's too late to go back now, though. I'm already on the rock.

"What are we watching?" Laura repeats. She's drinking bourbon from a silver flask.

Another of Laura Echols's secrets is that she keeps a flask hidden in the glove compartment of her car. The flask is engraved with her late alcoholic grandfather's initials, and it is the real deal. Laura hated her grandfather. The flask is a shiny piece of irony; Laura drinks from it to spite the old man.

The drinking is a secret, too, and so am I.

It's a little bit thrilling, to be one of Laura Echols's secrets.

"Hitchcock?" I ask.

Laura shakes her head, wincing against the bourbon. "I'm not in the right mood. I want something quieter. And, like, outdoorsy."

I don't know when we started going to the drive-in. It just sort of happened, and this is a game we play, watching imaginary movies on what's left of the old screen. We talk a lot about the exact sort of *feeling* we want to get from our moviegoing experience, and then we try to pick a flick to match the feeling. It's tricky business, hard to get just right.

"Bildungsroman," I say, hoping Laura will be impressed that I've remembered and employed one of Ms. Heslip's literary terms.

"Sorrow, but not *all* sorrow," Laura says, staring straight ahead. If she's impressed, she doesn't show it.

She passes me the flask, but I shake my head. I don't like bourbon unless I'm tasting it on Laura's mouth, in which case it is delicious and dangerously addictive. I scan her face for signs that she might be in the mood to kiss me today. It's not a thing I can bank on, and the ache of not knowing makes me feel drunker than the bourbon ever could.

I keep my eyes on what remains of the screen. *"Stand by Me."*

Laura considers this. Takes another swig. "Mmm. Maybe. But maybe *Moonrise Kingdom*?"

"We'll flip for it," I say, rummaging in my pocket for a coin. "Tails is *Stand by Me.*" I thumb a quarter into the air and slap it on the back of my hand. It lands Rhode Island–side up, an image of a sailboat and a bridge. It's this built-in instinct, the way I check quarters every time. It's like I can't *not* do it. My dad, touching base. I wonder what he thinks of Laura Echols—I mean of me with her in this car right now, if he can see us. I wonder too if this girl I used to know—this girl April, my old neighbor and the first girl I ever had a crush on, the last girl who ever knew my dad—kept up with the quarters. If maybe she's got Rhode Island somewhere.

"Tails," I say. "Pick a scene."

Laura thinks it over. "The part with the deer," she says.

We sit back and stare at the screen, and it's all there: deer, railroad tracks, woods. Wide-eyed boy, locked in this private moment, this secret he will keep from the rest of the world.

We have perfected the art.

I look over at Laura, and she closes her eyes. Beneath her lashes, tears shimmer. I have this urge to kiss her on the eye, and I'm reminded again of April from first grade, April who has my quarters. I can see her face as clear as anything, but I can't remember her last name to save my life. It's on the tip of my tongue but gets lost when Laura Echols leans over and kisses me, stealing it right out of my mouth.

GAVIN IN HIS REALM

(10:47 AM EDT)

The scene under the bleachers is out of control. Since when is there a *crowd* under the bleachers? Okay, so it's just two people, looks like from here, but still. Some kind of crazy #injustice, is what it is.

I've started to think in hashtags, #truestorybitch.

Man I do not like when my plans go awry. Under the bleachers is a ritual, like a necessary starting point of the day. Now, granted, I usually start my day way earlier than this, but you better believe that skip day means beauty sleep, bitches. I'd still be in dreamland, but Gina said I had to come for cupcakes, which, okay, cupcakes, but still! I require my morning time under the bleachers. It's where I think and ponder and whatnot, and now I can't think because there's a *crowd* under there, man. Like, who gave

« « «

you permission? What is this, this unauthorized elevensies-under-the-bleachers business? Come on, now.

So I'm all riled up and ready to bust on in there and lay some claim to my turf—but then I get closer and think maybe I'm seeing something I'm not supposed to see.

It's like I *feel* it before I see it, you know that feeling you sometimes get for no reason, like there's something messed up going on, like whoa, no lie, this shit is *not* right.

Been hanging around April too long, is what it is. You go to a movie with April and she's all watching the exits the whole time, waiting for some crazy mofo to stroll in with a Glock. She drives past the elementary school and it's like she can barely keep herself from busting in there and hugging every single one of those kids, like she'd sign up to be every single one of them's badass bodyguard if she could. But here's the thing about April. What it is, is that she lives in fear of all that, but also lives to look that shit right on up in its face, like #idareyoutoeffwithme, you with your Bushmaster and your outrageous rage. You with your Glock and your clown-ass face and your heart made out of nothing but evil.

During swim meets, man, April dives in like some kind of magical-ass fish; you should see her. And I don't know but it seems like she goes down *deeper* than everybody else, deeper than she's supposed to go, like she's down there for way longer than the other swimmers, like a year and a half longer, I shit you not. Gina and me will be in the stands screaming our heads off, truly decorating our pants, scared right on out of our minds, but then April will rise on up out of that water. She'll start swimming as smooth and graceful as anything, making it look easy, man, and every time, every *single* time, she will #effingwin.

What you should know about me if we're going to be friends is that if you're me, it is not wise to hang around when there's some kind of not-right enterprise going down under the bleachers. I'm getting the eff on up out of there before something starts. Maybe they didn't even see me. I don't think they even saw me. Which is good, because if you're me and you got two mamas and one's black and the other's white and you're just now getting comfy in your brown skin and green eyes that nobody knows what to do with but you still gotta check #other in every box on the planet 'cause nobody's very smart and you're about to haul ass on up out of Shitsville, Delaware, and run track and field for Yoo-Vee-Ay *where it's Edgar Allan Poesville, hey!* if you're me and you're looking your future all up in its beautiful face and what you do *not* want to do is eff any of it up, then what you do is this:

You run away like the very first bat outta hell.

I'm sure it's nothing. Just got my brain all warped from too much April, is what it is. April, she'll get you to thinking in a certain way. Take Monday, for example. You know where I was supposed to be on Monday? That's right, bitches, running in my first Boston Marathon. Only I had this stupid sinus infection from hell, cooking with fever, couldn't hear out of either one of my ears, was all dizzy and stuffy and whatnot, wah wah wah. I was going to race anyway — had trained forever, you know? finally I'm eighteen, you think I'm gonna miss my chance? — but April, she was all, Gavin, no. First of all, you're sick, and second of all, I've got this bad feeling about it for some reason. I mean, what! April and her *bad feelings*. Please. She's got bad feelings about everything. I tell her all the time that her "bad feelings," that's just her letting all those hateful effers win.

You're better than that, I tell her. Braver than that. You gotta live your life strong, live it bright.

April shook her head, though, and was like, no, Gavin, no. This bad feeling, it is for real.

This bad feeling I've got right now? Beholding the scene under the bleachers? Maybe I'm just being paranoid. I mean, it's a good day to be paranoid, right, what with all the nightmare goings-on in this effed-up world? It's just my imagination on turbo-speed.

Or maybe, you know what? Maybe I'm just hungry. I just need one of Gina's cupcakes, is all.

Still I'm gone like lightning, record-break fast, #licketydamnsplit.

SANDRA HESLIP, TEACHER OF THE YEAR

(10:02 AM CDT)

I am forty-one years old and on my way to the principal's office. I might as well be in sixth grade again, going to confess to the charges against me: *Yes, I did decorate Melissa Decker's desk with zit cream. I am that hateful, mean girl.*

There are lots of things people don't tell you about growing old, but the most shocking of all is that so many of the feelings are the exact same. The *click-clack* of these stupid heels on the floor — it's the same march of shame, only a couple of decades, one failed marriage, and fifteen years of honors English classes later. I'd still like to be swallowed by the floor, I'd still love to be loved, I still wouldn't mind having the answers to the universe wrapped up in a bow, please and thank you, I have to go now, get me out of here, see you around, *bye.*

« « «

There's a bench outside of Dennis's office, and I decide to sit down for a second. The first pinprick of a migraine is starting behind my left eyebrow; it won't be long before that wavy band of light starts to make its way across my field of vision, left to right, blotting out words on pages, on these pages in my hand, say. It was important to get it all in writing, and I hope I've gotten it right. I hope I've remembered correctly just what Adrian George said to me after fourth hour yesterday, and how he said it—in a terrifying whisper, so close to my face that spit from his quiet rage rained on my glasses.

It's harder for me to remember things these days. And what's that about, really? Short-term memory lapses, migraine headaches, varicose veins snaking their way around my ankles: I did not sign up for this. When did it happen? I look at my students and try to imagine them old, but it's impossible.

And impossible—as it should be; my career depends on it—for them to imagine me young.

There are moments, though. Moments of weakness when I am tempted to reveal just a glimpse of that girl on the inside, the one who would dance all night at raves and never get tired, who would tumble with her friends into the all-night diner at four in the morning, shoving herself full of pancakes and eggs, the music still thrumming through her veins. Everybody's parents worried about drugs, I am tempted to tell my students, but drugs were the furthest things from our minds then. The pulse of the music like a heartbeat, the thrill of night and a highway stretched beneath a moonlit sky, the electricity of a kiss if you were lucky enough to get one, the deliciousness of being alive and eating eggs — it was the only drug we needed.

She says, self-indulgent. Ancient and laughable in her outdated skirt.

But even then — even then, a million moons ago — I knew I wanted to be a teacher. Here it is, my dream come true, and yesterday a beautiful trainwreck of a boy named Adrian George leaned in as if for a kiss and told me that when the time came to shoot his teachers and classmates one by one, he'd be sure to spare me.

Nowadays the world is lit by lightning! Oh, Tennessee Williams, you have no earthly idea. There's so much lightning I can barely see the sky anymore. Here it comes now, a bright zigzag across my eyes, spelling nausea and defeat.

Dennis opens the door. "Sandy?"

I stand up, smooth my skirt, squint at him from behind the dizzying ribbon of light. I hold out the papers and try to find my voice.

"Dennis, I'm worried about —"

He ushers me in, a meaty hand on my shoulder, and cuts me off. "Do I understand that earlier today you let a whole class of seniors loose? Just invited them to leave?"

He's talking to me like I'm one of them. One of the kids, instead of the adult woman who once went out to dinner with him and decided it was never going to work. He's still acting like a wounded dog.

"Dennis. It's Adrian George. He—"

Dennis grabs the papers from my hand and tosses them onto his desk, where they'll be forgotten. "Right now we need to talk about why you thought it was a good idea to cancel your honors English class, Ms. Heslip."

Is he even being serious? The answer is obvious. The answer sums it all up, every bit of it. I close my eyes, wincing against the pain.

"They were wasting my time."

THE ASSASSINS

In the beginning there were forty-eight of them, one for each state in the Lower 48. In the beginning, they weren't even Assassins. They were just a bunch of ordinary kids who had been hurt and needed a place to vent, needed a place to find others like them, people who had been damaged too, who knew that specific brand of anguish and didn't want to feel alone anymore.

The online forum was harmless. Just a gathering place, is all. Safe as houses.

What does that even mean, *safe as houses*? Who came up with that garbage? Ask Utah what goes on in his house and he will be like: Dude. It is so not safe in here. Kansas used to have a house, but now it's gone. West Virginia never had a house in the first fucking place (*sic*).

« « «

In the beginning it was all pretty low-key, just this safe-as-houses-or-whatever place to find a friend. Everybody was super nice, super smart. Nobody was . . . crazy or anything. Wait, you know what? Just don't even use that word. *Crazy.* How about you just don't even go near that word unless you know exactly what you're talking about, which you don't. See if you can do it, if you can go even one day without that word.

That's crazy! you'll say when you see how you can't.

Nobody can.

In the beginning, the Assassins got along pretty well. Like before they were even Assassins, that is. Before the Plan.

Who was it that even decided about the Plan? Oh yeah, it was ~~me~~ the Mastermind.

But seriously, it was mostly like he was just joking. The Mastermind.

It wasn't really serious at all, the not-yet Plan. It was just this ha-ha thing that everybody on the forum made jokes about. *Wouldn't it be funny if—? Could you imagine just walking in one day and being like—?*

In all seriousness, it was all fun and games until it sort of wasn't. Then it got a little weird—like admittedly, a little tense. The forum wasn't the same after the Mastermind started all that joking around about the Plan. Georgia was the first to drop out, and Ohio bailed after a kid in his own state shot and killed three of his classmates. *This is getting old,* Ohio e-mailed by way of apology, or chickening out, or changing his mind. Whether his mind was changed by the genuine sorrow of what went down at a neighboring county's high school or by frustration at having his thunder stolen wasn't really clear.

These things just *never are clear,* are they?

The remaining Assassins—who at the beginning weren't even really *assassin*-assassins . . . more like a bunch of people playing a game together, just a stupid game, like any other game that you could just walk into Walmart and buy with your allowance—were banking on the Not Clear, the Not Predictable. But then—predictably?—real-life shootings kept happening. All the time. No: *all the time.* These things could barely get a WTF out of anyone anymore, such was their frequency. By the time summer came and Colorado took its worst hit since Columbine, things were looking grim for the Mastermind's burgeoning Plan. Not long after the mall shooting outside of Portland, the Assassin from Oregon decided he'd had enough. With a disturbing lack of fanfare or blame, he hanged himself in his parents' bedroom closet, and that was it. The end.

That right there? That was for real. That was awful. Haunting and unforgettable and nobody wanted to go near it. Suddenly, lots of people didn't want to play the Mastermind's game anymore.

Then the worst thing happened. The thing no one—not even the Assassins—could believe. The Mayan calendar predicted the end of the world on December 21, but a week before that, a gunman walked into an elementary school and beat the Mayans to it. Afterward, a bunch of Assassins—joke or no joke, they told themselves it was all a silly game, all make-believe, *how'd I even get here?*—bid farewell to their mission. Indiana took up Buddhism and decided to turn herself around; New Jersey got his shit together, started taking his meds again, and joined Habitat for Humanity, the better to rebuild his hurricane-stricken neighborhood.

It's called Perspective, New Jersey wrote on the forum, and that shocked and quieted everybody. *Over and out.*

Was he joking? These things are never really clear.

After the world stopped in its tracks on that December day, the handful of remaining Assassins had to sit back for a while, cool their heels. They had to really think. Then they had to cover their electronic tracks and rearrange the Plan to maintain the all-important element of surprise.

And what of these remaining Assassins? Who are they, what are they made of, that they remain unmoved by events that have the power to unhinge an entire nation and plunge it knee-deep in grief?

Look around, look closely. They are the bullied and the bereft, the mischief-makers and the malcontents. Their mean ACT score is thirty, but they're way smarter even than that. You'd be surprised at their grade point averages, what they wear, how they talk, how they just eavesdropped on your whole conversation and you didn't even notice, because of course you never do. You'd be surprised at how many of them have two actual loving, married (!) parents who feed them things like meat loaf and beets and (organic!) brussels sprouts in the evenings. You'd be surprised at the way they are provided for.

You might also be surprised to learn that some of them are girls. Goes against every prescribed notion you have of things like this, doesn't it? People think it's always boys, always video-game addicts, always the loners, or, no—what's that stupid phrase? Lone Wolf. It's those pesky Lone Wolves, each and every time. Right?

Wrong.

Among the very first players the Mastermind recruited was a girl named Phoebe, for instance. Phoebe from Idaho. He found her the same way he found all the others: in online news articles about kids who had been targets of one or another kind of cruelty, thanks to their awesome peers.

That was in the beginning.

Later, by some curious Internet sorcery that nobody can really put a finger on, people were coming to him. To the Mastermind. The original Delaware, for instance, defected long ago, following Ohio's lead. Then—just two days ago, as if fallen from the sky—a new Delaware arrived to take his place.

Phoebe, though, Idaho, she's one of the long-haulers. The article about her—TEEN CATFISHED—first appeared in what turned out to be her own father's newspaper. Once it hit the Internet, it was almost immediately reblogged by hundreds—thousands?—of people, people who had never met Phoebe, never heard her voice or touched her hair.

That the Mastermind was able to find and recruit Phoebe—or any of them—was a matter of simple probability, really.

Simple math.

Inevitable, you might even say.

THE GIRL'S NAME IS PHOEBE

(4:58 AM MDT)

But online she's Idaho.

They don't know one another's real names, at least Phoebe doesn't think they do. It's one of a bunch of questions she hasn't allowed herself to ask. In the beginning, the Mastermind assigned each of them a state name, clean and simple, so as to avoid confusion and mistakes.

In the beginning, Phoebe thought the whole thing was a joke: a strange invitation in her in-box, subject line *Are you in?* And like she was going to fall for that. Fall, ever again, ever, for anything presented to her by a person she had never met. Like she'd want a replay of *the Incident*. The press, her parents' rage, the way they made a thing out of it for all the world to know about—that stuff bothered Phoebe more than the Incident itself, which happened almost a year ago

« « «

now, although the humiliation still burns daily, hourly, minute by minute, increasing as Phoebe hauls herself out of bed each morning to face the charade that has been made of her life.

And yet. And yet—

Are you in?

Maybe she could find the answers in there.

Are you in?

Why not.

Phoebe knows deep down that Dylan Fisher isn't real (*was never real, never real, never real*), but there is a part of her—a small part, but the part that still feels like her truest self—that believes he is. It's the same part of Phoebe that can't quit the forum, even though the greater part of her knows that she should have given it up long ago. It's not an addiction—don't call it that. God, it's not like it's drugs or anything. It's more like . . . a compulsion. She checks it at least five times a day. Maybe ten or fifteen. Okay, so twenty-five times a day, tops. Thirty. She can't even figure out why anymore, but one thing is sure (although she's not sure she can admit this to herself—no, she won't, you can't make her): the forum has turned into her life. In its slow way—like poison; it's like this invisible poison, but *don't call it that*—it has steadily stolen hours from her life in such a way that now it *is* her life.

Phoebe also deep down knows, but can't seem to admit to herself, that she might have forgotten about the Incident long ago, might have let go of it and never looked back, if it weren't for the forum. The forum keeps it alive. The forum makes sure she matters. Does she want to let it go? She does, she thinks.

But she also wants to matter. She just wants to matter, is all.

Not that she'd tell any of it to you that way.

So now she's in, and today is the day. It is almost five o'clock in the morning, mountain daylight time, and Phoebe has not slept. A half hour ago she listened—motionless in her bed, teeth smashed together to keep her heart from escaping her mouth—to the sounds (familiar, devastating) of her father waking and moving about the house: his brief shower, singing through the pipes, his routine coffee and toast, a mug she can picture in her head, and the picture makes her want to cry. WALL DRUG. It's another place she's never seen and never will. There was a moment when Phoebe almost, *almost,* ran down the stairs to embrace her father, to say I'm sorry, I'm sorry I quit soccer, I'm sorry for everything, and I love you. I love you and I change my mind. She would have done it and almost did, but instead she lay in bed—forcing herself to stay there, biting hard on her own fist—and pictured her father's face. She pictured him folding his legs behind the wheel of his truck before heading to his job at the swiftly dying *Press-Tribune,* which, Phoebe knew, would soon be filled with the news of the Plan.

Would they even miss her?

No, Phoebe finally determined. They would not miss

her. What a relief it would be to them — rid, at long last, of the misery she had brought them all.

Five hours until showtime. Phoebe is as ready as she's ever going to be, although some bemused part of her doesn't *really* think this is all going to go according to plan. The Plan, after all, is techno-level, outer-limits crazy. Surely at some point — and he's running out of time, fast — the Mastermind will contact all of them to say Ha Ha, Just Kidding, Game Over, Adios, Suckers.

Phoebe is breaking out in a cold sweat. Suddenly, she's not so sure. A lot of things have changed over the past year, after all. Nobody has talked about the Incident in ages; it may even be that people have forgotten about it entirely. Things are better with her parents, too. She has even caught herself being swept away some days by that old familiar tug of magic in the air, a kind of buoyant, unnameable promise sweetening the breeze, the world bursting into life all around her. It dazzles her in spite of herself, the way the world wakes up in the spring.

Just a week ago, Phoebe's younger sister, Angela, was invited to the senior prom. This boy called her on the phone and Angela — a sophomore! — actually came *running* into Phoebe's room, so unexpected was this call, this invitation. She stopped jumping up and down long enough to show Phoebe the goose bumps pricking up along the length of both her arms. *Goose bumps!* Angela had said. *This is crazy!*

Now Angela's lilac dress hangs on the back of her closet door — another promise, a silken flower waiting to burst into bloom on the dance floor tomorrow night. It is hard, Phoebe realizes, much harder than you might think, to be entirely immune to such things.

Also, and don't tell anybody, but part of why Phoebe checks the forum thirty (okay, forty; fifty tops, but that is *it*) times a day is that she's been nursing a little crush on Nebraska. Lately the threads concerning the Plan haven't done much for her unless Nebraska chimes in, thrilling her, as he always does, with his elusive cybervoice. She detects in his words a certain reluctance to go through with all of this, and although of course it's too late now (is it too late now?), she still feels compelled to message him on her own and say, *Nebraska, dude, look. We gotta turn this thing around.*

Phoebe wonders if there are any secret alliances out there. If today maybe none of it will really happen, because, say, South Dakota has fallen for Mississippi and they've decided to call the whole thing off in the name of love. Maybe Texas has decided to call bullshit on the entire business and travel to the Mastermind's house and take him down, right there in his own stupid geek-boy base-ment laboratory. Phoebe knows better than to stereotype, but she likes her dream of Texas: he'll have spurs on his boots, and he will tip his cowboy hat by way of greeting and will squint amiably into the Mastermind's eyes and say in a thick molasses drawl, *Don't mess with Texas, bro.*

Nobody knows where the Mastermind lives, though, so that's impossible.

For all Phoebe knows, he too could live in Nebraska.

Nebraska! It's technically not that far, but to Phoebe it is as remote and far away as the moon. She presses her fingers to the space it occupies on her map of the United States, which she bought several months ago and which hangs on the wall above her bed. In recent weeks the map has become to Phoebe a source of romance, comfort, and strange possibility. Before, if you had asked her where she would most like to go in the world—anywhere, it could be anywhere!—Phoebe would have said the things that people say: Borneo. Italy. The South of France. Someplace romantic and distant. A place with brightly colored balconies perched on craggy shores, a place where people eat macarons and sunbathe naked, a place with a vertiginous view of the sea.

It occurs to Phoebe now, though, that her very own United States of America are imbued with their own secrets and mysteries. She now has proof of people like her, people her age, dwelling in the states on her map. The Plan has got her thinking about places like Kansas and Louisiana and Wyoming—places she never would have cared about before—and how each of those places has human beings *breathing* in it. Like her, the people get up in the morning and go to school and they do what they can to make it through the day.

Screw Borneo! She wants to go to New Orleans and hang out with the ghost of Marie Laveau. Not just New Orleans, but anywhere in the country. It's all fascinating; she'll take any of it—Virginia talks about all these mystical, haunted places, and Montana once got high in a sweat lodge, and Missouri has kissed a girl from the top of the Arch and there they were, floating, like nothing was beneath them but sky. Everywhere, no matter where you go, there is sky, proof that things keep going. Wide blue skies, cups of coffee with just a little bit of cream, midnight movies, songs threaded through with heartache—these things might be small, Phoebe thinks, but they are things worth living for. They are things people, even the worst of them, deserve. She wishes someone would *tell* her this; she wishes these weren't just thoughts in her own head, seeking validation. Her own thoughts aren't to be trusted; they echo around in her mind and wear her out.

The forum—and, later, the Plan—started as a way to say to hell with everything, to hell with all of them, to hell with anyone who doesn't understand. Oddly, though, it is having the opposite effect on Phoebe. She feels strangely connected to her fellow Assassins; she feels compelled to see through each of their eyes the world they encounter from day to day. The Grand Canyon, for instance. She's never seen the Grand Canyon! She's never seen the Hoover Dam, or Niagara Falls, or the Tomb of the Unknown Soldier. She has never been to Nebraska, home of the boy whose heart she can feel breaking through her computer screen. Nebraska. It's a myth, a dust heap, a place made up by Bruce Springsteen to sell records. Nobody actually lives in Nebraska! Today, though, Nebraska will rise up off the map and be for real, because, in the words of the Mastermind himself, this is going to be a wake-up call like nobody's ever seen. The Plan is saving them, right? It is saving them one by one, saving them from oblivion.

One Nation, Under the Assassins, Indivisible, with Revenge and Punishment for All.

APRIL IN THE LIBRARY WITH THE ~~CANDLESTICK~~ INTERNET

(11:17 AM EDT)

I'm figuring Dr. Angel will look all airbrushed and shellacked, a Ken doll with blinding white teeth, selling psychological drivel the way a schmoozy salesman might sell a used Honda. Surprisingly, though, I can't find a picture of him on the Web. This ups him a notch in my estimation. If he were a hack, there'd be a picture for sure.

I do, however, find some online sample tests, created by Dr. Angel to detect the potential for HSAM in ordinary people. They're organized by age range, and I can tell just by glancing at the questions that I'll have no trouble acing the quiz for those born after 1985. First, though, I do a quick scan of the room. It's study hall and I have every right to be in the library, but I don't want anyone to see what I'm doing. My brain is weird enough without advertising its weirdness.

« « «

A student volunteer is pushing a cart around the library, and another is sitting at the checkout desk, fanning a deck of cards from one hand to the other. "Hey, April."

I wave back. "Hey, Nate."

I've known Nate Salisbury since the sixth grade (the year the Amish girls were lined up and killed at their school; the year Madeleine McCann was stolen from her bed; the year of my cruelty toward a sleeping Leona Reece; *that year, that year, that year, checks and balances, connect the dots, your time is up*).

In the space of my quick exchange with Nate, I'm able to rewind six years and see him in gym class on the Tuesday before Thanksgiving break, 2006. It was the twenty-first of November, I remember, because that year Thanksgiving fell on my mom's birthday, the twenty-third. The air in our middle school was electric with the impending free-dom of the holiday, and Nate Salisbury was shinny-ing up the rope that hung like a giant blond braid from the ceiling of the gym. I can see him swinging up there for a second, then leaping from the rope onto the thick blue mat spread beneath him. When he landed, he sur-prised me by returning not to his seat on the floor next to Ben Higgins and Pal Gakhar and those guys, but to the spot next to me, vacated moments before by Gina, whose turn it was to climb the rope.

Boys were a mystery to me then, and I remember the odd way it felt just to have Nate so near my own body, the way he flicked his long bangs from his eyes and smiled at me in a way that made me worry, for some reason, that he might be about to say something mean. I remember, too, what he did say to me, quietly, so nobody else would hear: *Hey, April, do you think Gina likes me?* At that moment, Gina was halfway up the rope; she tried to jump from up high, the way Nate had done before her, but she fell in an awkward crumple on her ankle and had to limp to the locker room with one arm slung around the shoulder of Ms. Deevers, the gym teacher, who always smelled like licorice and sweat.

The following Monday, Gina returned to school on crutches. The lower part of her leg was wrapped in a purple cast, which everybody signed with a sparkly silver marker that Gina wore on a string around her neck. Nate Salisbury signed his own name on the back, where Gina wasn't able to clearly see the wobbly heart he drew until weeks later, when the cast finally came off. As far as I know, that was the closest Nate came to telling Gina what he had hinted to me that day in gym class, but I haven't forgotten it, the secrecy and sweetness of it, and I've wondered lots of times since then if Nate has carried his Gina torch all this while. It wouldn't surprise me at all — Gina is definitely the kind of girl who inspires torchbearers.

Behind the library desk, Nate has exchanged his cards for a rubber-band ball, which he is tossing again and again into the air. At one point he does a full spin in his swivel chair before the ball lands neatly in his palm, *smack.* He grins at me in triumph, and I grin back. I've always liked Nate.

Dr. Angel's online test consists of a series of questions about dates. Some of them are easy—Obama's inauguration date, the marriage of Prince William and his lovely Kate—but some of them make me wonder just what kind of crack my brain must be on. Why, for instance, should I have any business remembering the exact date of Heath Ledger's death? The guy was barely on my radar, but I remember exactly where I was on January 22, 2008 (another Tuesday; what is it with Tuesdays?), when word first started to hit the Internet that Heath Ledger's masseuse had found him dead in his New York apartment.

The news came to me straight from Gina, whose mouth was full of granola throughout the telling. It was after school, and we were sprawled on the furry white shag of Gina's bedroom carpet, enumerating every girl in our seventh-grade class, trying to guess who had started their periods (everyone but me) and who hadn't (freak-of-nature me). Gina, who had turned thirteen the day before, had been getting hers since fifth grade. I was still waiting for and dreading the advent of mine, which would arrive three days later during a surprise snow day: Gavin and Gina and I hauling our sleds to Beacon Hill and me bleeding through my favorite pair of purple underwear, although I didn't figure it out until I got home, where I sat in the bathroom and cried, sensing the loss of something bigger than whatever gain the dark stain in my pants was supposed to represent. When I called Gina to tell her, she picked up but said she couldn't talk because she was still observing her nightly vow of silence in honor of Heath Ledger. "I shouldn't even be talking to you right *now*," she said into the phone. "But I've got a ton of tampons over here if you need any."

Maybe it's not weird to remember that stuff. Maybe everybody does.

"Hey, Nate," I call.

"Huh?"

"Hey, when did Heath Ledger die? You remember?"

"You mean the Joker guy?"

I nod, watching Nate as he thinks it over. He is chewing the inside of his cheek and spreading his cards across the desk in a neat arc. Finally he says, "Hey, pick a card. Just say whichever one comes to your mind first. Any card in the deck."

"Nate! The Joker?"

"You can't pick the joker."

"No, Heath Ledger. When did he die?"

Nate gives the ceiling a one-eyed squint. "Like, a couple of years ago or something?"

Or maybe everyone doesn't remember. I feel a pang of envy at such bliss—at how Nate and the rest of the world can watch Heath Ledger play the Joker and not be completely hung up on how he died before the movie hit the screen; how the next movie in the series was haunted in its own way as well, thanks to the events of July 20, 2012, a date that should belong to Neil Armstrong and his magical 1969 moon landing but is now, like my birthday, an anniversary of something horrible. It's the thing I thought of on August 25, a month later, when Armstrong finally gave up the ghost: how I was sorry that some guy with a gun had to ruin July 20 for him. And for everybody in that theater. And for everybody else, all of us, everywhere. But Neil Armstrong, man. It truly sucks that he was still alive to have that awful knowledge on his radar, even if he did have only a month left on this earth.

So, yes, Dr. Angel, PhD, I know when Neil Armstrong landed on the moon, and I remember exactly when he died and got to finally return to that milky wonderland that was his heart's terrain. Check!

I can answer every question on this list, check check check.

I'm not sure, though, that I want to be Patient Number 22.

My brain is tied up with these dates, the pictures that go with them, neatly filed. I can close my eyes and find the file I'm after. Back, back. Way back, even before Gina and Nate and the rope and the cast. All day long, since the dream, I've been landing on this particular file: the file marked Lincoln Evans.

The computer eyes me with its steady white gaze. It's as easy as a few clicks. I could have Lincoln's eighteen-year-old face before me; I could match him to the boy in my dream-tree. I could know in an instant where he is, how he's doing, if he has a girlfriend, if he has a boyfriend, if he's looking at colleges, what books and music he loves, what he's planning on doing next Thursday, maybe even what he's doing right now, right this very second.

Why have I never searched him out before?

The urge to find him is so keen a thing it tastes like sugar on the tip of my tongue. I don't, though. Instead I log off and gather my things.

"Wait, April, what's your card?" Nate calls from the desk.

I turn to face him. "Ace of spades."

Nate closes his eyes and swirls his hand magician-style over the arc of cards. With a flourish, he scissors one between his fingers and holds it up to me without looking: the six of diamonds.

"Did I get it right?" Nate asks, face alight with hope.

"Almost," I say. I give Nate an offhand wave and am heading to the door when I stop, thinking better of it. It is, after all, April 19, and any number of things can happen in the course of any day in this world. It's not such a bad urge, is it, to gather joy when it's there for you?

"It's my birthday today," I say to Nate. It's a completely unnecessary thing to say — it's not like me to go fishing for attention like that — but the smile that breaks across Nate's face is worth it.

"That's awesome," Nate says in a voice that suggests that it is. He's leaning back in the swivel chair, goofy and good-natured, not at all unlike the boy who climbed the rope that day and gave me a teeny glimpse into the contents of his heart. "Happy birthday, April."

"Thanks, Houdini."

Nate looks stricken. "Naw, man! I'm going for Criss Angel. Hey, be honest, April—who's hotter, Criss Angel or me? Like, who would you go for?"

Criss Angel: Gina's famous tattooed magician, who is like the same age as my dad, dude. Nate Salisbury is way hotter, and I tell him so.

Nate beams. "See you in Physics?"

"Physics," I say. "Hooray."

On the other side of the library's double doors, I lean against the wall. The hall is empty and still. Two doors down, my sister Monica is sitting in French class. Through the rectangle of glass on her classroom door I catch a slant-wise glance of her being Monica. She's sitting cross-legged at her narrow desk, chin planted in her right palm. Her pencil is poised in her left hand, and I watch as she watches Madame Metcalfe, who I can't see but can hear talking in her smooth French lilt about the *passé composé*. I watch Monica as she takes notes. Something moves me about this—watching my little sister when she can't see me. The way I know the way she sits, the way she holds a pencil. The way I recognize that tilt of her head. She has a widow's peak just like mine. *Monica,* I think in her direction. *Look over here,* and she does. She glances up and smiles at me, just barely, like she doesn't want to get caught. I cross my eyes at her, and she crosses hers back. *Girls!* our mother used to shriek. *Don't do that! That's bad for you!* Once Monica and I tried out that whole urban legend about how your eyes can get stuck that way if somebody slams you on the back when your eyes are crossed. It didn't work, of course. Our eyes are fine. I wave bye to Monica, and she waggles her pinkie finger at me without lifting her chin from her palm.

My sister. She is so silly. She totally sucks at French, but I love her.

I'm thinking I might ditch Physics. Gina and Gavin will probably be waiting for me in our top-secret ditch-class spot, but what I really want is to swim a few laps. It's Senior Skip Day, after all, and the school is filled with a strange sort of hollow buzz, an unspoken loosening of the rules. Nobody will be in the pool.

First, though, I want to try something, here in the quiet, while I have a few seconds alone. It occurs to me that if my brain really is supercharged like Gina says, then I should be able to *do* something with it. Not just call up this Angel guy and have my head examined in California, either. I've heard of something called magical thinking. I don't know what the phrase is supposed to mean exactly, but I like the sound of the words. *Magical thinking.* Isn't that what just happened with Monica? Without my saying a word, she turned to see me in the window of her classroom door. Maybe that's just a sister thing, though—or maybe it isn't. Maybe it's magical thinking, and maybe, just maybe, if I think hard enough about Lincoln Evans, the thought will transfer to him, wherever he is and whatever he's doing, via the curious osmosis of enchanted thought. It's not like I have anything earth-shattering to say to Lincoln—this is just a test of my own mental broadcasting system. Maybe if I remember him vividly enough, he'll be able to sense it; he'll know—or maybe even *feel* it, in the tiny bones of his inner ear, say—that at that very moment he is being remembered.

I can see him plain as yesterday: Pokémon, blue sky, jar of quarters, yellow—*yes, it was yellow*—Ryder van, and all.

DELAWARE, WALKING

(11:17 AM EDT)

Delaware, walking dazedly down the empty hall with a pocketed gun, is thinking about *The Odyssey*, which Mr. Li's senior International Baccalaureate English class is discussing right now in Delaware's absence. There was this group assignment, and Delaware's team is probably in there right now giving their presentation on irony. Delaware, highly attuned to irony, feels weirdly regretful at not being in class to wax enthusiastic about the best part of the whole stupid story: the end, of course, when the only person who recognizes Odysseus when he finally gets his fatally flawed ass back to Ithaca is not a person at all but a dog. The *dog*, man!

"Oh, my God. *Where* have you been?"

Delaware pivots around to find Izzy Goff, her mouth hanging open and Mr. Li's famous hall pass (a plastic dinosaur the size of a shoe box) held aloft in her hand. Delaware can't help but laugh at Izzy trying to be mad while she's carrying Freedom, which is what Mr. Li named the dinosaur. Delaware's going to miss Mr. Li's sense of humor.

"Wait, are you *laughing*? Do you think this is funny?"

Delaware, fingers closing more tightly around the concealed secret, thinks she's talking about the thing. The great mistake. Surely this is all that anybody anywhere is talking about. Shame is already starting to spread, *head, shoulders, knees and toes, knees and toes.*

"I mean since when does 'group' mean Izzy, Izzy, Izzy, and Izzy? *You* were gone, *Lilly* was gone — Ty and I had to stand up there and do the whole stupid thing by ourselves! And I got all flustered and started talking about Tantalus when I meant to say Sisyphus. God, I hate group work."

Izzy is waving Freedom around in the air. Delaware, stupidly grinning, palm now sweaty around the gun, is enjoying this display. Izzy Goff is a complete pain in the ass, but Delaware, in this moment, admires her blustery outrage, her focused devotion to her GPA. She's got her own fierce kind of beauty going on.

"Did you make sure to talk about Argos? The dog?"

Delaware says the words out loud, but they're mostly a buffer to keep Izzy there in the hall. She is acting as a kind of tether — a link to a world where people talk about something other than the mistake that occupies Delaware's every thought.

"What!" Izzy snaps. "No, I didn't talk about the dog. I was in charge of talking about ironic punishments, remember? Tantalus and Sisyphus?"

Delaware — staring spacily now at a spot just over Izzy's head — tries to imagine Sisyphus's rock, the one he forged in life (oops, that little mistake is going to cost you, pal) and is cursed in death to push up the hill, watch fall, and push back up the hill again and again and again and again and again and again and again and again and again and again and again and again and again and again and again.

"How much do you think that boulder weighed?" Delaware asks (antiseptic walls now ebbing, now flowing, a bright-white blur).

Izzy looks stricken, squinty. "What?"

"Sisyphus's body is gone, but his soul is made out of stone. Isn't it supposed to be the other way around?"

Then Izzy, staring at Delaware for a good long second or two, does a crazy thing. She goes and places her warm palm on Delaware's forehead. "You don't look good," she says, her hip just inches from the gun.

"I'm fine," Delaware says, laughing. *No, no, no,* he thinks. *The boulder's not made of stone. It's made of shame.*

"I think you have a fever," Izzy says. She takes a few steps back and points Freedom at Delaware. "In which case, okay, I'm really sorry I yelled at you, but please do not breathe flu germs on me right now. I've got a huge debate in Dover this weekend, and —"

"I promise you can't catch what I have," Delaware says.

"Feel better," Izzy commands, turning now to head back to the girls' room. Delaware watches her go and has already resumed walking in the opposite direction when Izzy's voice rings back down the hall: "And, just so you know? The next time you ditch me on a group project, I will freaking kill you."

"Got it," Delaware calls back, fingers now sore from clenching the gun, which, like Delaware's shame, weighs practically nothing, but also weighs a thousand million pounds. Once again the hall is empty, and Delaware's inconsequential body could slip under the crack of that classroom door (French class: Madame Metcalfe's voice is carrying down the hall, *"J'ai entendu les nouvelles . . ."*) if not for the burden of the gun. Shame. Shame. It weighs more than sorrow, and much more than regret. Delaware can't even say what it looks like, because that's the thing with shame: After a while you might dare to open your eyes, thinking maybe you've managed to forget about it this time, just for a second — but no. There it is. Always there. It might once have been attached to whatever it was you said (or didn't say), whatever it was you did (or failed to do), but it is now its own dark creature, separate from and larger than the thing that gave it life. It keens its high, silver scream in your ears, the sound of echoing mirrors. It feeds and hungers and preens, and it will not go away.

Delaware leans against the wall — the cinder block so cool and solid; maybe this is just a fever after all, maybe that's all this is — half wishing Izzy (or anyone, really) would reappear. Delaware would like to tell her a story—no, a fable. A fable about water, and siblings.

That's when Delaware, hearing laughter coming from the library, crosses the hall to peer through the narrow window at Nate Salisbury, spinning in his desk chair beneath a clock covered by a metal cage. All the clocks in this place are caged, like time's going to escape or something—which, Delaware thinks, it is. Time's almost up. Hurry.

"Hey Nate," Delaware whispers into the cool cinder block's ear. Nate's a good guy, a good listener. He's as good a person as any to receive this story, so here goes. Delaware, eyes closed, will think it into Nate's ear:

> *Once upon a time, years and years ago, two siblings waded out together into the ocean. The older one, wild like the sea, wasn't afraid. The younger one, though, was accustomed only to the safety of pools, and was fearful of being swallowed up.*
>
> *"Climb on my back," the older sibling said. "I'll carry you out."*
>
> *"But—" the younger began.*
>
> *"Don't worry. If I wanted to, I could swim with you on my back for miles. Out there in the water, you won't weigh a thing. It'll be like I'm carrying air."*
>
> *"But I—"*
>
> *"I won't let you go. Just hang on, and I promise I won't let you go."*

*So together, the siblings waded out in the sea, and
what the older promised was true: the younger weighed
practically nothing at all.*

The gun, heavy as Delaware's shame, weighs practically
nothing at all. The ironic thing (Where is Izzy? She would
appreciate this.) is that the gun appeared at Delaware's
house only two nights before, after it became clear that the
fallout from Delaware's mistake might place the family in
the path of danger.

"This gun is not for me," Delaware's father had said, too
ashamed to look at his youngest child. "It is not for my life,
which I would give to anyone who wished to do me harm, if
it came to that, if it was so important to them. Take my life,
take it, if you must." Still, Delaware's father did not look up
from the floor. "But do not take the life of my wife. Do not
take the life of my child."

It was so easy, stealing the gun from its hiding spot. And
it barely weighs a thing. It is nothing, Delaware thinks, but
the shortest distance between two sorrows.

Above Nate Salisbury's spinning head, the second hand
of the caged clock makes its steady sweep. Delaware sways
from the wall and starts to walk again.

THE FORUM AT A GLANCE

THE PERSON I HATE THE MOST

<<PREV   1   2   3   4   5   6   NEXT>>

Texas   March 13, 2013, at 2:55 am

WEST VIRGINIA AND 3 OTHERS LIKE THIS

you mean today or in general lol? so today top of my shitlist is . . . um, my spanish teacher? fucked up my entire gpa thanks bitch

Louisiana   March 13, 2013, at 2:57 am   **TEXAS** LIKES THIS

My hatred for (codename!!!) still burns brighter than a thousand suuuuuuuunnns omg hands shaking too much Red Bull

« « «

Utah March 13, 2013, at 3:01 am   **TEXAS** AND 2 OTHERS LIKE THIS

Sorry about tu maestra Espanol ☹ ☹ ☹ Also Red Bull =
NASTY!! Also still hating stepdad (codename DICK)
the most the most the most UGH so who all can't
sleep? Entertain me I'm boooooooooorrrrrrrrreeeeeeed

Idaho March 13, 2013, at 3:05 am   **NEBRASKA** LIKES THIS

Sleep? What? What's that?

Nebraska March 13, 2013, at 3:07 am

IDAHO AND 12 OTHERS LIKE THIS

Sleep perchance to dream . . . dreams are good . . . just
saying . . . btw there's nobody else in this world I hate
half as much as I hate myself. . . .

Idaho March 13, 2013, at 3:07 am   **NEBRASKA** LIKES THIS

there's nobody else in this world I hate half
as much as I hate myself. . . .
↑THIS. THIS. THIS, FOREVER. <3 <3 <3 <3 <3 <3 <3

there's nobody else in this world I hate half as much as I
hate myself

there's nobody else in this world I hate half as much as I hate myself

there's nobody else in this world
I hate half as much as I hate
myself

there's nobody else in
this world I hate half as
much as I hate myself

there's nobody
else in this world

I hate
myself

I hate
myself

LINCOLN AND THE SIREN SONG

(10:17 AM CDT)

Laura Echols has her tongue in my ear. It's a strange, but not entirely unpleasant, sensation. I've wound my hand in her braid so I can pull her closer. I feel so lucky it makes me dizzy. Luckydizzylucky. Drunk on Laura Echols.

"Lincoln," Laura whispers in my ear, a thrill that travels straight to my pants, where her hand has suddenly wandered. "I have a secret."

No kidding, Laura Echols. Your whole life is a secret.

"Tell me," I say into her ear. Her earlobe has a diamond in it, and I'm willing to bet it's real. This girl is truly beyond imagination.

Laura pulls back, an abrupt jerk. In the space of an instant, some sort of cloud has passed over her eyes. "Later," she says. "I'll tell you later. First let's get out of here. I want to show you something."

« « «

Gravel flying crazily against the windshield, Laura wheels us out of the drive-in. My luck has turned to shame, and I can't figure out if that's what it is burning the back of my neck — shame? — or if it's something else. I've spent a lot of time at the drive-in with Laura Echols, but I've never felt afraid of her before. Now, for some reason I can't put my finger on, I want out of the car.

Two seconds later, as soon as she opens her mouth, I change my mind.

"I like you, Lincoln Evans," she says. She's got the Lexus on an even keel now; we're coasting along like whatever little storm just happened never happened.

"I like you, too," I say.

Laura gives me a sideways look that says I have no idea what I'm talking about. Like maybe she even feels sorry for me. "Aren't you sweet."

Thirty minutes later we're parked in front of a half-finished house in a suburban cul-de-sac filled with a bunch of other skeleton houses. I've never seen this place in my life, but Laura's acting like she comes here often. Abandoned drive-ins, empty houses: I'm starting to see a pattern.

Laura's on the front stoop, waiting. "Come on!" she calls. "Carry me over the threshold, just because."

What is it with me doing everything Laura Echols says? Jesus Christ. Before I even know what I'm doing, I'm lifting Laura, enjoying the miraculous heft and fact of her, and carrying her through the skeleton doorway of the house.

Sawdust is all over the place. I can feel the grit of it in my eyes, the sift of it under my shoes. Somebody has left a plastic Mountain Dew bottle on a dusty sawhorse, and there's a crumpled Hardee's bag on the floor. I find these signs of life oddly comforting and wonder where these people are, these Hardee's-eating house builders. It's the middle of the morning.

Hands on hips, Laura walks slowly around the room, assessing.

"Okay," she says, eyes sweeping the ceiling. "Okay. Let's say you're a serial killer and your targets are asleep in this house. Where do you go first?"

An involuntary laugh escapes my lips. "What?"

Laura flaps her hands. "Hypothetical. Just hypothetically."

"I'm not a serial killer."

Laura groans. "Okay, not *you,* then. Anybody. Any random serial killer."

I've watched plenty of *CSI* and *Criminal Minds.* I vaguely remember *In Cold Blood.* I should be able to answer this. I just don't feel like it, is all. Games have their limits.

"I don't know, Laura. What do you want me to say? I guess he goes for the kids first?"

Laura crosses her arms across her chest. "Who says the people in this house have kids? Who says the serial killer's a *guy?*"

I can tell this is one of those cryptic Laura-conversations that's just going to loop all around for hours and get me nowhere but frustrated, so I shrug and start back for the doorway. I'm in the yard and almost to the Lexus when Laura catches me with her voice. She's leaning in the doorway, a beautiful girl beautifully framed. It's insane what beautiful girls get away with in this world. What idiots like me let them get away with.

"If I were moving into this house, I'd pick the room closest to the stairs," Laura calls. "Serial killers always take out the person in the rearmost room first."

"Is that right," I say, turning.

Laura nods. "I can hear everything. My hearing's, like, off the charts. I'd hear it happening and be down the stairs and out the door before she could finish with victim number one."

"So you wouldn't try to save your brother? Or sister or dad or mom or whoever? You wouldn't even put up a fight?"

"It'd be too late." Her voice is *meh*, matter-of-fact, a smug shrug. "You gotta save yourself. Put on your own oxygen mask before you assist the children. God, Lincoln, don't you know anything?"

The Lexus chirps in reproach. Unlocked. I reach for the door, but before I can touch it, *chirp*, the door is locked again. Laura's still in the doorway, laughing and dangling the keys on one outstretched finger.

"Guess you'll have to walk home."

"Laura, let's go."

"I'm not ready yet. I like it here. Don't you like it here?"

The truth is — and the truth is sad, but here it is — that I like anywhere, as long as Laura Echols is there. I've been in this girl's thrall for so long I can barely speak in her presence, but that, I've decided, is over. Right now. This second. My heart is beating so fast I'm a little afraid it might fly out of my mouth. I'm a little afraid it might become a living, animated thing and pick up this big-ass rock from the ground and send it crashing through the windshield of Laura Echols's Lexus. Who buys their teenage daughter a Lexus? Who does that? No wonder the world is six million shades of miserable. Everybody's priorities are upthefucksidedown.

"What the *fuck,* Laura? Why are we here? Why did you pick me for this, whatever this is? I don't even know what this is. You tell me."

Laura Echols looks stricken. Good. Maybe that means I actually said the things I was thinking this time. Maybe that means she heard me.

"I don't know what it is." Laura shrugs. All pitiful, like she hasn't been dragging me around by my balls all year. "And don't talk to me like that. I like you, Lincoln."

I don't even have a response to that. Laura's sitting down now on the stoop of the half-finished house. Maybe she's crying, I can't really tell. It's possible I don't even care, or maybe I do care, and maybe I'm jealous. I can't remember the last time I cried, and I envy those tears, the flood of relief that comes with them. I'd give anything to cry right now, even with Laura Echols sitting right there. I'd pay somebody for some honest-to-God tears.

"Laura," I say. There's still this ridiculous expanse between us, but I think maybe if I try hard enough, we can be more honest with each other right now, across this stretch of gravel and dirt in the middle of nowhere, than we ever have been while twisted around each other's bodies in Laura's car. I lean against the Lexus and stare up at the sky, a wide and cloudless blue.

And that's when I remember the girl's last name, the neighbor from first grade whose eyelid I kissed on a day when the sky turned to flames and my dad flew away.

I like to think he was one of the ones who jumped. Like, in my mind, he jumped, and in the middle of that awful descent he grew wings and lifted right back up, right back to the sky and whatever's up there, like he never hit the ground at all. In my mind he doesn't burn and doesn't fall. He just flies, gigantic wings spread wide.

April Donovan. Her last name was Donovan, first name April, as in now, this spring, this month, this hour day minute second heartbeat. April with freckles, laughing with two gaps for front teeth. Her face appears in my mind with such suddenness and clarity, such a feeling of missing and having missed, that tears start to rise in my throat. I gave April Donovan my quarters.

I try to imagine Laura Echols in first grade, and it's impossible. Girls like Laura skip everything from infancy through puberty; they're mermaid-born, complete with waist-length hair and car keys and silver flasks.

No wonder she picked me. No wonder.

"What?" Laura says, bringing me back around. Sunlight glints on something she's got in her hand, although I swear she left that silver flask in the still-locked car.

"Laura Echols," I say. My voice sounds like a caught thing, begging. "Tell me something true."

THE MASTERMIND

(7:30 AM PDT)

The Mastermind's mom is late for work. That, for the moment, is the most immediate of her problems, which are about to increase at an exponential rate. She didn't have twenty extra minutes to search for her keys, and how on earth did they get in the freezer? It's one of a million little mysteries that she's handed on any given day: How'd the keys get in the freezer? Where'd I put my mind? Who is my son, and what goes on in his head? The Mastermind's mom, who is an expert at being attentive and worried when it comes to her son—her only child—is exhausted. Her attention, her worry: they have replaced anything else she might have to offer.

The Mastermind's mom doesn't know this, but it was he, the Mastermind himself, who put the keys in the freezer. A little thing he did for his own amusement, and to distract

» » »

his mother. The Mastermind's mom also doesn't know that he only pretended to get on the bus this morning. A senior in high school, still riding the bus, still two years away from legal driving age.

It's not Asperger's, he wants to shout. Do they really think a thing like Asperger's syndrome just appears, just *shows up* all of a sudden when a person is fourteen years old? It's a little late for all the tests, people. Yet. He's about to be hauled off for tests — extensive, expensive tests that his mother cannot afford — to determine just what it is that makes him not want to leave his room. As usual, he's a few hundred steps ahead of the game, enough to know that it's not Asperger's. He is now an expert on the subject, and he is prepared to assert that Asperger's syndrome is not the same as the innumerable ill effects of sending your ten-year-old off to high school when he has barely finished the fifth grade.

Skipping middle school, it turns out, does not equal skipping the humiliation that comes with being caught like a fish between here and there. The Mastermind knows a thing or two about humiliation. Imagine a fourteen-year-old senior, smart enough to enter MIT in the fall. Preternaturally gifted with a knack for numbers who has various overeducated, authoritative types — his therapist included — convinced he might have late-onset Asperger's. This is what's wrong with people, the Mastermind thinks. People always have to put a name on something. People feel like they understand a thing if they can name it. If they can name it—if they can Google it, more importantly—then people can control it. Oh, it must be Asperger's. Voilà! Problem solved. Now that we've named this problem, we can hand it over to some other overeducated, authoritative type for fixing. Carry on, carry on.

Everybody thinks he's so far ahead. But he's not, the Mastermind. He's way behind. There is so much catching up to do.

There was a while there, at the beginning of all this, when the Mastermind thought he might be finally catching up. It was junior year and Wendy Neely, who had just gotten her driver's license, was failing Calculus. In exchange for rides to and from school for a month, the Mastermind would spend Tuesday and Thursday afternoons helping Wendy wrap her brain around tangents and derivatives.

That month of riding in Wendy's car was the sweetest of the Mastermind's life. She drove a beat-up Taurus whose odometer clicked over the two-hundred-thousand-mile mark on the first Tuesday of the calculus tutoring. The Mastermind was in the passenger seat, taking this in, and also enjoying the chance to pay attention to Wendy while she was paying attention to the road. He noticed that she watched the rearview mirror constantly; she seemed way more interested in what was behind her than in whatever might lie ahead.

"Are you named for Wendy Darling?" the Mastermind asked.

Wendy grinned from behind her sunglasses, which were

the same bright orange as her fingernail polish. "I'm not named for anybody, I don't think."

The Mastermind nodded. "I like the name Wendy. Did you know J. M. Barrie came up with that name himself? His *Peter Pan* Wendy was the first Wendy, pretty much."

"Really?" Wendy said.

"Yeah," the Mastermind answered. "Take a left up here."

Wendy turned left into the Mastermind's cul-de-sac, and they got out of the car and went into the house, where they ate microwave popcorn and talked about calculus. This was when the Mastermind discovered that Wendy wasn't just a girl like any other. She was different. When he talked about calculus, she paid attention, even though she didn't love it. Even though it didn't come naturally to her. The things that did come naturally to her were many, and they were things that the Mastermind himself never could have done. Stuff like student government, like decorating the gym with a big painted mural of the shimmering world and their tiny place in it: Irvine, California. Wendy was even in a play — she had been cast as Amanda Wingfield in the drama department's spring production of *The Glass Menagerie*. Sometimes they'd take breaks from the math and the Mastermind would help her run lines. He liked the groove that appeared between Wendy's eyebrows when she was remembering what to say. It was the same groove that would surface when she was concentrating on calculus.

"What do I even need calculus for?" Wendy said on that

first Tuesday afternoon. "This has nothing to do with anything I want to do with my life, ever."

"Oh, but it does," the Mastermind told her, sensing that he was going to have to teach it to her in a way that was different from the way he himself learned it, which wasn't so much learning as a refining of something that already existed deep in the marrow of his bones. He realized, in that moment, that this was his chance: only he, the Mastermind, could clearly explain calculus to Wendy Neely. It was a job for him and him alone; nobody else could even come close. All his wild genius, flying around in his head with no place to land—here it was. A place to land. It would be like giving Wendy Neely a gift, and she was going to be grateful, so grateful.

In that moment, the Mastermind's unique brand of obsession—his secret, dark fever, the thing everybody tried to name but couldn't name—transferred from the things that had occupied it before (games, drawings, hastily scrawled plans, never before anything with an actual soul in it) onto the hapless Wendy Neely, blithe and sunny Wendy Neely of the orange fingernails, who had not a clue in the world of what kind of dangerous spark she had ignited in the Mastermind's astounding brain.

"Don't think of calculus like it's the study of numbers," the Mastermind said to Wendy, who in his mind was already his girlfriend, already body-soul *his* and nobody else's. "Think of it as what it really is."

"Well, what is it, really?" Wendy asked, sunny as ever.

The Mastermind grinned, an involuntary response to the tidal shift that had happened within him, which was happening still, and was surely happening to Wendy, too, right before his eyes.

"It's the study of change."

GAG, BUT MISSING THEIR A

(11:47 AM EDT)

Gina and I are in the broom closet eating some more of those red-velvet cupcakes from April's birthday, and April should be in here with us because this is how we roll and all, this is one of our official and top-secret meeting spots, but April is nowhere. April's up and gone #MIA, and it's making me nervous. She's probably just in physics class, but hey, what if her weird-ass April mind somehow knew something about whatever it was I maybe saw or didn't see underneath the bleachers this morning? What about that?

"Stop worrying," Gina says.

"Dude. I didn't even say anything."

"Whatever. I can hear you worrying, like, from inside your head. That's how loud it is. Who even was it?"

"I couldn't really see," I say, which is the truth, and which is half of why I'm worried about it in the first place.

» » »

April and Gina and me have known everybody around here since birth, and April always promised we had nothing to sweat, that nobody at our school is the shoot-'em-up type, but then what about that one guy? What about that effer, effing with a school that wasn't even his? An elementary school, man, don't even talk to me about it. Don't even talk to me about how there's nothing in this world as innocent as a first-grader. Since then April's had a whole nother layer of paranoia. Since then it's been *good guy with a gun wtf!* at the school entrance every day and it's been periodic trips to the Lockdown Closet, which let me tell you is one tiny-ass claustrophobia-making hellhole but you can fit twenty-eight seniors and one teacher in here, #ishityounot.

Only right now it's just me and Gina, ditching Government.

There's a thirty-six-pack of generic toilet paper in here and about twenty bottles of Pine-Sol and that yellow bucket thing with a sour mop in it and this whole place smells like antiseptic cleaner mixed with the total ass smell of filthy mop and I could just about gag, so I'm shoving a cupcake in my mouth to keep from retching, that's how gross it is. The light above our heads is all fluorescent-nasty and is flickering like to give a person a seizure and it's all sort of greenish and makes me and Gina both look like we're about to puke, which I think maybe I could, like any minute now, look out.

"Man, where *is* she?" I wanna know.

"I've texted her eight million times," Gina says. "Relax."

Relax. Right. In the Lockdown Closet. Because this is the world now, ladies and gentlemen. Every day of high school is a game of #russianroulette.

Gina's actually painting her nails. In the Lockdown Closet! Because it's not like we can breathe in here already or anything like that. The polish is this awful shade of throw-up green. Gina wants to do mine but I'm like, are you kidding me?

"We're almost out of here," Gina muses. "Pretty soon you and April are going to go off to your fancy smart-people schools, and then what? What's going to become of me?"

Gina's going to the University of Delaware, and there are lots of days when I wish I were going with her. Newark is far enough to feel distant but close enough to feel like home. It's a #bestofbothworlds scenario, is what it is, but Gina's a little irritated that it's not Hollywood.

"You'll be the hottest Blue Hen around, is what will become of you. Maybe after graduation you'll end up an assistant for that washed-up magician of yours. Who knows? The future is a big place, Gina Marie."

Gina fans her nails in the air, spins neatly around so I can rub her back. "I'd study magic if I could," she says. "I totally would. Learn how to turn the world on its ear, learn how to disappear. Those are some freaking marketable skills right there."

Gina! She kills me. She goes around rhyming without even trying to do it. Girl is made of rhythm.

"Honey," I say, "let me tell you something. There's not anybody in this world doesn't wish to God they lived at Hogwarts. Come up with something new to bitch about."

Gina laughs, all sad but happy, then turns around to look at me. "I've got an idea," she says, like she's never had such a great idea before, like this is the #bestoneevah. "Gavin! Let's go to prom."

Man, I knew this was coming. Sooner or later everybody caves and decides they want to go to prom. "Like you and me together? Like ironically or for real?"

"You and me and April. The three of us as dates. Totally un-ironic. You can wear two boutonnieres and we can thrift shop for some old-school prom gear and it will be epic and please please say yes, Gavin. Do this one thing for me, please?"

Of course I have to act all put upon and offended, so I roll my eyes and pretend the world's ending. The truth is, though, that I can't wait. Deep down I have always, always wanted to go to #prom.

"Okay," I say, and already I'm dreaming about it.

It's not more than three seconds later that we hear the first round of shots, and three more seconds after that Mr. Goodrich's physics class—April's physics class, only she's nowhere, nowhere, and this kills me—is piling into the Lockdown Closet.

Only this isn't a drill. You can tell because Mr. Goodrich

doesn't even ask Gina and me what we're doing in the closet. You can tell because somebody turns off the light, and in the dark nobody's laughing, and also nobody's screaming because by now we all know the rules for survival, and the most important very first rule is this: #nobodymakeasound.

JUST AN ORDINARY OBJECT

(10:47 AM CDT)

"I'll tell you something true," Laura Echols says. Then she raises the flask to her temple, only I see now it's not a flask. The thing in her hand is a gun.

"Laura," I say, choking on my own adrenaline. How, how, how did I land in this moment?

"Laura, no." I hope I've said the words out loud; it's hard to tell because fear has clogged up the highway between my brain and my vocal cords. Everything is slowing; everything is speeding up. I'm dizzy and think I might fall.

Laura lowers her hand and lets the gun fall to the ground, where it glints dangerously in the sunlight. It's just a thing, I say to myself. Just an ordinary object, but it's as sinister a thing as I think I've ever seen. Never in my life, not ever, have I touched or held a gun. I wouldn't know what to do with it if I did. My brain on its crazy slow-down-speed-up

« « «

loop returns again to the girl from first grade, my old friend April, and I'm remembering how for a while after that day on the playground she couldn't stand the sight of an airplane crossing the sky, how a glimpse of that ordinary thing—an airplane, how common is that?—would be enough to make her cry.

We were first-graders. Six years old. I thought my life was over then, stolen at six, but the slow-down-speed-up loop keeps zooming, and now I'm thinking of *those* first-graders, the ones whose lives really did get stolen in a classroom in Connecticut, and the ones who had to carry on. How do you carry on?

"Don't worry," Laura says. "It's not loaded. It's not mine, either. It was his."

His. I have no idea who she means, but I'm walking slowly now toward Laura, toward the gun. I watch her watching me, and think that as long as I can keep her eyes locked with mine like this—as long as I can keep her with me this way—I will reach her, I will get all the way there, I will touch a gun for the first and last time in my life and throw it into the nearest river and hope that it never surfaces, ever again.

The gun is beautiful, in a weird way. Its weight in my hand is solid and cool, satisfying. There's some kind of fili-gree on the handle, and there are initials engraved on it, too: *SEE.* These same initials are on the flask. This is Laura's grandfather's gun, and there's no river around for miles.

"Just get it away from me," Laura says. She sinks to the

stoop of the skeleton house and presses the heels of her palms against her eyes. I stand there not moving while she cries. This cry is wringing her out; at one point she starts hiccuping, and then she does this weird bark sound that might be a laugh. Is she laughing? What the hell part of this is funny?

"Laura?"

"I'm serious. Get it away from me. Throw it as far as you can."

Like a person well trained by a lifetime of TV, I use my T-shirt to wipe the gun clean before I walk to the edge of the ghost property, which is skirted by a dense half circle of trees that go on for who knows how far. Far, I hope. *Far,* I think.

Then, like a kid making a penny-wish in a fountain, I screw my eyes shut tight and throw that gun as hard and far as wishing will make it go.

As I turn around to head back to the house, there's a panicked second when I don't see Laura. How easy it would be for her to get in her car and drive away, leaving me here in this sad patch of nowhere by a wood now haunted by that awful gun. The panic reminds me that I'm still afraid of her; that I'm at the mercy of someone who scares me; that it might be better if I took off through those woods and kept running until I came to whatever might be on the other side. There has to be something on the other side, right?

I'm about to turn and go when I catch sight of Laura, a

ribbon of her blond hair flashing like sunlight between the trees. She's still there, and I approach her carefully, like she herself is a bomb that might go off at any second.

"Is it gone?" she asks.

When she drags the back of her hand across her runny nose, I get a split-second image — *there* — of the little girl she must once have been. She had to have been six once after all, and the proof of this is what makes me scoop her up once more, all of limp and faraway Laura Echols in my arms, and carry her to the car, where I reach into Laura's hip pocket for the keys and open the passenger-side door and lift her into the seat, reach across her chest and lap to secure the seat belt, shut the door, and walk around to the driver's side.

Because somebody around here needs to be in charge. Somebody needs to drive the car and put as many miles as possible between us and that skeleton house and the woods where the very worst of all of Laura Echols's secrets is lying there, waiting to be found.

TEACHER'S PET

(10:47 AM CDT)

The landline at Adrian George's house has been disconnected. Coming at me through the phone is an automated voice, which I find strangely comforting: *You have reached a number that is no longer in service. If you feel you have reached this message in error, please hang up and try your call again.*

I've listened to the recording six or seven times now, and the words are simultaneously losing their meaning and gaining significance; the singsong refrain is taking on a sort of magical lilt, like these words right here might be the very ones responsible for unlocking the secret to living: maybe this isn't the right career path for you after all? *Hang up and try your call again!* Your marriage didn't work out, despite the best efforts of everyone involved? Don't worry: *You have reached this message in error.* You're afraid Adrian George has

« « «

not only got your number but the number of everybody, every single life, at this school? Never fear: *You have reached a number that is no longer in service.*

Poof! Adrian George is gone, just like that. No longer your problem.

I can't help it. The absurdity and truth of it all makes me laugh. I'm sitting here on the bench outside Dennis's office, laughing silent tears with a phone pressed to my ear. Where, oh where, is Adrian George? Maybe he just skipped the light fantastic out of town. Those words from the play keep looping around in my ear: *He was a telephone man who fell in love with long distances; he gave up his job with the telephone company and skipped the light fantastic out of town.* When Bruce-as-Tom-Wingfield read them out loud in class, at first I thought he'd gotten them wrong. These kids, they're so careless with words; they say things and don't think about what they're saying. Did Adrian George hear himself say the things he said? Did Bruce even try to get Tom Wingfield's lines right? *Trip* the light, I thought it was. "*Trip* the light fantastic," a phrase I thought meant dancing, not leaving. *Skip* the light makes me think of that song, the one about the light fandango and cartwheels. Oh God, that song. It comes on the car radio out of nowhere, and there I am, back in Jefferson High School's gym, my head on Eric's shoulder, swaying to that song with my belly so full of butterflies I'm almost all the way sick with love. It was 1990, but the people in charge of the dances couldn't get enough of Procol Harum and—on account of that movie

Ghost, which I pretended to hate but secretly loved—the Righteous Brothers. "Unchained Melody"—that was the other one, the other anthem that unraveled us all.

Maybe that was the problem: Eric and I had been together since high school; there was never anybody else. How can anyone or anything stand up under the weight, the freight, of all that history and memory? No wonder Eric skipped the light. Eric, Mr. Telephone-Man Wingfield, Adrian George's father . . . they're all out there somewhere, skipping the light. Jump-roping with a string of stars. Standing somewhere on a gossamer bridge above a beckoning expanse of water, skipping stones made of soft white light, promises glowing bright as they skim the surface of the water. *Ha, that was a good one,* one of them might say. The image of them is so clear it makes me laugh again. Out loud. Right there on the bench outside the principal's office.

Then, as if conjured by my laugh, Adrian George appears in the hall. Greasy dark bangs aslant across his face, backpack slung lazily over one shoulder. Clutched in his hand is the same book I had to take away from him in class last week when he refused to lift his eyes from it and give me his attention, *Life After Death,* an autobiography of a guy—this guy Damien Echols, only a couple of years younger than I am—who was sent to death row on a murder charge when he was eighteen (Adrian's age; you think these things are lost on me?) and whose teenage self could be Adrian's twin.

I know all this because after confiscating the book, I devoured the first three chapters on my lunch break over cold coffee and a Hot Pocket. Then I took it home and lost an entire night's sleep reading the rest of it. I wonder now if the book has contributed to my impression of—my worry over—Adrian George. I've judged students for less than idolizing the subject of a riveting book about a guy stolen from his teenage years and sentenced to the death penalty for murders he clearly didn't commit. Adrian, Damien— the names sound kind of the same, don't they? Same enough to jigsaw my memory, to get everybody mixed up and confused. It's *Adrian* George, not Damien; it's Damien Echols, no relation to *Laura* Echols in my senior honors English class, although both of them seem haunted. Today in class, when Laura was reading aloud, I heard it in her voice, some heartbreak or other. What a surprise it was, hearing that—is it possible I had thought her immune to sorrow on account of her grades and her face? Inexcusable, but possible, yes.

"What's so funny?" Adrian asks.

"Adrian," I say, and I hope he doesn't hear in my voice that I've just been thinking about him. I mean to stand and ask him why he skipped my class, where he's been all morning, why his landline has been disconnected, but as I rise from the bench, I realize my foot's asleep, and I have to sit down again and shake it back to life. The phone clatters from my lap to the floor. Adrian follows it with his eyes.

"Expecting a call?"

This is all so flustering—my skirt's too tight, I keep dropping things, I am afraid of this boy, the things I want and need to say to him have taken flight from my mind.

An onlooker would be unable to determine just who is in charge here.

"Adrian. I've been meaning to talk to you about—"

"Oh, that," Adrian says. He rakes a hand through his hair. "Look, forget it. I was just shitting you."

Just shitting you. Ohhhhhhhhhh, okay. Never mind, Sandy. I don't really want a divorce. I was just shitting you! Never mind, folks, as I stand here in your classroom waving this automatic weapon around; I'm just shitting you, after all. The world's not really going to hell in a handbasket, everybody—just shitting you!

I take a few steps toward Adrian. "Walk with me," I say.

I start toward my classroom, and Adrian lopes behind, a reluctant, shaggy-haired dog. I'm in charge, I realize. Also my leg is still asleep and the migraine is now gnawing at my eye sockets. People ought not *shit me* when I'm in this sort of state.

We're walking. Twenty paces ahead of us is my classroom, where we, Adrian George and I, will sit down at a pair of desks designed for people way smaller than us (than we, than *we,* Sandy—don't let your anxiety mess with your grammar; these things matter!) and hammer this out, start to finish. We'll figure out just who's been skipping the light fantastic around here; we'll get to the bottom of this misplaced rage right now; we'll do what we can to fix it, with me, Sandra Heslip, in the role of Sensitive Teacher Who Makes a Difference in the Life of a Youth.

"Have a seat," I say to Adrian.

Adrian, obedient, sits.

"Now why don't you tell me what's going on?" I say.

Adrian smirks, casts his eyes to the ceiling. He's not going to tell me a thing.

Only, you know what? He does.

He opens his mouth and starts talking. Just like anybody, everybody, else, Adrian George has a story to tell, and this time he's not shitting me.

Only what Adrian and I don't know in that moment is that the dominoes are starting—have started—to fall. After this talk with Adrian I will feel relieved, will feel once again assured that being a teacher is not just a job but a calling, that my years spent in this building have been not only worthwhile but meaningful, as in *full of meaning,* as in it means something, sometimes, to just give one bereft kid fifteen minutes' worth of your time, your ear, your hard-earned forty-something wisdom.

This buzz of peace and satisfaction will last all of three minutes, long enough for me to excuse Adrian George and walk to the teachers' lounge, where I will check my phone to find it's full of the same messages that have been pouring into the in-boxes of teachers all over the East Coast, where dread is unfurling at a sickening rate, where people are starting to connect the dots: two injured in a classroom in Maine, shooter in custody in Vermont, police on the scene in a New Hampshire high school now on lockdown.

This, of course, is only the beginning, and from where I'm standing, nobody can guess at an end.

PHOEBE = LIGHT

(7:03 AM MDT)

Phoebe has been awake so long that she's starting to see things. She's feeling dizzy and frantic and ill, there in front of her computer screen, and she has to run to get to the bathroom, where she dry heaves into the toilet until tears fill her eyes. The bowl is cool and solid; she rests her cheek on it and tries to get a good deep breath. Wallpapered in an innocuous pink and trimmed with a waltzing parade of voyeuristic Disney princesses, this bathroom is what separates her room from Angela's. Their mom calls their third-floor domain the Sweetheart Suite, as in, *Girls, you're not going out until I can see the floor in the Sweetheart Suite. The bathroom in the Sweetheart Suite needs some attention, stat. Calling all denizens of the Sweetheart Suite! Dinner awaits and grows cold, Your Royal Highnesses.*

« « «

Until this moment, all that stupid talk of her mom's has mostly gotten on Phoebe's nerves. She and Angela aren't little girls anymore, after all. Proof of this is all over the bathroom. The surface of the sink is strewn with the sisters' teenage-girl stuff. Phoebe's side of the double sink is a mess: a brush nested with hair, toothpaste crusted in the bowl and flecked on the surface of the mirror. Phoebe's clear plastic retainers — hundreds of dollars' worth of protection against her new and worrisome habit of grinding her teeth at night — are two pieces of a broken smile among a tangle of elastic headbands, the kind Phoebe uses for soccer practice.

Only she hasn't worn her retainers in weeks, and she quit the soccer team after the Incident, and the hair caught in the brush is longer than the hair on Phoebe's head.

Just last week, Phoebe stood before this very mirror and chopped off her hair by herself. Holding her thick, ash-blond ponytail in her hand had been an odd experience — here was fourteen inches of her signature beauty, clutched in her fist and miraculously apart from the body to which it had been attached just moments before. It took only a few seconds to make that change, Phoebe had marveled. A decision and then a result. An action and then a consequence, all in the space of a minute. Although at first she had been struck by a nauseating wave of remorse — she had been growing this hair all her life! — it didn't take her long to succumb to the feeling of adrenaline-laced power at what she had done. It was so much easier than she would have thought, had she given herself time to think about it.

And that was the key: don't give yourself time to think about it. Just do. Just go. The change, the lesson, the message: that's the thing.

Now Phoebe heaves again into the toilet, trying to remember what the message is supposed to be. She doesn't know. Last week it occurred to her to send the ponytail to Locks of Love or one of those places, but she didn't do it. The ponytail is spiraled neatly into a flat white box now hidden in the cabinet under the sink, where the girls keep their stash of tampons and pads. Phoebe can't remember when she last had a period, but that's par for the course—her body has always been lithe, unpredictable, too constantly in motion to be slowed for any length of time by the burden of menstruation. She can always get by with the superlight tampons, while Angela has to suffer the huge kind, to accommodate the monthly nightmare that sometimes makes her miss school, that's how bad it gets. That makes sense, it occurs to Phoebe now; Angela has always been so much more the *girl*-girl. Her side of the bathroom is testament to this: six different kinds of sweet-smelling lotions lined neatly in a plastic caddy, curling iron and straightening iron and blow-dryer hanging from pink hooks on the wall. Taped to her side of the mirror is a picture torn years ago from *People* magazine: a shirtless Taylor Lautner, sporting this ridiculous six-pack that Phoebe always thought completely missed the point of his face, or his face missed the point of his abs—whichever, whatever, they didn't seem to match. Angela had once upon a time loved Taylor, though, so Phoebe had drawn a little bubble from his mouth, encapsulating the words *I'm on Team Angela,* heart heart heart heart heart. They used to do funny little things like this for each other all the time, the sisters, but lately Phoebe has lost interest.

The Incident really wasn't such a big deal. Phoebe keeps telling herself this, just as she keeps telling herself that probably nobody even thinks about it anymore, but none of that matters because Phoebe thinks about it, and she thinks about it all the time. It was—is—a big deal for her, and it's not going away. The shame of it feels like a persistent rash, threatening on some days to become the whole of her skin.

What happened is that Phoebe got catfished. Catfishing, it turns out, is an actual thing, a thing that has nothing to do with freshwater sport, a thing that Phoebe didn't know about until it happened to her. *Catfish,* as in a verb made out of a noun, an elaborate ruse created by someone—or someones—who still haven't revealed themselves.

That's the worst part, the reason why Phoebe can't let go. Someone saw fit to be cruel to her, and she still doesn't know who it is. Because it could be anyone, it has become, for Phoebe, everyone, and that's why all she wants is out.

It happened last spring, when Phoebe's soccer team played in the state finals against a team from Coeur d'Alene.

Hey star forward, said this boy who called himself Dylan Fisher, appearing from nowhere to comment on a picture Phoebe had posted. The photograph—snapped seconds after Phoebe's winning goal, all thrill and triumph and flying ponytails — captured one of the best moments of Phoebe's life. How pure and uncomplicated her joy had been. Afterward, pizza and laughter at this hole-in-the-wall place in Coeur d'Alene. The shining faces of her teammates, whom she loved. Fatigue settling pleasantly in her calves on the night ride home, lulled by the rumble of the school bus, happy in the private cocoon of the dark and the music pouring through her headphones.

Nice victory, said this boy called Dylan Fisher.

In Dylan's profile picture, a boy with a tiny gap between his front teeth grinned from behind a pair of sunglasses. The boy's hair was golden, spiky with chlorine and sunlight. The gap kept him from being perfect and — as Phoebe's mental image of him deepened and sharpened over time — made him beautiful.

My cousin plays for Ventura, said Dylan Fisher of the gap-toothed grin. *I saw you at the game and couldn't look away.*

Dylan Fisher had an answer for everything: *Seventeen. Homeschooled. Used to play soccer but tore my ACL, still recovering from surgery. The dog's name is Pavlov. I can't today. Mom needs the car.*

Pavlov the dog — bloodhound with droopy eyes, droopy ears stretched across the arm of a blue sofa in Dylan Fisher's living room. Pictures and pictures — the dog, the sofa, the eyes (behind the sunglasses, hazel and flecked with light), the physical therapy.

It was real. It was real.

Only it wasn't.

So, Phoebe has been asking herself ever since, what *is* real?

The answer rises to her mind in her mother's voice, lines from a childhood bedtime story that has never lost its pull on her: *Real isn't how you are made. It's a thing that happens to you.*

So this thing happened to her, and now here she is, a girl with her arms thrown around a toilet bowl as she contemplates throwing away her life.

"Feeb?"

Angela's standing there, framed by the open doorway that leads to her room.

"Are you okay?"

Phoebe, dazed, regards her sister, who is wearing her glasses and has her hair piled into this loose bun on top of her head. The glasses lend Angela an air of vulnerability that seizes at something inside Phoebe. She thinks of all the times — thousands of times? — she has stood at this very sink and watched her sister put in or remove her contacts. Like all contact lens wearers, Angela performs the act without thinking; it's a thing she does with practiced grace and ease, the way Phoebe used to slide an elastic from her wrist and whip her long hair into a ponytail, or the way both girls can remove their bras without first taking off their shirts, unhooking them with swan wings folded behind their backs and yanking them out through their sleeves.

It occurs to Phoebe now that to watch another person do

such a thing—put in contacts, yank a bra off sleevewise—
is a privilege and a wonder, the sort of intimacy that belongs
to shared family life. This other person, standing barefoot in
her glasses and rumpled Gonzaga T-shirt and sleep-creased
face, is Phoebe's *sister*. The only person in the world with the
same two parents, the same exact set of living circumstances,
the same long history filled with lopsided birthday cakes
and summers at Yellowstone and cringeworthy embarrass-
ments at the pool and all the lines from movies and songs
and learning to drive stick and pages ripped from magazines
and taped to the mirror above the sink.

Phoebe has never kept anything from her sister, not ever,
and yet for months she has harbored the dark secret of the
forum, and the Plan. Probably if she had just told Angela
about it, right from the start, the desire to be involved would
have evaporated into thin air. For Phoebe, a thing isn't really
real until she has told her sister about it. So maybe the Plan
is real, but some essential part of Phoebe has wanted all this
time to think it really isn't. Like the Incident wasn't real; it
was just a stupid little drama that played out in the ether.

Some days Phoebe comes away from the screen feeling
as though her skin has gone ashen and gray. At first she
blamed the phone for her compulsion; maybe if she just
got rid of that thing, she'd quit looking at it. Checking it
again and again, wondering who's whispering about her,
wondering if Dylan will somehow return and turn out to
be real after all, wondering if the truth will surface, wondering what's happening on the forum now and now and

now . . . but now the phone is at the bottom of Little Spangle Lake (stupid, stupid) and she is still checking and checking, only now she's checking on her laptop.

Some days Phoebe's back hurts from standing hunched over her desk, her laptop, because she has told herself that she's not going to sit down in the chair. Sitting in the chair equals committing, pledging the time and energy, getting sucked once again into the forum. So she stands, hunching, and gets sucked in anyway, sometimes for a whole hour on her feet, bent over, and then her back will scream at her all night long. On such days the sky comes as a surprise. No kidding. The sky! How huge it is, how opposite a thing from the narrowing that has become her life. Real, not real, a thing that happens to you, a thing that's happening now, Now Trending, I Like This, Breaking News, and then it's this news, and then this, and now this news, and all the news is bad. There's no running from it.

Angela in her glasses is breaking Phoebe's heart.

"Feeb. Are you okay?" Angela asks again.

Phoebe shakes her head no.

I see you when I dream, said Dylan Fisher. He of the charming tooth-gap and torn ACL and droopy dog and birthday on Valentine's Day and soccer trophies and quiet, homeschooled brilliance and little brother whose Legos are everywhere, all over the place, all over the blue couch in a living room with a grandfather clock and a braided rug. Dylan Fisher of the half-moon cuticles and chlorinated hair, Dylan who can't because he's grounded, because he's sick, because he's visiting his grandma in Boise, because he has to watch his brother, because he's got physical therapy, because and because and because.

But I want so much to touch your face, said Dylan Fisher.
You are beautiful.

How can I miss you so much when I've never felt your skin?

Soon, he said. And said and said and said. Months of saying *We'll meet soon.*

No, Phoebe is not okay.

The sky is falling.

THE MASTERMIND'S MIND

(8:25 AM PDT)

The Mastermind is walking away from what he has done. His computer has been smashed to a million trillion bazillion blithereens. Poof! Like magic. Lost to the air.

He could take the bus, but he'd rather walk. The university's not that far. So close, actually, that the Mastermind wonders that he has never ventured there before. All this time, his father has been right there. His father! Contributor of one Y chromosome. Owner of brown eyes, which carry the dominant gene. The Mastermind has brown eyes, too, and can fold his tongue and stick it out almost far enough to touch his own nose. Perhaps his father can do this, too. Perhaps his father can whistle, or wiggle his ears. Perhaps, after he eats asparagus, the Mastermind's father's pee smells like that, like asparagus. Wendy did not have the

» » »

asparagus-pee gene; they tried this out once during calculus tutoring.

Wendy was prone to dominant traits.

Wendy also had a birthmark near her left elbow, a reddish-brown splotch shaped like Arkansas.

Wendy was double-jointed.

Wendy had freckles, also known as angel kisses, although this Angel, this boy, this Mastermind, is not someone she felt compelled to kiss, because *It's not like that,* because *I like you, I do, just not in that way.*

Just in the calculus way.

Freckles. Angel kisses. The Mastermind has fashioned a pair of wings and has strapped them to his back so that he will not be missed when he flies past the window of his father's office, which is on the fourteenth floor (which means the thirteenth, probably; the Mastermind is not one to overlook the power of superstition and how it might figure into his mission) of an office building that contains twenty-one floors in all. He imagines that he is Icarus. He imagines, as he makes his winged walk northwest toward the university (sixty-four steps, sixty-five, sixty-six, sixty-seven, sixty-eight) that the stares he is drawing from passersby have everything to do with how unusual it must be for these people to be encountering Icarus, right here on the sidewalk on this twenty-first-century April morning. *Crazy!*

In the story, it is Icarus's father who fashions the wings for his boy. So it's the fault of Daedalus, really, that Icarus meets his end the way he does. It's nobody's fault but the father's.

In the story, Wendy Darling can fly! Peter's youth is a thing she so desires, so wishes to be near, that under his spell she can fly, even without the use of wings. Why would she walk away from that? Wendy is a fool, the Mastermind thinks.

In his dreams, the Mastermind can fly. He can soar on outstretched wings over his neighborhood, his house, the high school, the university, the great wide expanse of the Pacific Ocean. He can fly wherever he wants, and when he wakes, his limbs still feel buoyant with the sensation of flight. His body remembers the way that feels. It's muscle memory, the kind of thing you employ to remember phone-number digits on a touch screen, or how to inject yourself with insulin, or how to send a basketball swishing neatly through a net from midcourt.

Three hundred eighty-nine, three hundred ninety, three hundred ninety-one.

Walking is such laborious tedium; what sweet relief flight will be!

The backpack nestled between the Mastermind's make-shift wings contains two handwritten letters (that word *manifesto*—it chafes and offends, a bedfellow of *crazy*). The letters are twelve pages each; one is addressed to Dr. Angel, and the other is addressed to Wendy Neely. The only other item in the backpack is a granola bar that the Mastermind wants—that he needs right now this minute; he can feel his blood pressure plummeting—only it's too early for a snack. He has already planned where snack time will happen: at a bench four blocks from here.

Four blocks to go and he can have his granola bar.

Five hundred eighty-two, five hundred eighty-three, five hundred eighty-four, -five, -six, -seven, -eight.

APRIL UNDERWATER

(11:59 AM EDT)

This is one of my favorite things—having the school's pool all to myself in the quiet of the middle of the day. Ours is the only public school in town with a swimming pool. Swimmer kids from all over town sign up for Hayes High's magnet programs just for the access to this pool, which right now is shimmering in the sunlight filtering through the glass dome of the ceiling.

The dome is why it's called the Bubble, and it's where I first learned to swim.

When I was three, maybe four, my mom brought me here for these kid-mom swim classes. Maybe there were lots of other moms and kids in the class, but if there were, I don't remember them. What I remember is me and Pal Gakhar and our moms, and the memory of being here with them—here in this pool—is one of my first ever. It's also

» » »

one of the few memories I've got from the Time Before; that is, the time before that day with Lincoln Evans when all the turbo-remembering began.

I had this yellow bathing suit with a duck on the front. Pal had orange trunks and a hooded towel with dragon spikes on it. My mom wore a blue tank that tied in a knot behind her neck. I held tight to the knot and mouthed her freckled shoulder while she bounced me in the water, then we went under together and her hair swirled around her face like slow-motion seaweed and we lifted pretend tea-party cups to our lips and we laughed. That's what I remember most and best: the tiny trail of bubbles that rose from our mouths as we laughed together under the water.

Even when I was a tiny girl, I felt safe and at home in this pool.

This moment right here, too, is one of my all-time, favorite-ever things: I'm poised on the block, on the brink, and I can actually feel the pull of the water on my body, like in the pool is exactly where I belong. My toes ache with wanting in there. Sometimes at meets I get afraid of jumping the gun because the pull of the water is so strong. Crazy, but I can feel my body sluicing through the lane before the gun sounds, before my hands even break the surface. It'll be like I'm standing there on the block, watching my body as it leaves my body and dives on ahead of me into the pool.

It's never not new to me, is what I'm saying. It's never not a wonder.

I stay on the block, feeling that delicious pull until I can't stand it any longer, and then I dive in.

The sunlight has reached all the way to the bottom of the pool, where it wavers and dances around like some living, magic thing. Down here I'm weightless; down here all the things that shame me about my body—my too-wide hips, my huge feet, the angry line of acne that claws at my hairline no matter what I do—disappear, and, just for a moment, I'm perfect. Even my memory leaves me alone for a few seconds—I have never been mean; I have never faltered—and I'm free to float unburdened in a tiny, precious sliver of now.

Usually, when I'm down here, that's what I come for: that bliss. That *now.* But something about today, about that crazy dream, has me feeling a Lincoln Evans–shaped ache in my chest.

Eighteen-year-old Lincoln Evans is sitting cross-legged in a circle of light at the bottom of the pool. All around him are quarters, some drifting and some motionless, winking in the light like wishes set aflame, like we're at the bottom of a well and this is where the wishes have gone to come alive. The ripple of sunshine—the way it moves in the water— makes me think of that line in the play we read in English: *skip the light fantastic.* I imagine that this right here, this ribbony sunbeam, is the light fantastic, and somehow by skipping it Lincoln Evans has beamed himself here to be with me. For some reason, he has dressed up for this affair. He's got on wingtips and is wearing a tie that floats around his head. *Happy birthday,* he mouths, and a stream of bubbles escapes his grin. In his hand, pinkie finger lifted, he holds an imaginary teacup. I lift the imaginary teapot to his cup and fill a cup for myself and we do a little clink, like, *Cheers, haven't seen you in a decade! What's been going on?*

There's a reason why in movies people are always making out in pools and bathtubs and showers and in the rain. Water is its own kind of silk. Liquid abandon, where stuff like your overdue math homework and your countless shortcomings don't really matter. You're a part of something vital, the same essential stuff that makes up more than half of every human body. That's how things got started between me and Drew Bennett last fall. It happened one afternoon after swim practice (Thursday, October 11: it was 10/11/12, and my bathing suit was navy blue, and I was coming down with a cold, and Vice President Biden had left Delaware for the debate against Paul Ryan), when everyone else had gone. Two minutes, Coach Danforth had warned, arms full of kickboards on the way to the equipment room. Okay, I'd promised. It was something I had done a hundred times — stay after for a couple extra laps to get my muscles quieted down. That day, I hadn't noticed Drew was still there until I reached the wall and started to climb out. There he was, toweling his hair into spikes, the pool-pruned soles of his feet a stark white against the tan of his legs.

"Let's take a jump," Drew said, and cast his eyes across the empty pool toward the high dive. "Together. Just for the hell of it. Just because. Want to?"

I laughed but climbed out, self-conscious and dripping. Even though I wasn't cold, I shivered all the way to the ladder, where I followed Drew up. I was being so careful not to touch his feet, but at one point my wrist grazed the back of his heel and I could see the damp hair on my outstretched arm stand on end. He looked back, grinned, flicked water from his hair. The boys were always doing that, shaking their wet heads like dogs, and it made them look so cocky, I thought. So smug and almost mean.

I was about to climb back down — Coach would be back any second — when Drew made a half turn and reached for my arm. He pulled me up, and together we walked the plank, Drew first, his arms behind his back and me holding on to his hands. The diving board bounced slightly beneath our weight, and I almost lost balance, but Drew held on to me until we jumped, shrieking laughter that went bouncing against the high glass dome and seemed to fill the whole room with our surprise. Drew hit the water first, and I followed. Underneath I was embarrassed; my suit had shifted around and I didn't want him to see. I yanked things back into place and was swimming to the wall when Drew caught my ankle. I thought to kick him away, but instead I turned, and under the water he reached for my face and pulled me to him and kissed me as together we rose to the surface, stunned.

At least I was stunned.

Five seconds later, an oblivious Coach Danforth came whistling back into the Bubble and told us to go home already, we were burning daylight.

Outside the pool (in the halls, or the rest of the real world, in the backseat of his car not withstanding) Drew Bennett is another person. I don't even know that guy. Gina and Gavin want that guy officially out of my mind and off my radar. They're tired of hearing about that asshole, and have put an outright ban, effective immediately, on any future backseat forays. Meanwhile, I can't help it: I keep waiting to get a glimpse of Drew from underwater, where, I swear, it was this whole other story. The true, real-life, underwater story of Drew Bennett. It's a thirty-second miniseries, fraught with drama and highly charged romantic possibility. I've had it on repeat in my head for so long that it's starting to break.

This underwater tea party with Lincoln Evans, though? This is different. A memory in reverse, because this is a thing that hasn't happened to me; this is a thing that has yet to happen, or is happening now for the first time, even though this wry, wingtipped Lincoln Evans seems to know everything about me already. He's got my whole history in his pocket, I think, and before I can finish the thought, he downs his tea, reaches in his actual pocket, and produces a purple sneaker. It's faded and covered with grass stains, and there's a knot in one of the laces. I recognize the shoe as mine, but it's impossibly small. Exactly the length of my palm. I tip the shoe and out spill dozens of quarters, a shiny rain of coins.

The sight of the shoe makes me think I'm running out of air.

What are you doing here? I ask Lincoln in a rush of bubbles, hurrying.

He smiles, reaches into his pocket again, and offers me something else: another quarter? No. It's something sharp and triangular—a broken piece of glass, maybe? A shard of mirror? No, I realize as I accept Lincoln's weird gift. This thing he has handed me is a sliver of blue sky.

Then Lincoln puts his finger to his lips, like, *Shhhhhhhhh. Quiet.*

I close my eyes, thinking—hoping—Lincoln might kiss me like Drew Bennett did once, right here in this pool, only this kiss will be better because Lincoln Evans apparently knows me from the inside out.

Flip a coin: heads he'll kiss me, tails he won't.

My eyes are closed, and I've been underwater for much too long when I hear it—or feel it, really, at first: that familiar crack, and a tremor that says it's time for the next heat to dive into the pool. Only there's no other heat, this isn't a meet, and the cracks keep coming, *bam bam bam bam bam,* and when I open my eyes the quarters are gone. Lincoln Evans is gone.

When I open my eyes and look up through the water to where the sunlight is still filtering steadily through the dome, I see what I can't possibly be seeing: that rain of coins again, only this time they're falling from the ceiling. And wait: it's not quarters, but glass. Glass.

In that split second, it looks exactly like the sky is falling.

LINCOLN, THE GREAT EMANCIPATOR

(11:15 AM CDT)

Laura Echols sleeps all the way east on I-80 into Omaha. Odd and terrifying as this day has been, I'm still thrilling a little at being in a new city. God, the world is so huge. This is all anybody needs to keep on going, I think: a daily reminder of just how huge the world is, and how small we are — how small our problems are — in comparison. Don't laugh at me, either. Don't laugh. This is not me talking some sort of manufactured inspirational nonsense. This is me trying hard to tell the truth about something, and the truth is that I couldn't not be in love with the world if I tried. And I've tried, too — I've tried to feel sorry for myself; I've tried to affect a brood. I can't do it, though. It's like I'm physically incapable. Sooner or later I always get bowled over by what appears to be my genuine affection for the world. It's like I can't help it, and it doesn't even take

« « «

much. Like a song'll come on the radio, some song I haven't heard in a while or whatever, and, *bam,* there I am, taken by surprise, right back in love with my life. Music does this to me all the time. Music, and that part of the day just before the sun disappears, and cherry Twizzlers, and, most of all, freedom. Any kind of freedom at all.

I swear, freedom is completely wasted on people with actual cars and driver's licenses. I wish so hard I could just keep going and going, which is all well and good, but the Lexus is almost out of gas. The tank has been running on fumes for the last fifteen miles, so I'm relieved to be pulling into a gas station. Only I don't have any money for gas, so I have to wake Laura up.

"Laura," I say, and touch the back of her hand. Touching her has not lost its appeal.

"Hmmm?" Laura says, as if she's been underwater. She blinks in the glare of the sunlight and swipes at her eyes with the back of her hand — another gesture that makes her look like a little kid. "Where are we?"

"Omaha," I say.

"Omaha," she repeats.

"Listen, we're out of gas."

Laura rummages in her purse before I have to ask. Which is good, because the shame of having to ask is awful. She hands me a shiny gold card. "Here."

Laura curls up and closes her eyes again while I pump the gas. It makes me feel a little ill, watching the numbers climb as the tank fills with liquid gold. Jesus Christ, wanderlust is expensive. I'm amazed by it, just as I'm amazed that there's a little TV screen at eye level above the gas pump. Seriously? For real? Some talking head is going on about the weather, and then, no warning at all, the story changes to breaking news about the lockdown of schools all across the country.

For what feels like the hundredth time today, my adrenaline spikes to dangerous levels. I scan the lot of the gas station for signs of panic, but everything seems normal: A tired-looking mom-type is pumping gas into her Volvo while her kid hangs out the backseat window and whines for a slushie. A guy leans against his truck and chews gum. A bell signals the opening of the store door, which pours forth the smell of hot dogs and a forty-something couple carrying Mountain Dews and cigarettes. Just people going about their business. Just an ordinary day.

The ordinary is equal parts reassuring and ominous.

"Laura," I say. "There was this thing on that TV just now—"

"Shh, I know," Laura says quietly, like she's still half-asleep. She takes the gold card from my hand and returns it to her wallet, which I notice is fat with bills. What does a girl like this have to worry about? What could possibly be wrong in her world?

"Just keep going and I'll tell you a story."

So I keep going. East, Laura points, toward Iowa. Because this is apparently a long story.

"Start at the beginning. Don't leave anything out."

I'm merging again onto the interstate when Laura Echols

lolls her head to the side and says to me, "Lincoln Evans, do you know why I love you?"

What? Laura Echols loves me? Her words lift every hair on my arms. I'm aware that something is very wrong with this day, with the country in general, but still these words out of Laura's mouth make me feel like the world outside this car is nothing but a rumored mirage.

"You're the only one at school who doesn't know every little thing about what happened to me."

I look sideways at Laura. I mean what could be worse than what's happening right now, am I right? This must be about her grandfather. Mr. Asshole Flask-Man. Hovers like a black cloud over every single one of our drive-in movie adventures. That guy's like the plague.

"About what happened when?" I ask.

"That night," Laura says, impatient, a shift and a shaky exhale, *let's get this over with.* "That night at Rachel's. It was—before. Before you moved here. Before everything."

What is she even talking about? Which Rachel? Rachel who?

Laura sits up straight in the passenger seat and begins.

Once upon a time there was this girl, this girl Laura Echols? You'd have liked her. You'd have liked her if you were a boy, that is. Boys, man, they think Laura is great. Girls? Eh. Not so much. She's got everything, after all. Brains, that car, that stupid cello, that outrageous fucking hair. And God, she's so *nice.* WTF! She's never done anything wrong, never gotten a B, never not been perfect, never not looked perfect, blah blah blah. Whatever. The hair makes her look like a horse, some girls say, and her face is sort of horsey, too, if you really stop to look at it. *So* not a big deal, that face. Laura Echols needs to get over herself. She's — she's *cold,* you know? One of those girls who can't make friends with other girls. Like she's so above everybody else. I mean, come on, she totally had this coming. She signed up for this waaaaaaaay back in eighth grade when she got those boobs and started showing them off, like, ooh, look at me, worship at my altar, only don't touch! Oh, no. Laura Echols would neeeeeeeever let anybody touch her precious Ice Queen self.

The plan had an online code name: Horse Race. Everybody was in on it, but the party, the actual event, was at Rachel's house.

Rachel was all, *Hey Laura, why don't you come over before so we can do our hair together? We can make strawberry daiquiris! You can spend the night if you want.*

Meanwhile online it was all, *The horse is out of the gate!* Laura, of course, would never see it because she's above social media, just like she's above the whole rest of the world. Her thigh gap is only that wide because she always has that stupid cello between her legs — ha! — like she'd rather have sex with that cello than a guy.

The worst was that Laura had loved hanging out with Rachel before the party. Laura had always gotten along well enough with her classmates, but it's true, she had never really had close girlfriends — or not the kind of friendships where they'd hang out at each other's houses or whatever. She always had cello practice or youth orchestra rehearsals, and there was never really time for that kind of thing.

Rachel's kindness was as startling to Laura as the unexpected privilege of finding herself inside a house that wasn't her own—a house where the parents were gone for the whole weekend. Laura's own parents were never away. She was the sun around which they orbited, and although she knew she was lucky, the weight of that responsibility had started to make her feel hungry for a little air. Hanging out with Rachel, getting ready for a party together—it all felt new to Laura, an overdue initiation into a world that seemed to come automatically to most people. She was running out of time to make things like this count.

Rachel let her borrow a dress that scooped so low in the back that Laura could feel the ends of her hair swishing against the bottom knobs of her spine. She didn't recognize herself in the mirror and blushed at the curve of her own hips. Strange—she had always felt sure of herself, but now she wasn't sure she felt sure.

Just have another drink, said Rachel, and *vroom* went the blender all frothy with pink.

Just have another.

And another.

Playing the cello is all about precision and control. Music is not unlike math that way, and this girl Laura—this girl you would have liked, back when her life was still her own—had always excelled at both. She's good at control, and if there's one thing she's always known, it's that alcohol is not her friend. Her parents never touch it, and her grandfather's sick legacy hangs in her house like a shroud. Laura's the kind of girl who knows her facts and statistics, like that it takes at least three generations to shake the poison of addiction out of a family's bloodline. It's just that Laura never thought she had that snake in her veins. She's not the kind of girl to do something just because other people are doing it, and it's never really occurred to her to drink.

But. Three strawberry daiquiris—what's the harm in that? It's mostly fruity nothing. Mostly actual food groups. Girl stuff.

Only these daiquiris were extra-special ones, and it didn't take long for this girl Laura Echols to be completely out of it and spread out naked on Rachel's basement floor. How many people were at this party? Hundreds? The whole school? Who even knows. They all had phones, though, so even the ones who weren't there got to see everything— *everything*—online in real time. Laura walked around school for two days, confused by the looks she was getting, before she realized the pictures had even been there.

And of course by that time they were long gone.

This girl Laura Echols, who you would've liked, remembered nothing past the third daiquiri. She woke up the next morning in Rachel's canopied bed, wearing a pair of Rachel's pajamas, her mouth gauzy and crusted with sick. Later, Rachel would be praised for having taken such good care of her new best friend. She offered Gatorade and

Tylenol and rinsed the puke from Laura's hair. She drove Laura home that morning and gave Laura a sideways hug across the console of her car. *Let's do this again sometime, sweetie!*

Yeah, Laura Echols had said, her head pounding its own furious warning.

Let's.

#WHATHOPELOOKSLIKE

(12:02 PM EDT)

You know people always say stuff like you don't know how you'd handle a situation—a gun in your face, a hurricane bearing down on your house, the sky falling on your head—until you're in that situation, and I'm as shocked as anybody right now that I have not shit my pants, right here in the Lockdown Closet. I am like eerily effing calm, like even though my heart feels on six different kinds of speed, my head is full-on cool calm and collected, like I've got this feeling that we're all going to be okay. Gina has been grabbing onto my arm for so long that the circulation's cut off. Did you know that crocodiles can, like, actually close off a chamber of their heart and conserve their energy that way? I saw that shit on TV and right now that's what I am. I'm an #effingcrocodile, man. I have closed off a chamber of my heart, the one that belongs to Gina and

« « «

April and my moms. Nobody's allowed to touch that part of me, nobody's allowed to come close, so you better back off, whoever you are out there. That part of my heart is on reserve right now and it's what's going to get me out of this closet. I'm gonna get out of this closet and go to prom with Gina and April and dance until my ass falls completely off. I'm going to eat so many effing pancakes, you just don't even know. Watch.

I know the Moms are outside. They're at this church across the street with a bunch of other parents. I got one text from Mom Leslie before the airwaves got choked up and it was #allcircuitsbusy. Leslie's text said: *We love you every minute.* And you know what? I know that they do. Even if I wasn't in this effing lockdown closet, they'd be loving me so hard. I bet you Mom Resa is over at the church right now in her scrubs, holding people's hands, talking them down from their trees. God Grant Me the Serenity, and all of that. The Wisdom to Know the Difference. Not crying, because I know her, and she won't shed one tear until she's got me safe in her arms, and then it'll be Niagara. Resa is short for Theresa, and that woman, she is some kind of #bonafidesaint. Works for hospice and has learned to recognize when somebody's truly about to go. She's been there for moments like that—can you even wrap your brain around such a thing, to be there when that gate swings open? I used to think, what if she fell in? What if Mom Resa slipped through that gate?

What I want to tell her now, what I wish I could say to

her is, I'm #notabouttogo. I've got the wisdom to know the difference.

Mom Leslie, now, she'll be the one crying like to lose her head. She's got all the emotions, like me. Tenderhearted, she says we are, her and me. Which sounds nice and all but is way more true of Leslie than me, because let me tell you, I can be a real bitch sometimes and I know it.

I bet Leslie brought sandwiches to that church. I bet she's running around feeding everybody, and I bet she's all covered in paint, like she came straight from the studio. Maybe she's got Valentino out in her truck. Valentino, he's so regal, he'll go and break your heart. Here I've been sitting with no circulation in my Gina-arm and my heart chamber all cut off and I'm thinking about my moms and what's about to make me lose my shit is thinking about Valentino. How Leslie brought him home to me from the greyhound rescue when I was just ten and said, *Look at this, baby. I got you a running partner, only thing in all the world that can maybe run half as good as you.*

That dog. Has running built into his heart, just like me. His knobby old head, I can feel it in my hand, regal, regal. He's going with me to Charlottesville in the fall soon as I get out of this effing hellhole, and sweetheart, we are going to live like the #royalty we are.

Right now, though, we're all holding so still. Everybody linked. Hanging on tight. Nobody makes a sound for the longest time, and I swear I can hear everybody's heart beating, only it's like one big pulse, like one big heart going *please, please, please.* Please let this not be for real. Please let me get out of here and see the sky, my moms, my dog, the grass. My life? It's awesome and it is huge and I am lucky and also the world's biggest pain in the ass for not knowing just how lucky every minute hour second of the day. Just this morning I acted all like a bitch when Mom Resa tried to make me eat a bowl of oatmeal. Oatmeal, man! What did I even say to her? I don't know. I don't know. Some useless shit. It wasn't I love you. It wasn't thanks for everything. More like where're my headphones? Have you seen my headphones? I'll never bitch about anything ever again not ever just please get me out of here please.

There's a sound outside the door. Movement. Somebody out there is talking to us, saying he's the police. A badge appears under the door, gleaming like some promise from God. Only everybody's frozen; everybody's scared to touch it. Mr. Goodrich lets out a breath and reaches for it, slowly, slowly. His other arm, the one not reaching, is held back toward all of us, like stay, like don't move. The way you do when you're driving, you know, and you have to stop too fast and Gina or April or whoever is in the passenger seat and you reach out your arm like it's gonna save them or something. Human seat belt. Mr. Goodrich is doing #humanseatbelt, man, and it touches me. I mean I am legit moved by that gesture. What do I even know about this guy? Nothing. Except now here he is, human seat-belting his physics class plus Gina and me like he'd give his life right now for any of us, and I know—I know it, all of a sudden, without a doubt—that he would. Mr. Goodrich with his gut all hanging out over his belt, with his nasty old coffee breath, with his hair all wispy and graying and sticking up all sad on the top of his head—dude would die to save us, I shit you not.

"You're safe now, but you need to stay where you are," the officer tells us through the door. "Don't open this door until you hear my voice again."

In the dim light I can see Mr. Goodrich clutch the badge and wipe his eyes with the back of his hand. He nods, even though Officer Safety Guy can't see, then pushes the badge back through to the other side. We wait, and everybody is quiet. It's just us and the faint buzz of some radiator somewhere and people breathing and that one big heartbeat, *thud thud thud.*

"Hey, Mr. Goodrich," somebody ventures after a while. The whisper hangs there in the air, and when nothing bad happens, we all let go of our breath a little, like maybe it really is okay now to breathe.

"Yeah," Mr. Goodrich says. His voice is a little shaky.

"You got kids?"

The voice belongs to Nate Salisbury. Nate's a nice guy—I know him from track and from the rest of my whole life. He's a good runner, Nate, only he doesn't have a competitive bone in his body. Just as soon run for the hell of it, just for the good way it feels to have your lungs all full up with clean air, and hand the trophy over to some other team. Also he's got an epic thing for Gina.

"Two," Mr. Goodrich says. "But they're not kids anymore. One's about to have a kid of her own, any day now."

"So are they, like, physicists?" Nate asks.

You can sort of hear Mr. Goodrich smiling. "Nope, neither one."

It sort of seems like Mr. Goodrich wants to leave it at that, like he just can't talk about his family right this second, but you can hear it, the way he loves these grown-up kids of his. This grandkid on the way. Makes me sort of have to rearrange my picture of Mr. Goodrich in my mind, like I've got to make room for this notion that the guy's an actual person, like he's probably got a shitload of his own stuff on his mind right now.

"That's cool," Nate says. His voice is the way it always is, easygoing and warm, a little spacey. It occurs to me that he's a generous kind of guy, Nate, and man, it occurs to me also, in addition, that I just want him to keep on talking for like a hundred more hours. His voice sounds normal. Not terrified. Nate, I'm thinking, sweetheart, you could just read me the phone book right now and I would hang on to every single word like an #effinglifepreserver.

"Hey, Gina," says Nate's life-preserver voice, all cheery as can be, I'm not even lying. God, I love Nate Salisbury. He's keeping this whole physics class from going into shock.

"Yeah?" Gina whispers, like she's daring herself to talk.

"I'm gonna tell you a secret."

Everybody waits. Gina doesn't say anything, but her grip on my arm tightens.

"Are you ready?" Nate asks.

Gina can't help it; she laughs. And man, her laugh is like a miracle, one of about sixty-five thousand things I can think of right this minute that I don't want to give up on, or miss, or forget, or be deprived of, ever.

"I'm ready," Gina says.

"Okay, here it is," Nate says, pausing to make sure he's got everybody listening. "Gina, I've loved you for five—no wait, six? Yeah. Six years. A third of my life on Earth, Gina Marie Morales. You and nobody else. What do you think about that?"

Gina lets go of my arm and goes to cover her face, even though it's dark in here. I can't tell if she's laughing or crying. "I think you're crazy," she says.

"Awesome," Nate says. "Let's go to prom."

"I've already got a date."

"No, she doesn't," I say, and I am smiling. Right here in the Lockdown Closet, full-on emergency happening in my midst, #shithittingthefan all over the place, I am smiling. "Gina's officially going to prom with you, Nate, and as soon as we get out of here you and I are gonna go pick out our tuxes together."

And then I'm thinking about April again. My other date. Where's April? My heart kicks back into gear, *thud-a-dud-dud,* and I'm picturing her out there, maybe shot. Gina and Nate are whispering back and forth now, but I'm like, Shhh. Shhh.

"Gina. What about April?"

"April's fine," Gina says, holding tight again. "She has to be fine. You know she is. Think good things, okay?"

So I start thinking good things. Like us at Brandywine Creek, like us throwing a Frisbee around, falling asleep on a blanket out on the lawn with Valentino, the insides of his ears all glowing pink in the sun, pink like the inside of a shell. I think about April, and April's sister Monica, and April's mom and dad, who still go on actual dates. They are like this excellent family, man, the good kind. It's April's birthday, too. It's her birthday, so then my mind starts wrapping around all this stuff April told me and Gina once—the way her effed-up mind works, she knows this stuff, man, it is nuts—about how she heard somewhere that if you die on your birthday, it means you've come full circle, like you've lived a full and perfect life, even if your life was short. That is one morbid-ass way to think, I told April then, but she was all, No, man, think about it, Ingrid Bergman! William Shakespeare! George Washington Carver! They all died on their birthdays, and those were some perfect lives right there, you can't say they weren't.

Only, okay. I am not letting that shit happen to April. I am not. I'm keeping her with me right here, right now. Brandywine Creek. Windows rolled down, the Sky Drops blaring, everybody's fine, everybody's whole, everybody's heart's alive and beating.

When Mr. Goodrich speaks again, his voice is different from his teaching-physics voice. It is the kind of voice the Moms use when I've had a bad day, or when the news isn't good, or when they're caught off guard by whatever the world has decided to hand us.

"You know," Mr. Goodrich says, "people might say to you kids that your generation is spoiled. Entitled. Too wrapped up in yourselves."

The collective heartbeat goes *thud thud, please please.* Our palms are sweaty from hanging on so tight to each other. Mr. Goodrich swallows and goes on. "I heard this stuff too, you know, that my friends—my generation—that we didn't know hardship because we weren't drafted. Because what we knew of war came to us from the TV, right? A televised drama happening half a world away in a desert we couldn't imagine if we tried."

Mr. Goodrich stops. I don't want him to cry, I don't want him to lose it, because he's supposed to be in charge of this ship and if he goes down, we all go down with him.

"But this thing," Mr. Goodrich says. "I mean, what is this? Nobody can tell me that you kids aren't fighting a war all your own. Jesus Christ, nobody can tell me that."

PHOEBE AND (ANGEL)A

(7:15 AM MDT)

Phoebe must have blacked out for a second, because when she blinks her eyes, she sees, blurred before her in a kind of wavy whoosh, her mother. Her mother and Angela are all crowded up in her face, and her mom is holding something to her lips. Something fizzy and cold. Sprite.

Phoebe's eyes fill with tears. Here is her mother, administering Sprite and pressing a cold washcloth to her forehead. Somehow she still deserves her mother's love. It's unimaginable.

"Mom," Phoebe begins, but her voice gets stuck in her throat. How long has it been since she has spoken to another human being out loud? A million years, seems like. A billion.

» » »

"Baby, don't try to talk. Just sip on this."

The Disney princesses pirouette around the ceiling. Taylor Lautner grins from the mirror. The bathroom tilts on its axis.

"Nebraska," Angela says, pushing her glasses up the bridge of her nose in a gesture so familiar to Phoebe that once again she chokes on a sob.

"You were talking about Nebraska, and then you were out."

Phoebe closes her eyes and lets the tears swim.

"Phoebe," the girls' mother says. "Here. Come here."

The girls' mother's name is Christina. For a while there, Phoebe and Angela went through a phase when they called her Christina instead of Mom. They thought they were being hilarious until one day when Phoebe was like, Hey, Christina, what's for dinner? And Christina—their mother, who was standing at the stove in her nurse's scrubs and clogs, doing something wholesome with chicken after a double shift—surprised them by quietly turning off the burner, dumping the contents of dinner into the trash, and turning to face her daughters, who were so stunned that they did a horrible thing: they laughed.

"Nothing," she had said, calm as anything. "Nothing's for dinner, that's what."

And then she—Christina—had surprised the sisters even more by blinking back tears. "You know, you two girls are the only people in this entire world who can call me Mom. Now that might seem stupid to you, but it matters to me, okay? It matters. Fix your own goddamn dinner, how about."

Now Christina lowers the lid on the toilet and sits down. She holds Phoebe's head in her lap, strokes her hair, and says, "Phoebe, Phoebe, Phoebe. What is going on with you? What?"

Christina is wrapped in a depressing green bathrobe. Her feet are bare, and Phoebe notices that her toenails are unpainted — they look thick and yellow and in need of a trim. When did her mother stop painting her nails? It was a thing they used to do together, the three of them. Christina's hair, usually vibrant, hangs limp around her shoulders. She looks so small and broken, she could be a teenage girl. She could be one of her own kids. This kid. The one on the bathroom floor.

Phoebe buries her face in the green bathrobe and manages to say, "Mom. There's this — this bad thing. I'm sorry."

Phoebe's thinking now about this trick she and Angela used to be able to do. Phoebe would close her eyes and say, Okay, I'm thinking of a movie. What is it? And Angela would squeeze her eyes shut too, and they'd try as hard as they could to pass the thought between them. They'd do it with movies, songs, books, people at school. It was like their own private ESP. They could communicate without talking. They could shine, like in *The Shining*.

Phoebe lifts her eyes to her sister. Please, she is saying in her mind, please hold on to me. Please, Angela, get me off this floor and back into the world.

Angela goes to her sister and holds on. Here are the three of them in this sad heap, being spied on by the Disney princesses. Phoebe wants to close her eyes, just for a second. Just for a second she wants to be held like this, just one minute, please just let this one tiny minute pass without anything bad happening in it.

One minute.

One minute was long enough for a gap-toothed avatar to pop up on Phoebe's screen and change her life forever. The avatar had a voice on the phone, too: rich, caramel-flavored. Whose voice was that? Whose? Every day she strains her ears, yearning to catch the specific, familiar vibration of it. This caramel-flavored voice does not belong to anyone at her school. It does not belong to the guy behind the counter at the drugstore, or to the driver of the bus, or to the mailman, or the FedEx delivery guy, or the stranger boy she passes on the sidewalk (she makes it look like an accident, but bumps right into his shoulder, just to hear him say sorry—and no, that's not the voice, either). She has to get very, very quiet, the better to listen for the caramel-flavored voice, which can only belong to those freckles, that spiky hair, the vocal cords of one Dylan Fisher, who may not have shown up when he said he would, but who (still, still, still) is real until proven otherwise.

One minute.

Long enough to fall for a voice.

Or to win or lose a soccer game.

Did you see me after school today? I saw you in your green sweater, watched you walk across the field, but didn't feel like the moment was right.

One minute.

Long enough to realize she'd been had, that she was nothing more than the butt of somebody's joke.

I have never felt like this about anyone before.

I have never felt like this about anyone before.

Long enough to chop off her hair.

Long enough, say, for a tornado to rip an entire house from the ground. Or a bomb to go off, or a shot to ring out, and for nobody to be the same, ever again.

Phoebe knows she can't do it. She can't go through with the Plan. Some part of her is broken, unfixably broken, but the fixing is not going to come this way.

"Phoebe, take another drink. You're staying home today."

Christina moves to disentangle herself from her daughters. Phoebe knows that her mother is once again running late, and that she can't afford to miss any more work. How much, Phoebe wonders, has she cost her parents? The thought topples her with a fresh wave of nausea and remorse.

"I need to get in the shower," Christina says, straightening up. "Angela, stay with your sister for a minute. I'll be right back."

Angela stays. "Here," she says, reaching out her hand. "I'll pull you up."

And here's the weird thing. Phoebe and Angela can read

each other's minds and almost hear each other's thoughts, but they've never been the touchy-feely kind of siblings. This lopsided embrace-thing they've just done on the bathroom floor? Not at all the way they usually roll. They love each other, but they're not in the habit of saying so out loud. They're not in the habit of hugging.

So it's a very unusual sort of thing when Angela helps her sister rise to her feet and keeps her hands on Phoebe's shoulders as she steers her around to face the mirror. It's unusual for them to stand so close to each other and stare at their reflections like this.

"Phoebe, talk to me," Angela says to the Phoebe in the glass. "Start talking, starting now."

Phoebe looks hard at herself, at her reflected image next to Angela's. There was a time—as in, most of their lives—when they looked so much alike: same thick, ash-blond hair, same wide-set eyes and freckles. When they were little, people would always ask their mother, Are they twins? They may as well be, their mother would always answer, sounding exasperated but mostly happy, rounding the corner with her grocery cart, both girls bobbing around illegally in the basket with the juice and bread and milk. Once, Phoebe bit a hole into a package of sausage—just for the good way it felt to gnaw into that plastic and watch the pink meat splurt out, just because it would be so funny to dare Angela to eat some (which, obedient little sister that she was, Angela did). Their mother worried that her girls would get sick and die of E. coli, but they didn't. They were fine.

They have always been fine.

People wouldn't think they were twins now, Phoebe knows. In the mirror, she looks older than her sister by about a lifetime. The skin beneath her eyes looks dark and papery, like she could be somebody's teacher or grandmother. Angela's skin glows, but Phoebe's is grayish and drawn. Her freckles have faded into smudges that make her face look dirty.

"You look scary," Angela says.

And then she stares at Phoebe's reflection some more and says, "You look like somebody I don't even know."

SANDRA HESLIP, TEACHER FIRST AND FOREMOST

(11:08 AM CDT)

Back there in the classroom, when I was sitting at a desk opposite the desk where Adrian George was sitting, I noticed for the first time that he has one brown eye and one green.

"There's a name for that, isn't there?" I asked. The word I wanted blipped briefly on my mental radar, then escaped.

"Heterochromia," Adrian said.

"Right," I said, although that wasn't the word I was thinking of. The word floating around in my head was *hyperthymesia,* a totally unrelated thing I'd heard about on 60 *Minutes.* It's where you can remember even the smallest details of all the days of your life. Can you even imagine? If pressed, I think I'd choose death over that.

"Heterochromia," I repeated. "Right. Doesn't David Bowie have that?"

« « «

Adrian grinned, apparently surprised that I knew who David Bowie was, even though who was the ancient one in the room? I swear, sometimes I think my students truly believe they invented the world and everything in it. Sarcasm, the Internet, David Bowie — you name it, they thought of it first. Try convincing them that Honors English is worthwhile.

"No," Adrian said. "Common misconception. Christopher Walken's got it, though. He's the guy —"

"I know who Christopher Walken is."

Adrian slouched back in his seat, hands shoved into his pockets. In his earlobes he wore those things — what are they called? Those things that stretch your lobes into holes big enough to toss grapes through. Or plums, even. I could've gotten smallish plums through Adrian George's earlobes. I didn't want to stare, but why else would you do such a thing, if you didn't want people to stare? I almost couldn't look. It was fascinating, but also made me feel woozy and off-balance, seized by an involuntary twinge in my groin, arousal and disgust competing for attention.

"How long did that take?" I asked, touching my own lobes. Tiny pearl studs I wore every day, a long-ago anniversary present from Eric. I thought of the me who used to go to all those raves, how her favorite earrings were these long silver fish bones that glinted in the light and swished against her neck as she danced.

Adrian shrugged. "Coupla years."

"Wow. That's a pretty serious commitment."

"Yeah."

"What else are you committed to, Adrian? Anything?"

"Plenty of things," Adrian replied, not missing a beat.

I crossed my arms across my chest and sat back. "Such as."

Adrian chewed his lip and narrowed his heterochromatic eyes. When he didn't answer, I returned my gaze to his stretched lobes.

"What happens if you change your mind?" I asked.

Adrian smirked. "I'm not going to change my mind. This is it. This is who I am."

And here's the thing: when Adrian said it, he made it sound absolutely true. That's the other thing about my students: they walk around like they've got it all figured out, like nothing fazes them.

"So who are *you,* Ms. Heslip?"

Adrian's question burned. I could have probably gotten him thrown out of school for talking to me like that, for looking at me the way he did. What would he care, though, if he got thrown out? Only a handful of weeks left to go, and he's been biding his time for months. He would remain absolutely unfazed. And who am I, anyway? Ah, it's a good question, one I ask myself daily.

I'm a teacher; that's who I am, first and foremost. That's what I say to myself when I need reminding. *Teacher daughter sister friend.* I also used to be a wife, once upon a time, and once upon a time, for a precious and heartbreaking couple of hours, I was also a mother. The baby had a name, a cap of dark hair, ten perfect fingers and toes, and a heart beating on the outside of his body. He was born in the spring and, had he lived, would be turning eighteen today.

Today.

All morning long I've waited to hear from Eric, who always touches base on this day, to say hello and *I remember,* to acknowledge our shared history. It's a thing I dread and also cling to with everything I've got, Eric's call, which in recent years has turned into a text: *Hello. Hope you're doing well.* Our boy would be eighteen today. All school year long I've been looking at the senior boys in my class, the way they're growing into their long limbs, the way their huge white athletic shoes look like boats, the way they flick their hair from their eyes and look away when the girls steal glances at them. Maybe he would have looked like that, I've thought. Or that or that or that. Maybe a hallway littered with hockey gear and soccer cleats packed with dried mud and a backpack spilling over with paintbrushes and sketch-books and novels, Tolkien and Kerouac and Vonnegut, the usual suspects. Maybe there would be marks penciled in a doorway somewhere in the house — a chart to measure how much the boy had grown over the years. Maybe by now he would be tall like his dad, taller than I am by a foot. Maybe he would have Eric's laugh, or my dimples, or — Jesus God — earlobes stretched all to hell and an eyebrow pierced into a permanent smirky arch by a tiny metal barbell.

"I'm your teacher," I said to Adrian George, who could be my son. This is what I tell myself about all my students when they're getting on my nerves, when everything seems in ruins: *This is somebody's daughter. This is somebody's son.* "I'm your teacher, Adrian, and it's my job to help you."

Adrian laughed at this and shifted in his seat. "Ms. Heslip, man, I appreciate that and everything, but I don't really need your help. Help somebody who needs help, do you know what I'm saying?"

I stared at Adrian, willing him to go on.

"Look," Adrian said. "I know I shouldn't have been shit-ting around with you the way I did the other day. I was just—"

"Watch your mouth," I warned, a tired reflex. "Have some respect."

Adrian sighed. "Sorry. My apologies. Anyway, about the other day. I was just seeing if you were paying attention, is all. I just wanted to get your attention. It worked, right? I mean, here we are."

Adrian George, prophet of the ages. How smart is this smart-assed boy? We all want attention. Every single one of us. We're all starved for it, and anyone who says they're not is a liar. The root of all evil? I don't think it's money, like the saying goes. I think maybe the *actual* root of all evil is the constant need for attention on the part of every single human being on the planet, myself included. We are all just bottomless pits of need.

"You have my attention, Adrian. Now why don't you tell me what I've been missing?"

Adrian slouched again in his chair and shook his head

wearily, like he'd suddenly decided that it was no use, that whatever he wanted to tell me wasn't going to register with me at all.

"I'm waiting."

"Listen, Ms. Heslip. I love your class. I guess that's what I really should be telling you, what I was really trying to say. That's all. Just, you know, thank you."

In spite of everything, Adrian's words made tears start behind my eyes. But I didn't want to lose him; I couldn't lose him now.

"Adrian. Who is it? Who needs my help? Some friend of yours?"

"Ha," Adrian said, a word like a slap. "You've never met any of my friends, okay?"

My mind shuffled through my students like so many cards. Hope and innocence smiling from the pages of the yearbook, senior quotes borrowed from pop songs. Just yesterday I was in the teachers' lounge looking at the yearbook, newly minted and not yet distributed to the students. I wondered that a thing like this should even matter anymore. A yearbook! It's a relic from a bygone era. I imagined that it would apply to my students about as much as an abacus might, or a rotary phone. A stack of shrink-wrapped yearbooks sat atop the table in the lounge, and while nobody was looking I unwrapped the stack and spent an entire free period poring over the pages, imagining futures for my kids. I know a teacher shouldn't pick favorites, but I have mine, and my heart breaks for him just about daily.

This kid Lincoln Evans, he's been moved around a bunch of times, one of those kids who don't seem to have roots put down anywhere. One of those kids who seem impossible to reach. Here's a kid who has so much to be mad about, so much to resent, and still he goes around with this look of stupid wonder on his face. And he's smart. Lincoln Evans is an English teacher's dream, only his grades would never tell you that. In the yearbook where his photograph should be, there's a generic black-and-white silhouette and the words MISSING IN ACTION. At the end of the seniors section, his name appears on a list of other MIAs; CAMERA-SHY SENIORS, it says. If you flip to the index in the back (Evans, Lincoln: p. 116), you'll be redirected to a blurry photo of the French club. Only the top of Lincoln's head is visible in the picture, the only yearbook proof that he was ever part of this graduating class.

"Lincoln Evans," I said to Adrian. "Do you know Lincoln?"

"Sure. Lincoln's cool. He wasn't even there that night. It all happened before he moved here."

That night.

"What night?"

"Rachel's party. It was forever ago. Last year."

I nodded and watched Adrian's face as he watched mine, trying to figure out how much I knew. I knew nothing, of course, and worried that my ignorance would cost me, that something bad was my fault.

"You know Laura, right?"

Laura Echols. Yes. People talk about her like she's a lightbulb: *Bright, bright, bright.* To me, though, she's more like a distant star, a remote planet. Faraway and unreachable. Sometimes I catch her looking at Lincoln, and just for a second I can see the two of them—my pair of bright, unreachable planets—orbiting each other, watchful. There's something there.

"So you know what happened to her at Rachel's, right? Last year?"

I shook my head no. It has always been my policy not to concern myself with what goes on with my students outside of the classroom. If I did, I don't think I'd ever get out of bed in the morning. My boy, Eric's and mine. Maybe he would be a soccer star or an academic wonder or an art protégé—but it could just as easily have gone another way. Nights I can't sleep, I am haunted by the endless ways the world is fraught with peril for any child: freak accidents, drowning, leukemia. Or worse, the ways children can turn on each other. Turn against the world, against themselves.

Maybe he would not be turning eighteen today after all. He might not have made it past five, or twelve, or fifteen. In my mind the Fates aren't wizened hags, as literature would have us imagine them. In my mind, their faces are young and smug. The one with the scissors is the meanest, most beautiful one of all. She wears tight jeans and a slick of fruity lip gloss and keeps a list of all your failures hidden in her bra. Item 82B: *Melissa Decker's desk is covered in zit cream. You know anything about that, Sandy?*

The one with the scissors is you. The thing she cuts is you, too.

There in the classroom, opposite Adrian George, I made a mental note to use that as an essay question for next year's *Odyssey* unit: *Were Penelope's suitors brought low because it had been decided by the Moirai when they were born, or did their ultimate fate come in direct proportion to their wicked deeds? Discuss. Be sure to cite concrete examples whenever possible.*

Adrian George, leaning forward on his knees, was still talking.

"Big party, Laura's passed out, pictures all over the place, shit goes viral . . . you're saying you really don't know about any of this?"

How long had Adrian been confiding these things? What else did I miss? Was this the beginning of the story, or had we reached the end?

"No," I said, snapping back, feeling the weight of what he was saying. "I didn't know about any of that."

"The whole world knows, but not you," Adrian said. "Huh."

I could see Adrian's interest waning before my eyes. He started to gather up his stuff—his bag, a set of keys attached to a chain jangling from his pants, that book with the hollow-eyed, unjustly accused guy staring out from the front.

"Adrian, wait."

Adrian looked at me with something like pity. "It's a

little late," he said. "A little late for all this talk, don't you think?"

There was an instant when I almost told him everything. I have never spoken a word about my boy to anyone at this school — not my fellow teachers, certainly not a student, not a single person with ears to hear — but there I was, about to spill the story to Adrian George, who could be my son. Just as Lincoln Evans could, or Bruce Franklin, or any boy in any high school in America who might wake up some morning so wounded and full of sorrow that he feels the need to spell out his rage with gunfire.

Instead, I told Adrian what I hoped was — is — the truth.

"It's never too late. Is it?"

That was twenty minutes ago. Past tense.

Too late.

THE FALL OF THE MASTERMIND

(8:43 AM PDT)

The Mastermind is sitting on a bench, eating a granola bar. He chews each bite thoroughly before swallowing and wishes he had brought something to drink. His throat is too dry, and he worries he might choke. Not long ago, he choked on his own saliva — he was just swallowing like normal, but his throat caught on something and seized up — and was barely able to recover himself. He was alone in the house, and when it became clear that there was no breath going anywhere, that he was seeing flashes of light behind his eyes, he ran through the front door and flailed his arms at the guy mowing the lawn next door. The guy was shorter than the Mastermind but was able in an instant to step behind him and circle his arms around the Mastermind's middle and squeeze, four practiced thrusts. The whole time

« « «

the lawn-mower guy was saying something in Spanish, fast, but the Mastermind missed most of it. The air came back, the world zoomed once again into focus, and just like that, he was fine again. Embarrassed. He was embarrassed that the man had put his arms around him like that; he was embarrassed that he had lost control so easily, that he had panicked when he knows how important it is to always, always stay calm.

Here's the other thing that so haunted the Mastermind about the choking episode: the grasping, involuntary desperation with which he struggled to get his breath—his life—back. That certainly came as a surprise. He should learn better control of his own body, he thought at the time.

Now he is practicing that control. The chewing calms him. Everything is still going according to plan, although his wings are bothering him a little. They are heavy and awkward, and they still smell faintly of superglue. The Mastermind shifts on the bench and watches as a bus wheezes to a stop in front of him and releases several passengers, including a man in a wheelchair who is lowered to the curb by some sort of electronic device. The driver has come around to help the man, who shakes his hand and thanks him.

"Have a good day, now," the driver says.

"Most days are good," the man in the wheelchair replies, and for some reason this gives the Mastermind a pang in his chest. How could this guy think any days were good? He's missing a leg, and he's gaunt, sickly looking. The

Mastermind frowns at his granola bar as the bus lumbers away from the curb. He doesn't want to stare.

"Hey. Wanna trade?"

The Mastermind looks up, startled. He thinks the wheelchair guy must be talking about his granola bar, but no. The guy's pointing at his wings.

"My chair for your wings. How about it? Even trade?"

The guy chuckles amiably at his own joke, but the Mastermind looks down, ashamed. The back of his neck is prickly with heat; the day is growing warmer. If he wants to stay on schedule, he needs to leave now — he needs to leave two minutes ago — but something about the man in the chair has unnerved him, and he finds himself rooted to the spot.

"Where you flying to, son?" the man asks. His eyes are a watery blue, and on his right arm, the one poised over the chair's controls, he has a faded tattoo: a pair of outstretched wings not unlike the ones bound to the Mastermind's back. Beneath the tattooed wings, in curly script, is a girl's name.

The Mastermind squints at the man. "I don't know," he answers. "Where would you go?"

"If I could fly?"

The Mastermind nods.

The man laughs and runs a hand over his face. "I expect it wouldn't much matter where I went to. The flying itself would be thrill enough, I expect."

Thrill enough.

"Who's Lorna?" the Mastermind asks, eyeing the man's

tattoo. The question is out of his mouth before he can stop it.

"Lorna's my angel," the man says. "My little girl."

The Mastermind squints again in the sun, which has risen fully and is now a hot, white orb in the sky, melting everything. There are so many different kinds of angels, he thinks. It could mean so many different things. He's really hot now. It's time to go.

"Angel's my last name," the Mastermind confesses after a beat. He hopes that this will somehow prompt the man to tell him more about Lorna. A daughter, the Mastermind thinks. She has to be a daughter. He has particular vested interest, the Mastermind does, in relationships between parents and their children. *How come Lorna's on your arm but not standing right here right now?* He wants to ask but doesn't. Instead he says it again. "Yeah, Angel. It's my last name."

"Is it, now?" the wheelchair man says. "Well, what a coincidence."

The Mastermind does not wish to be having this conversation. He wishes to go back and delete the moment when he accidentally contributed his part, so he starts a low hum in his throat and dares himself to stare at the sun. When he can't look any longer, when the hum seems finally to be erasing all other sounds, he closes his eyes. Everything swims in cool and astonishing green. There. He still knows how to get to this quiet place.

"You know what they say about coincidences, right?"

This wheelchair man, he will not stop talking. His voice has cut through the hum and the green and is growing steadily louder, as if it's being boomed through a megaphone the size of a truck. "They say that coincidences are God's way of keeping anonymous. Now isn't that something?"

Oh, how this needles at the Mastermind's skin, a fine, shocking sensation that pricks at his epidermis and burrows all the way through to the subcutaneous layer, where the heat of his body is rising. "Remaining," he corrects.

"Beg pardon?"

"*Remaining* anonymous. And 'they' didn't say that. Albert Einstein did." The Mastermind has started to perspire, and worries that the wheelchair man can sense the change that is happening in his body.

"Ah," says the wheelchair man, grinning. "Albert Einstein was a genius."

"He was also an atheist," says the Mastermind, eyes back on the sun. It is time to go. It is time to go. It is time to go go go go go go *hummmm.*

"Well. I do like a good coincidence every now and again. Always feels — fortuitous."

The word seems strange, coming from the wheelchair man. The Mastermind is starting to wonder if maybe the man isn't real. Maybe he never got off that bus; maybe he's just a figment of the Mastermind's own warped and sleep-deprived imagination — a weird manifestation of his own fight-or-flight response to the events he has planned for so long and, just this morning, just now, set in motion.

Just like that, his quiet place is gone.

Fight or flight: the Mastermind knows exactly what that means. He can close his eyes and envision the way it looks in his brain and how it will show up in his body—in his pupils, say, which are dilating now. He knows that the response begins in the amygdala, triggers the hypothalamus, and hits the adrenal gland, which will then rev up the production of epinephrine, which will in turn produce cortisol, which is the thing that will make his heart beat faster, and will shut down his immune system, and will make him, officially, afraid.

This is what being afraid looks like, the Mastermind thinks. And he thinks, as it is happening to him, as his blood quickens in his veins, little highways he can see as on a map from up above, where he can hover above himself like that, outside looking in: *I am afraid.*

FRIDAY, APRIL 6, 2007

(APRIL'S MENTAL MOVIE REEL,
FRAME ONE)

"Fortuitous," **Ms. Gregory says, overenunciating, hissing** on the *s*.

It's sixth grade, the year of Gina's broken ankle. The year of hating Leona Reece. The year of that one spelling bee, which has come down to me and Pal Gakhar. Pal took the prize in elementary school, but that was just practice. Now we're in middle school and eligible for the citywide bee and this is for real and here we are: just me and Pal. The silence in the room buzzes. Somebody coughs, and as someone else stifles a giggle, a third voice goes *shhhhhhh*.

"Fortuitous," Ms. Gregory says again, peering at me over the half-moons of her glasses.

My palms are prickly and damp. I know this word, I know it, but Pal is making me nervous. Out of the corner of my eye I can see him shaping his mouth around the

« « «

syllables. If I get it wrong, the word will volley back to him, and he will do that thing where he uses the pointer finger of his right hand to trace invisible letters on the palm of his left. Then he'll ask for the etymology and to hear the word used in a sentence, even though he already knows the origin and could use *fortuitous* in a sentence right now, as in, *How fortuitous that I've just been given such an easy word.*

"*Fortuitous,*" I repeat. "*F-o-r-t . . .*"

The word hovers at the edge of my line of vision, just out of reach. In a front-row desk, just feet away from me, Nate Salisbury is busy drawing something in his notebook. Nate is the best artist in the room, but he doesn't seem to know it or care. It's just this thing he does. Now, hearing me pause, Nate stops his pencil and looks up, waiting. He smiles and something loosens in my chest. Behind him, two rows back, Gavin is sleeping, a line of drool connecting his cheek to the desk. A row over from Gavin, Gina is glaring at me. She knows I know this word. Her eyes say, *What's your problem? Girl, hurry up!*

Just like everybody else, Nate and Gina want me to win, not necessarily because I'm their friend but because it would be interesting—an unexpected development, a surprise—if somebody other than Pal or Izzy Goff went on to the city-wide bee. They are excited about it the same way we all get excited if there's a storm or a fire drill in the middle of the day: here is a departure from the predictable norm.

Next to me, Pal shifts his weight from one foot to the other. He smells like he always does: spicy-warm and close, like an overheated room. And, God, he's so skinny. His khaki pants, cinched at the waist with a belt, are too short, missing the tops of his shoes by a couple of inches. Embarrassing. But his eyelashes are thick and long and make me think of deer. It's weird, but Pal's lashes, they stir something in me — something that makes me feel excited but also sick, like I'm waiting in line for a roller coaster. Once, I sat behind Pal and reached out to touch his hair — glossy, thick, dark. So much hair he didn't even feel the brush of my fingertips. Excited, queasy, ashamed, thrilled: the roller-coaster wait, the sudden urge to pee.

Pal glances at me sideways, then looks away. Tiny beads of sweat have appeared on his upper lip, where he already has a line of downy dark hair. I think of way back when, swim lessons at the Bubble: even as a little kid in the pool with his mom, Pal's back was covered in fine black hair that pointed into a V at his waist. We would sit on the side of the pool together, shivering, me in my yellow duck bathing suit, Pal in his orange trunks and strange fur, our moms bobbing like buoys in the water before us, holding on to us by our knees.

Pal knows this word. I know he knows.

"O," I say, even though I know it's a *u*. "O-t-o-u-s. *Fortuitous.*"

Ms. Gregory blinks at me, even though we both understand there's no going back. I stare right back at her. Nate flops his head on his desk and sighs, air going out of a tire.

"That is incorrect," Ms. Gregory says. I start to head back to my desk, but she stops me, holding up a hand to remind me that I'm not out until Pal spells the word correctly, which of course he does, quickly, without even asking for the language of origin. I look from Pal to Ms. Gregory as she issues Pal the final word, the one that will determine the winner.

"*Schadenfreude,*" Pal repeats, voice cracking on the third syllable. I watch as he swallows the word and traces it on his palm. In my head it appears clear as day: *schadenfreude.* Noun. A combination of the German words for damage and joy. A word for which there is no English equivalent, at least not where language is concerned. There's a moment when I worry that Pal doesn't know it. I can almost see his mind tripping over that *eu:* which way does it go? I try to will it silently into his ear, *eu, eu.*

"*Schadenfreude,*" Pal says again, and now my heart is racing. I can't look at him, so I concentrate on the floor, flecked with a pattern that makes my eyes swim if I look at it in just the right way. I imagine myself underwater as Pal delivers each of the letters in the proper order, *e* before the *u.* When he's finished, he says the word aloud again, a rush of sounds, a wash of relief. My eyes are stinging now from all that staring at the carpet.

"That is correct," Ms. Gregory says, and when I lift my eyes to her voice, I see it's me she's looking at, not Pal, not the winner. She gives me an apologetic grin and nods her permission for me to return to my seat.

"Can you spell *stupid*?" Gina whispers as I make my way to my desk. "What just happened, April?"

The walk to my desk is miles and miles long. I have to pass Leona Reece. It has been almost three months since we invited her to Gina's birthday slumber party, where we waited until she was asleep, submerged her limp hand in a bowl of warm water, and watched, stifling our laughter, as the pee leaked from her body all over her sleeping bag. Plain, stained, a flimsy gross brown thing borrowed from her Boy-Scout brother; like so much about Leona, her sleeping bag was all wrong. It wasn't like the furred, fluffy, jewel-colored bags that Ailynn Leonard and Emma Davidson had, and that Gina and I coveted. Three months ago, we wanted everything those girls had. We wanted to *be* them, so when they dared us to trick Leona like that, we did it without thinking.

Only we didn't know then that the trick was also on us, that the slumber party was the beginning and the end, something Ailynn and Emma probably dared themselves to do, just for fun. We didn't know then that Leona would finish out the year and switch in the fall to the Montessori middle school, that we wouldn't see her again until ninth grade at Hayes High, where we would barely recognize her.

Now Ailynn's and Emma's glossy heads are locked together in a whisper across the room. I can't look at them, the way Leona can't look at me when I brush past. How hard would it be to apologize? For weeks, the apology has been caught in my throat, where it will stay lodged for years.

Pal is still standing in front of the room, scrawny arms dangling at his sides like he doesn't know what to do with them.

"Congratulations," Ms. Gregory says, rising to face the rest of us. "Class, let's give Pallav a round of applause."

Nate Salisbury gets to his feet and starts to clap, and we all join in, and I look right at Pal. I even give him a thumbs-up and mouth the words *good job*. For the longest time he just stands there looking terrified.

Finally, after what feels like forever, he smiles at me.

THE FORUM, ANY GIVEN DAY

Maine January 29, 2013, at 2:16 am **VERMONT** AND 13 OTHERS LIKE THIS

I. Am. Completely. Alone.

« « «

LINCOLN ON THE BORDER

(TOO LATE, OR RIGHT ON TIME CDT)

THE PEOPLE OF IOWA WELCOME YOU, says the sign. Underneath that part there's an image of a sun rising over a hill. IOWA: FIELDS OF OPPORTUNITIES. I'll take it. Gimme some fields, man. Sign me up! Right now, though, it's not fields. It's the Missouri River, rushing along beneath us, mirroring the sun. A thousand beams of light, sparkling on the surface of the water. *The light fantastic.* That's what it looks like, and here we are, skipping it, crossing over. I'm holding my breath—an involuntary thing I do whenever I cross bridges or walk in cemeteries. My dad taught me that when I was little, before he made like that telephone-man-slash-dad in the play and *skipped the light fantastic out of town* and then—poof, good-bye—out of the world altogether. Dude! I should have been Tom Wingfield. I'd have been a good one, getting all spellbound and moved just driving

» » »

some brokenhearted girl's Lexus across a bridge. Writing poems on shoe boxes. Ms. Heslip should have picked me to do Tom.

Laura stirs as we rumble across the bridge. I'm relieved to see she's alive. She's gotten all narcoleptic on me, falling immediately into these insta-deep sleeps, like she's been drugged or like this is the first time she's slept in weeks. Either scenario seems plausible, given what she has just told me about the party at Rachel's and what happened there and how she will never be the same, not ever. I've worried more than once that she is on actual drugs; I mean, if she's carrying around a flask and a handgun in her purse, who's to say she doesn't have a bunch of illegal narcotics in there, too? And we've just crossed a state line, which for some reason seems to up the danger ante, like now I'm not just Laura Echols's chauffeur but I'm all of a sudden also her *accomplice,* which, okay, thanks, but since when did I sign up for this?

Back there, when we crossed the state line, I beeped the horn. *Bee-bee-be-beep-beep, beep-beep.* Another thing my dad used to do. The guy ghosts around after me all day long, I swear he does. I swear he's been in this Lexus with me all day, sitting in the backseat in his business suit, flipping quarters: *Heads or tails, Lincoln? You choose.* I didn't have the Iowa quarter. That one hadn't been released yet. I wonder if April Donovan has it, or if she's ever been to Iowa, or if she's even still alive. I mean, so yeah, chances are she's fine and she's eighteen or whatever, but what if she didn't make it that far? There are no guarantees. I hope she's fine, though. I do. I liked April. *April,* I say, talking to her in my head like a freak. *I'm in Iowa!*

"Welcome to Iowa," I say to Laura, nudging her. "I need a bathroom."

Laura nods, dazed.

"Do you want anything? Are you hungry? Want something to drink?"

Laura shakes her head. "I'll wait here." She squints at the squat Iowa Welcome Center building and opens her mouth to say something, but catches herself, starting over. "Hurry up, okay?"

I make sure to pocket the keys. It takes forever to pee, like I can't stop going, and I worry that every second I'm in the bathroom is a chance for Laura to make her escape. She could just walk up to the highway and park herself in front of an oncoming eighteen-wheeler. I can see it so clearly: Laura, calm as ever, smiling serenely as the *whoosh* of the passing traffic lifts her hair and sends it swirling around her head. I pee for what feels like a thousand years, wash my hands with no soap, dry them on my jeans as I jog back to the Lexus, where Laura is — thank you, God — still slouched in the passenger seat, gazing blankly out the window.

"Let's take a walk," she says, just as I'm sliding back behind the wheel.

I look around. "Now?"

"Yeah, now." Laura's out of the car, walking like she

knows where she's going. I'm starting to think this is bullshit, this business of just puppy-dogging around after a girl like this, trying to save her from herself. What am I doing in Iowa?

"Wait," I say, a useless delivery to the wind. Laura Echols waits for no man. I jog to keep up, and Laura tells me that we're going to go across the bridge, even though didn't we just do that? Jesus, what a mess.

"The pedestrian bridge," Laura clarifies. "There's something I want to show you."

We walk for a while in silence. It's clear that Laura has been to Council Bluffs before; she knows her way along the river. She smiles at strangers as we pass, even says hello, like there's nothing at all wrong with her, like we're not out here running from something. I still haven't figured out what we're running from, or toward. With most people it's usually one or the other or both. That much I've figured out. Here's a concept: enjoy where you are for a second. Pay attention to the air filling up your lungs, and just be still and shut up. This is becoming a thing I want to scream to everybody — to this guy passing us, for instance. He's wearing headphones that cost hundreds of dollars, and he looks completely enraged.

Not everybody looks that way, though. A couple of girls our age, carrying huge iced Starbucks drinks, are laughing as they stroll past us. Why aren't they in school? What about Headphones Guy? Where's he going? It's weird, all these people out here in the middle of the day. There's so much happening, so much going on, so many people crowding into the streets and buildings and schools of every town in America. I think about it all the time, how many people there are, how there can't possibly be room on this earth for all that love and confusion and longing and fury. Where are you supposed to put all that? Where's it going to fit?

"Listen," Laura says as we approach the bridge. "You can hear it singing."

It does sound like singing. Or like we're treading on the lip of a silver bell. The bridge is huge and shining, cables reaching like slanted rays of the sun into two high peaks, pointing skyward. I've thought about it all day, how sometimes a sky this blue and a sun this bright can be so beautiful that it hurts. This day is so gorgeous that it physically hurts me. This sky is perfect 9/11 blue, end-of-the-world blue, and there they are again: April Donovan, my kiss on her eye, the crash and burn of airplanes in the sky. My father, briefcase in hand and wings at his back, nodding at me to go on. Both of them ghosts, following me and Laura around. It's like I can feel them tiptoeing behind us as we move forward across the bridge.

"You should see it at night," Laura says. "See all the lights?"

I manage a nod. The height, the silvery cables, the river gleaming beneath us; they've got me dumbstruck. I don't even know what to say, so I grab Laura's hand and hold her tight as we walk to the middle of the bridge, where Laura stops. She keeps my hand in her hand, though.

"Look," she says. "I've got one foot in Nebraska and one in Iowa. Two places at once. Two states at the same time."

I turn to face Laura and thread the fingers of both my hands through hers. My feet are spread so that I'm in two states, too. I'm in Nebraska and in Iowa, kissing Laura Echols in two places at once. On the one hand (the Iowa one?), it feels wrong: this girl is on the verge. The world's falling to pieces all around us, and here I am following my hormones into the danger zone. On the other hand, who's to say that it's not this—our two mouths, our hands trembling, this bridge singing beneath our feet—that keeps us alive, anyway? You find what's worth living for, and right now Laura's mouth is high on my list. I can save her like this, one breath at a time. It's like CPR, I swear to God.

"Laura," I say, her face in my hands. "Please, please tell me what is happening here."

Tears fill Laura's eyes. She's not saying anything. Oh, the huge rush of things I want and need to tell her, so many words they don't all fit in my mouth; they get stuck there so I can't say a thing. I can't say, Laura, the thing you don't know is that it gets better. I didn't think it would get better, but it does. It does. Sometimes the better even goes too far—like sometimes I think I'm losing him, the memory of him, the shape of his face or the way he walked, those things. Then—you know what, Laura? You know what I do? I close my eyes until I can hear his voice. If I still have his voice, I still have him. The voice comes first, then the eyes, the face, the hands. It starts with a voice. Find a voice you love and then keep it, keep it in your ear, this voice you love—

"What do you love?" Laura asks.

Have I said those things out loud? It's possible that I said them out loud, that I didn't just think them. My mind is too full; my throat is too full with all the words. Maybe they fell out of my mouth and my ears were too full to hear them falling.

"Lincoln. What do you love?" Laura asks again.

Cherry Twizzlers. Graveyard drive-ins. The world and this ridiculous blue sky. You.

"So many things I can't count," is what I say. It's the truth. It is. "What do you love?"

Laura shakes her head. "I don't even know."

"Yes, you do. You love your cello, don't you? Don't you love music?"

"I'm good at the cello. I'm proficient. That's a different thing. Somebody else's dream for me."

Laura's still holding my hands, holding me steady with her eyes. It's like she wants *me* to tell *her* what she loves. It's like I've got to guess, and our lives depend on my guesses. The river is fifty feet below us, glinting like a blade.

"Your family?"

This makes the tears spill. Laura shakes her head hard, casts her eyes toward the water. "Yes. I mean, no. Yes, I love them. I do. I just don't know them. Or wait, I do, but they don't know me. They don't know any of it."

This is what I'm talking about. This right here, this business of how Laura talks to me in these weird riddles. How she can't be silly with me or laugh or talk about anything meaningless and ordinary—shoes, tacos, bowling, grasshoppers, fractals; I can think of tons of different boring-ass, fascinating things that I would love to discuss. It's like we're always in the deep end, like it's always high drama-stakes, like I can't get us out of the wilderness of this heavy, heavy shit, like I can't get Laura out of her own head, like she refuses to let go of misery, like she's *this* close but just won't let me in, won't let joy in, won't let any of this magic between us be real. I'm way out of my element here, way out of my league. Laura needs a dog, is what she needs. She needs a dog and some counseling and—I don't know—like a close girlfriend or something. Somebody to do with Laura whatever it is girls do to get shit out of their systems, get things into perspective. I've seen how the girls at school, they hug each other after being separated for an hour during class—like they are genuinely thrilled to see each other in the halls, these girls. Their friendships are made out of *passion,* man, out of devotion. Out of secrets I can't even begin to fathom. It makes me sick with jealousy sometimes to see it, to be near it. *That's* what Laura needs.

I'm not what Laura needs, not at all, but I had better be. I had better be, starting now.

"Close your eyes," I say, and just to be sure, I cover Laura's eyes with my hand. "Listen."

We stand there for a second, listening to the song of the

bridge. The sun is warm on our faces and our hands. Laura Echols, she is astonishing. I just want her to be happy, just for a minute. A minute is a start.

"Laura, what do you love? Don't think. Just say."

Laura bites her lip, stifling a grin. "The drive-in. With you."

"Good. Me too. What else? Go. Don't think, just say."

"Beginnings," she says. "New pencils."

Laura Echols also loves board games and the ocean and crème brûlée and her cousins and the way it feels to put on clean, dry clothes after you've just gone swimming and your muscles are still trembling from the water. She loves summer and fireflies and her mother's marshmallow brownies. And she does love her cello, most of the time. She loves her parents, even though just last night she told them that she hated them, that she wished they would go to hell and leave her alone. She loves Ms. Heslip's English class and the way it felt in class to climb into that other Laura's skin for a minute—Laura Wingfield, Blue Roses, broken girl, fragile as a glass unicorn, who—God—has it way worse than the real Laura, Laura Echols, who also loves Vassar and can't wait to get to Poughkeepsie and start over, if only she could get there, if only she could make it these last few months, but she doesn't know if she can; each day feels like a glass wall that she crashes against, her reflection staring dumbly back at her, wondering, *Who in the world is that girl? What has become of Laura Echols?*

Laura, she's still in there somewhere, and she still loves

tangerines and carnivals and the cool of the silver flask on her lips and also this magnificent silver bridge, the one currently holding us up, keeping us from falling into the river below. Laura, it turns out, loves lots of things, and anyway it doesn't matter what exactly the things are, although I'll remember them, I'll carry baskets full of tangerines to Laura Echols's house every single day of the world if I have to. What matters is the love, and love is always good. It's a start, a tether. It's enough.

Behind Laura, stretched between the silver cables of the bridge, is a spiderweb like you wouldn't believe. Hugest spiderweb I've ever seen, shimmering in the light. At the center is this tiny green spider, waiting. Laura still has her eyes closed, and I take her by the shoulders, steer her gently around.

"Check it out," I say, and Laura draws in a breath when she sees it.

"She's so little," Laura says. "How'd she even fit all that web into her belly? Her spinners, I mean. Whatever."

Seriously, this spider's web is about ten times the size of what you'd think this teeny spider would want or need. It's a phenomenal architectural feat, is what it is. I could look at it all day. I could stand here all day and wait for the lights of the bridge to come on and make this thing glow.

"What time is it?" Laura asks.

"I don't know," I say, because I never wear a watch.

"Huh," Laura says dreamily, still staring at the web. Then

she turns to look at me, a new Laura, one I've never met before. "I'm pretty sure, Lincoln, that I'm supposed to be dead by now."

I shrug. "Yet here you are."

"Yep," she says. "Here I am."

GAVIN'S SYNAPSES

(12:07 PM EDT)

What you should know about me if we're going to be friends is that there's no part of me that likes sitting still. How long have we been in this effing closet? Where's Mr. #goodguy Policeman? Nobody knows. What I know is that my calves are twitching. Atrophying and whatnot. Atrophy and adrenaline, man, they do not mix. I'm like this cocktail of insane twitchy get-me-out-of-here nerves, all of them about to propel me right through that door and to wherever April is. I could run five marathons right now. I could run to Baltimore and back again; I could run circles around the moon. Watch.

"I gotta get out," I say, making like to move, but Mr. Goodrich sticks out his human-seat-belt arm and goes, Gavin, no, stop. Sit down. Everybody just stay put.

« « «

"You think we don't all want out of here?" somebody says, I don't know who, doesn't matter. "We all want out, Gavin. We all love somebody out there. We all want to be a fucking hero. Just shut up and sit down, man."

Well. What else is there to do?

So I sit back down, go back to the only place there is to go, the last place I want to be: inside my own mind. It's getting dark in there. I want to shake these thoughts out of my head the way Valentino shakes himself free of a fly on his ears, ripple ripple shake shake, a tremor that moves from the tip of his long nose to the end of his tail, a wave passing over water, sleek and smooth like that, beautiful, I can hear the spangle-jangle of his tags in my ears as I'm thinking about him doing that ripple-shake. Get me out of here. I want my dog.

What's in my mind, man, it's not what you think; I know you think you can see us in here, filling up this tiny space with tears, apologies, confessions. You're thinking somebody's got their phone video going, that it's all testimonials and apologies and promises and last words. Let me tell you what: we are past all of that. We are way beyond. This feeling I've got in my thud-a-dud heart, and in my twitchy achy atrophying calves, it's this feeling — no, this *knowledge,* a thing happening in my synapses — that we're getting out of here, that we'll be free as soon as #officergoodcop gets his ass back here and lets us out. I am sure of it.

So the thoughts in my head, they have gone past fear and regret and worry. They're focusing and narrowing zoomwise, and they are landing on the thing that everybody else in here is thinking and not saying, only somebody does. Somebody whispers it into the room.

"Who do you think it is?"

Mr. Goodrich says, "Shhh. It's not anybody. Let's get quiet."

Yeah, well. I can smell Mr. Goodrich sweating from over here. You know he's thinking the same thing, wondering which of his students is out there playing God. You know he's sitting there sweating his brains out and wondering how he could have missed the signs, or how he could have made a difference. You can feel the elephant weight of the guilt crushing him from across the closet. Which makes me so mad, man, and so sad, because Mr. Goodrich isn't any more responsible for that stupid elephant than anybody else in here.

Gina shakes her head, hard. Against my arm, the brush of her hair—all that familiar goodness, how many times have I taken a nap in it? We have this thing we do, Gina and April and me, called Gerbil. Gerbil is when we all go over to somebody's house—usually April's, where the snacks are better and there's April's dad's old record player and a shit-ton of Otis Redding—and we pile on the bed together all curled up #gerbilwise and talk and listen to music and fall asleep and whatnot. Gerbil, man, is an excellent way to spend time. I could go for some Gerbil right now.

"I don't think it's anybody we know," Gina says, eyes

pinched shut against even the thought of it. "It can't be anybody we know."

"Bullshit," somebody says. Devon Heath, this guy who never says anything. It's interesting, how this scenario, this weird dark, is bringing people out into the light. You never know what's going on inside somebody's head, somebody's heart.

"Man, isn't it always somebody you know?" Devon continues. "Maybe it's somebody you forgot about, or someone you haven't talked to in a while or maybe never talked to at all, but the person's always been right there. Always right there in front of you."

"Shut up, Devon," somebody says, but not in a mean way. More uncomfortable than mean, because the truth always itches like that, doesn't it?

"Quiet!" Mr. Goodrich warns again. "Keep quiet, all right? I'm sure we'll get the all-clear soon. I'm sure there's been some sort of mistake. Everybody just—just, please. Quiet. Sit tight. Okay?"

So we're quiet. Everybody weighing elephants, trying to figure out where the scale tips, who the finger points to. Gina leans into me again, and I feel her tears on my neck.

"In sixth grade," she whispers, "my birthday sleepover, we invited Leona Reece just so we could be mean to her. Just so we could be cruel. Have I told you this story?"

"Gina, shh, come on. Stop it."

Yeah, I've heard the story. Over and over, I have heard

this story, how Gina and April were just trying to impress these bitches Ailynn Leonard and Emma Davidson, who, guess what, are still bitches. Who will grow up to be grown-ass bitches with #evilbitchspawn if they don't start getting their act together pronto. And really, if I stop to think about it — and what have I got to do in the Lockdown Closet but think my own brains out? — it's not so much that they're bitches, Ailynn and Emma. It's not so much that they're mean — I've even seen them be pretty nice or whatever, when they feel like it — but that they're . . . *dumb.* Not dumb, even — just, more like completely unable to think for themselves. Totally effing incapable of original thought. Which, really, is worse than being dumb, or being a bitch. You can be a dumb bitch all you want as long as you do it with #originalflair. If Ailynn and Emma haven't figured that out by now, I'm not sure there's hope for them.

But it was forever ago, man, that stupid middle-school slumber party. Leona has probably forgotten (Who am I kidding? No, she did not, and won't ever), and anyway, now Leona's this genius-goddess, so who's getting the last word? Leona Reece is not the one out there, dude. She has way too much going on. Anyway, Gina and April apologized forever ago. They're friends with Leona now, even if that chapter of shame is always going to be wedged in there between them.

"Gavin, man, I'm sorry."

This voice belongs to Jacob Hull, who may or may

not be capable of original thought. Like I said, you never know what the inside of somebody's head looks like. There's always the possibility for buried treasure, and today of all days, I am optimistic.

"What are you sorry for?" I ask.

"For all that stuff I said about your moms," Jacob says.

What stuff? I don't even know what kind of #crazytalk this is. I'd rather not know. I'd rather stay ignorant and blissful, thanks.

"It's cool," I say.

"No, man," Jacob says. "It's not cool at all. It's the opposite of cool."

All the elephants in the room have gotten up to rearrange themselves, to start taking shits all over the place.

"Your mom—the taller one?" Jacob starts tentatively. I hear the question in his voice; I get it a lot.

"Yeah, I say," saving him the trouble. "Mom Resa. I call them both Mom. And they're each other's wives. That's what they call each other. My wife, Resa. My wife, Leslie."

"Yeah," Jacob says. "Resa. She was with my aunt when she passed. She was the only one with her, you know?"

Well. I don't know. I didn't know, but now I do: Jacob Hull's got a dead aunt. Cancer, probably. Cancer is the biggest, meanest, dumbest bitch of all, no original thought whatsoever. I'd ask what happened if I wasn't so full of adrenaline and atrophy. I can't be thinking about dead aunts at this stage in the effing proceedings, so I don't ask. Maybe that's mean or whatever, but self-preservation? That shit is #forreal. So what I say to Jacob Hull is what I know to be the bona-fide truth:

"If Mom Resa was with her, she had safe passage, man. Your aunt had safe passage. I'm sorry."

"I'm sorry, too," Jacob says.

Sorry sorry sorry sorry sorry. Who's not sorry for something? We're all sorry. I'm sorry, for instance, for all the times I've thought Mr. Goodrich was disgusting and moldy and a sad old sack of nothing but physics. So maybe Jacob Hull talked shit about my moms. Most people around here, they look at my life and don't bat an eye, because guess what, here is what the world looks like, and it's a beauty. There's always at least one Jacob Hull, though, and if he's sorry, I'll take it. I'll take it, because now he knows Resa. Now he knows one family like mine from the inside out.

But what Jacob Dipshit Hull or anybody else should know about me if we're going to be friends is that people can talk all the trash they want about my moms and it's still not going to turn me into the sort of person who completely loses his shit and brings a gun into the equation. It's not my job to fix all the ignorance in the world, first of all, and second of all, the world, even with its shit-ton of ignorance, has got too much gorgeousness to offer. *I've* got too much to offer, bitches. I don't have the time or the inclination to get all #vigilante on your ass.

FRAILTY, THY NAME IS PHOEBE

(6:21 AM MDT)

"Come on," Angela says to Phoebe-in-the-mirror. "Get your clothes on. Get it together. We're going for a run."

Angela stands there, arms akimbo like some gym teacher from hell, and watches Phoebe lace up her shoes, a pair of neon Sauconys that have been languishing in her closet for months.

"I know how to put shoes on," Phoebe tells her sister.

"You think I'm gonna leave you alone in here so you can be all hunched up in front of that laptop before I even turn all the way around? No way. Welcome to your personal barnacle, my friend. That's me. Barnacle Sister. Barnacle Sister says let's go. Only first, fix your shirt. You've got it inside out."

The sleeping eye of Phoebe's computer swells and fades, an ominous glow. She wants so badly to just flip it open,

» » »

log on to the forum, say I'm out, say I can't. Her whole body is flooded with panic, icy-sharp. *Nebraska, Nebraska, Nebraska. Come with me, away from here, away from this whole thing.*

"Don't even look at it," Angela says, following Phoebe's gaze. "If you look at it one more time, it's going out the window, I swear to you. You will find it in pieces on the ground, Phoebe."

Angela's voice is trembling. Phoebe can see that behind this gym-teacher-drill-sergeant routine, she is worried and afraid. "Look at me," Angela says. Again, louder: "Phoebe. *Look at me.*"

Phoebe looks at her sister, long and hard.

"I'm going to think of a song. Or, no, a movie. I'm going to close my eyes and think of a movie, and you tell me which one it is, okay?"

Phoebe nods at Angela and watches as she closes her eyes. This is all so silly. Over the years they've played this game so many times that the novelty and fun are gone from it—they always think of the same things, not because they're mind readers, not because they can shine like that, but because they've lived together all this long while and their pool of shared movies, songs, books, moments, everything, is only a fraction of what exists in this wide world. Only a tiny, insignificant part. How stupid they've been, to think they could make their minds perform magic. All it is, all they've been doing, is coughing up their own inconsequential past. It's really nothing special at all. Nothing is ever half as special as you think it is.

"Okay," Angela says. She opens her eyes and grabs a pencil from Phoebe's desk. She scribbles something on an old receipt, shoves the scrap in her pocket, and shuts her eys again. "I've got it." Behind Angela's glasses, behind closed lids, the balls of her eyes quiver, traveling back and forth. The movement makes Phoebe uncomfortably aware of fragile things like Angela's optic nerves, her bones and her veins and her cuticles. We're all just this mass of parts and cells, right, so what is it, what *is* it, that makes Phoebe's sister so dear to her?

"Are you thinking?" Angela asks. "Make sure you're thinking. Concentrate."

Phoebe closes her eyes and tries to get her mind in that place, but her mind, as always, is noisy and crowded. Crowded with shame, and with Dylan's face—a face she's never seen in real life, that doesn't even exist. *Whose face is that? Whose voice?* And there are other voices, too, created out of words on a screen, words belonging to Nebraska and the Mastermind and the other Assassins. The Assassins. How'd they turn into assassins? It didn't start that way. Who said that, even, the first time? Whoever it was, they had to have been joking. Like ha-ha, like that game Phoebe played one summer at soccer camp. It was called Assassin, and how it worked was that you were assigned somebody's name in secrecy, and it was your job to "assassinate" that person with a toy gun, and then you'd be assigned that person's target, and then that person's target, and so on and so forth until there would be only one assassin left standing. It was such a stupid game. Stupid and innocent as hide-and-seek. Phoebe can't even remember who won it that summer at camp. Or if they even finished playing. It was just a game — just toys. Surely they got bored with it and moved on to something else, as easily and mindlessly as you might change a channel on a screen.

It occurs to Phoebe that so much of what she knows and feels about this whole thing has come to her on a screen. Movies and news stories about kids killing other kids, kids killing themselves. It's a thing on the periphery of her life, a shadowy piece of *other* that simmers beneath the everyday goings-on of her world. It's as if this is all one big movie, directed by the Mastermind, who has handed out scripts and assigned his chosen actors their roles. Real, not real. It's so mixed up. *Does it mean having things that buzz inside you and a stick-out handle?* Yes, Phoebe thinks, that's exactly what it means, or what it has meant to her over these long months. She has so many things buzzing inside her that she doesn't know where to put them all; she tried just now to heave some of them into the toilet, but nothing came up. She may as well have a stick-out handle, the way she's been manipulated into believing so many stupid, stupid things: *I know that I could never love anyone, anything, the way I love you.*

In Phoebe's head, where he will never not be real, Dylan

has a slow smile to match his low voice. There has been some mistake. He was supposed to meet her at the lake, and when she got there to find no one—to find nothing but a beat-up old portable CD player, spinning a disk on which was recorded the ongoing sound of cruel laughter—there must surely have been a good reason. Who knows why the recorded laughter was screeching through the trees? It was somebody else's. Not Dylan Fisher's. It was a coincidence. A coincidence, too, that afterward Dylan Fisher disappeared. There is an explanation. Somewhere, an explanation.

He's hiding. He's hurt. There's a secret she doesn't know.

I have never felt like this about anyone before

Phoebe at the edge of the lake, spinning around to spot him, here or here or here—and the laughter. It didn't sound human. It sounded like the high-pitched shrieks of gibbons or loons or hyenas. She couldn't even bring herself to go near the thing producing the sounds.

I have never felt like this

"Angela," she says, because the shine isn't working; she doesn't know the movie because, as usual, nothing is in her head except her own awful humiliation, "I don't know. I don't even have a guess."

Angela shakes her head at the ceiling. "I know this is dumb," she says. "I know how dumb this is. Don't you know I know it's dumb? That it doesn't matter? But Phoebe, oh my God, something needs to start mattering to you. Something real needs to matter, starting now, because it's getting to be like I don't even know you anymore. What is going on with you in front of that screen? I mean what is *happening*? Whatever it is, it must be fascinating, and it must be stronger than cocaine."

No, Phoebe wants to say but doesn't. Nothing fascinating about falling down an Internet rabbit hole for an hour, two hours, three hours at a time, reading about mindless stuff she doesn't even care about: So-and-so's postpregnancy look. Cellulite in Hollywood. This guy who shot a couple of his classmates and showed up in court with a smirk on his face, blah blah. If it's on the same page as the cellulite and the smack talk, what's the difference? Who draws the line? Phoebe can't even draw the line anymore. She loves to laugh at her own First World problems even as she is wallowing in them, just as she is letting them absorb her until her ass falls asleep and feels like a three-ton block of numb, prickly cinder that somebody put there in her chair while she was busy taking an online quiz—who knows why? just because—about "What Color Is Your Aura?" Online her aura is golden, but here, here in this room, her sister going all evil gym teacher on her ass, her aura is—what. What? It is the color of the bottom of an eel with an oozy wart going all ashy-gray-bleedy in a pool of muck. Her aura makes her sick. Ashy, warty eel shit, that's the color of her aura. That's the approximation of her actual self-worth. Ha! That's really good. It's hilarious. She cracks herself up and should post that brilliance so that she can crack others up, too. So many people she has never met IRL think that she, Phoebe, is really, really funny. These people, they are Phoebe's own personal laugh track; this is convenient because Phoebe is free to enjoy their laughter while she sits in the dark of her room and cries. Phoebe and these people, they can sit around and (virtually) pat each other on their ashy, warty backs in the privacy of their own dark rooms, where the screen glows its own soothing blue aura and everyone *out there* can still believe that Phoebe's own personal aura is gold. Gold! She is Rapunzel (sans the hair; the hair is in a box under the sink at the moment), smack in the middle of her own sad fairy tale. What is she even looking for? What secret message does she think is going to be revealed to her in some viral video about how to flatten your abs in fourteen days? Maybe the real Dylan will appear in that video, or that one, or that one. She has all day; she'll wait. She'll wait until the message comes (*ping!*) or the truth is uncovered or the real Dylan comes forward to please state his real name.

> *Come forward and state your name, please.*
> *State your name, name, name, name, name*
> *What's in a name*
> *Frailty, thy name is Phoebe*
> *Hallowed be thy name*
> *The name of the father, son, and holy spirit*
> *Name, father, father, name*
> *My name is Inigo Montoya. You killed my father*

"Princess Bride," Phoebe says to her sister. She is weary and says it wearily, but she knows this is the right answer. The knowing, the whooshing way it comes to her, brings her back to herself for a fraction of a sliver of a moment. Something inside her—Heart? Ear? Jugular vein?—still works. She is still here, not yet gone.

Angela unclenches her palm to reveal the crumpled slip of paper. It is damp with sweat when Phoebe plucks it between her fingers and unfolds it to reveal what she has just guessed, what she already knew. It's so dumb, but this dumb thing, this weird shine, is enough to get Phoebe to lace up her shoes, get her shirt outside out, move down the carpeted stairs behind her sister (their little-kid, gap-toothed faces smiling from frames on the wall, their four feet on the steps: *thup thup thup thup thup*), past the bathroom where their mother—*theirs* and theirs alone—is currently showering, steam gathering in a familiar, fragrant fog behind the door.

Behind the front door is the morning, still silky with new light. And there is that sweetness in the air, the thing Phoebe thought she caught the other day, just for a second. Whatever is in the air, it tastes weirdly like memory—or no; it feels like a memory that can cartwheel forward and in the turning change to something bright and new. Phoebe gulps in as much of that sweet air as she thinks her lungs can hold. She thinks of her map; she thinks of Nebraska; she thinks of New Orleans and jazz and getting her palm read. Here is her sister, owner of contact lenses and a beautiful lilac dress.

"Are you ready?" Angela asks.

"Let's go," Phoebe says, and her heart picks up, and her feet lift one by one off the ground, and at first it hurts, it hurts—Phoebe's body has forgotten how to do this—but before long her breath gets measured and starts to match her sister's, the two of them breathing together like this, in, out, in, out, in, out, in.

Phoebe grabs for Angela's hand. She doesn't care if she hasn't held her sister's hand since they were little girls. She doesn't care if they look stupid, hands clasped while they run. Who can see them, anyway? All the world is still asleep. The day hasn't yet fully begun, and there's still time.

Phoebe thinks of the soccer field behind the school, how at early morning practices and dusky games the sun will sometimes shine in this just-right way that makes everything look soft and dreamlike. There will be ponytails flying and girls laughing and calling to one another, girls high-fiving, girls lifting one another up, the ball sailing into the net, the sun shimmering just right all around, making everybody glow. There's this old couple—they aren't grandparents of anyone on the team; nobody knows who they are—who like to watch the girls practice in the late afternoons. Even when it's hot, the man wears one of those wool patchwork caps, like he should be a sheep farmer in Ireland or something. The woman always wears skirts with her bright-white walking shoes, and she holds on to the man by his elbow, gallant. This gallant old couple, they have a routine. They walk the trail that winds behind the soccer field, and then they make a slow loop around the track, and then they stop to get a drink at the water fountain, and then they settle into the bleachers and hold hands and watch, always smiling, never not smiling, as the girls — the teammates — sprint as fast and as hard as they can, up and down the field.

"Don't let go of me," Angela says, breathing hard.

"I won't," Phoebe says. She squeezes her sister's hand. Her lungs are burning, her mind keeps spinning, but she keeps going. She looks straight ahead, holds on with everything she's got — everything she has left — and keeps going.

SATURDAY, APRIL 24, 2010

(APRIL'S MENTAL MOVIE REEL, FRAME TWO)

It is freshman year, and we're at this party at Jacob Hull's house. In the backyard there's a pool, but right now there's no water in it, only a huge, leafy limb, torn from Jacob's poplar tree during the crazy storm that just passed through. The limb is so big you can sit on parts of it; people are down there with their Solo cups, lounging around on the branches. Tree house in a pool: it makes the world seem topsy-turvy, which it certainly feels today. There's weird weather everywhere, all the time, seems like. Earlier today, this tornado tore through Mississippi and killed ten people. We don't usually get tornadoes around here, but if I've learned anything, it's that anything is possible in this world. It's starting to get dark, and I can't tell if that's because the sun is on its way down or because there's another storm brewing. The air feels thick, electric, but that could just be because a few

» » »

minutes ago Drew Bennett came over and put a drink in my hand and our fingers brushed for just a second and there was this weird current between us, a thing that surprised me because I've been swimming with Drew for a million years and he has never been anything to me but maybe mildly on my nerves. Surprise, surprise.

"What even *is* this?" Gina asks, frowning into her cup. Her drink came from the tub in the upstairs bathroom, where Jacob dumped several bags of ice and the contents of whatever he could find in his parents' liquor stash. It tastes like gasoline. We dump our drinks onto the grass, and Gina asks if we can go. We walked here from her house, which is three blocks away.

"We should wait for Gavin," I say, nodding toward the pool, where Gavin is bouncing on a tree branch and throwing his head back, laughing at something somebody said. Above him, the stripped limb of the poplar glows pale in the dim light. It looks so wrong, like a gaping wound, and I feel this stab of sadness for the tree.

Gina groans. "We're never going to get him out of here."

"I know."

"I'm going to go give him a fifteen-minute warning. Then I'm going to the bathroom. Meet me out front in twenty, and we're out of here, whether he's with us or not. *Comprende?*"

"Got it," I say. I watch her go, and then I watch the sky, where the clouds are picking up speed.

It's then that I smell the pot. On principle, I've never smoked pot before, but that unmistakable fragrance—earthy, rich, mysterious—always makes me want to. Just a little bit. Just once, just to see.

Behind me, at the edge of Jacob Hull's yard, is one of those weeping cherry trees, full of new pink blossoms. They drape against the ground like curtains, or the bottom of a swishy ball gown. This tree, too, is glowing in the weird, waning light. It looks alive, which of course it is, being a tree, but what I mean is that it looks like it's breathing.

Underneath the tree, leaning against the trunk, is Nate Salisbury, and in his hand is a joint. I'm always stupidly surprised when I see someone with pot or beer or whatever. I mean, how do people get this stuff? No, I mean, I know how they *get* it, but I'd like to know the actual logistics and dynamics of such an enterprise. At my house we have Cheerios and instant oatmeal and Listerine and stuff like that.

Next to Nate, also leaning against the tree, is Pal Gakhar. I see that I have interrupted them midconversation, and I turn to go.

"I was just leaving," Nate says, getting up. He's looking at me like he knows something I don't know. His smiling eyes, goofy smile, easy gait: Nate reminds me of a spaniel. It's hard not to hug him. He waves the joint at Pal and me, and when we both shake our heads, he shrugs and slips out beneath the veil of blooms. I'm feeling a little dizzy and wonder briefly if the whiff of secondhand smoke has made me high, or if something else is going on.

"Hello," says Pal, all sort of formal. Like: not *hi.*

"Hello," I say back. At some point over the past year, Pallav Gakhar has become beautiful. He is tall now and lanky, carries himself with this sort of foxy grace. Not hot-foxy, but like-an-actual-fox foxy. As in, sly. Watchful. Slinky languid smart quiet, and also with these hip bones, graceful knobs on which his pants rest, belt jangling beneath a wisp of dark T-shirt. What is it with me and the sudden boy urges? Drew Bennett and his plastic cup, Pal Gakhar and his hips. I have found myself wondering what it would be like to place my palms on those hip bones. This isn't the kind of thought I have all the time. I mean, I thought it only once or twice at most. But I've thought it.

I definitely accidentally just got high.

"What brings you here?" Pal asks. His voice has deepened this year, too. It comes as a surprise every time.

I laugh a stupid, nervous laugh. "Nothing, I guess."

"Ah," he says, grinning. "Fortuitous."

The word. He remembered it. Did he remember it? Maybe he's just saying it because this is an appropriate context in which to use the word *fortuitous.* No; he remembers. I can tell by the tilt of his smile. It has been three whole years, and here he is with that word on his lips. Suddenly I want to kiss him — just really quick, just this once — and get it back. I'm so moved, so thrown off-kilter and stirred, that I'm afraid for a second that my knees might buckle.

Other words from that spelling bee rise to the surface of my mind, and I'm tempted to weave them into sentences designed expressly to impress the newly impressive Pal Gakhar, but I'm not thinking fast enough and my mouth lags behind my brain.

Later that night, lying wakeful in bed, staring at the glow-in-the-dark stars on the ceiling, I'll come up with a good one. Me, standing in the pink glow of that dreamy weeping cherry: "Isn't this scene oneiric, Pal Gakhar? You, me, the tree?"

Oneiric. Adjective. From the Greek *oneiros.* Dreamlike; of or related to dreams or dreaming.

I don't think of that until later, though. I always think of the good things to say when it's too late. In the actual moment, I'm struck dumb, just as I am when Pal's friends part the branches of the tree like a curtain and step laughing into the space where Pal and I are watching each other. As quickly as it was conjured, the spell is broken. Pal's friends — Dan Gregorios, Heath Steineke, and Ben Higgins — are smart and funny, and together they make this smart and funny quartet. Another subtle shift has happened since middle school: the smart boys are now the cool boys. Pal and Dan and Heath and Ben are the smartest boys in our grade. Always have been, always will be. All about them there's this air of irony and nonchalant brilliance, evident in everything from the all-new spin they've put on Ultimate Frisbee to the music leaking from their expensive headphones to the posters and newspaper they create with Ben's dad's old printing press. The newspaper is this wild-minded thing called *Kafka's Thorax*. Dan and Heath draw the comics, and Ben and Pal write the columns — satires of everyone and everything at our school. The only thing worse than being a subject of one of their columns is not being one — I admit to secretly wishing that these boys would notice me long enough to put me in their pages. What would they say about me, I wonder?

I like to watch Pal and his friends because they are this little world unto themselves. They get together and there's this kinetic energy, this sparkle. Sometimes before school, they'll spread out on the front lawn and throw the Frisbee around in accordance with whatever rules they've established to suit their unique version of the game. More than once I've found myself staring at their shared concentration, their rhythm. They can talk and laugh and throw the Frisbee all at the same time; it's all one motion, fluid and uninterrupted. Fascinating and lovely to watch.

I'm an interloper here, beneath the cherry. I'm the one who doesn't belong. Dan and Heath and Ben are all, hey, April, how's it going, but I know I'd better go. When these boys get together, magic happens, and I don't want to ruin whatever the surprise might turn out to be.

"See you later," I say, and as I'm ducking through the pink blooms, going off to find Gina and Gavin before the sky splits wide open, Pal says something that makes me know for sure that he did say *fortuitous* on purpose, that he remembers those words we passed back and forth so long ago.

"Later, April," Pal says. "It's been numinous."

Numinous. Adjective. From the Latin *numen,* which translates to something like "divine sway." Awe inspiring. Evoking a sense of the transcendent, mystical, or sublime.

I'm walking back toward the pool, smiling. Enjoying my moment of divine sway.

THE MASTERMIND AND THE EMERGENCY ANGELS

(8:46 AM PDT)

The Mastermind is rattled. That guy with the angel tattoo rattled him. He's wondering now about the significance of the exchange, and what the chances are that he should encounter, on this of all days, a perfect stranger with his own "angel" inked across his arm. One in a thousand? One in six thousand? Coincidences interest the Mastermind, and not because of the disturbing thing that the wheelchair man had to say about God's anonymity. What interests the Mastermind about coincidences is that they can usually be explained through simple math. So they're really not coincidences at all. It's just mathematical probability, beautifully and logically unlocking the so-called mysteries of the universe. Cause and effect, cause and effect.

« « «

The opposite of God.

Sometimes, though, the Mastermind has to wonder if there's some other, strange force at work. Some coincidences are just too startling to ignore. For example, there's this weird phenomenon that seems to happen to him all the time — this inexplicable thing where he'll be reading a word (in a book, on a screen, on a billboard) and at that same exact moment he'll hear (on the radio, rising up from the background conversation in the room, from a person on the bus or on the street) that very same word spoken aloud. It doesn't just happen with common words like *and* or *but*, either. It happens with words like *iguana* and *barbecue* and *convenient.*

It happened to him just a moment ago, before the tattooed man in the wheelchair left. The Mastermind had been looking at an approaching bus, at the words EMERGENCY EXIT, and someone somewhere behind him, just a person passing on the sidewalk, had uttered at that exact moment the word *emergency.*

Okay, so it's a pretty common word, but still. Emergency. Angel. Emergency angels. What are the chances? What is the exact statistical probability? If he thinks long and hard enough about the number of words an average person reads in an average day (upwards of four thousand?), he can figure it out and explain it away. The Mastermind is considering all of this as he trudges beneath the weight of his wings toward the university. He is keeping his head down so as to avoid unwelcome eye contact or the appearance on signs of words that might suddenly come floating out of the mouths of random passersby.

Yes, the Mastermind guesses, the average literate person probably encounters at least four thousand written words a day, whereas the average person no doubt speaks more than double—maybe even triple; in some unfortunate cases quadruple—that many words. People just talk talk talk talk talk. They never shut up. Right now, as he's thinking about it, the voices of surrounding strangers are rising up in a cacophonous racket that makes the Mastermind's eardrums trill and burn and shakes his brain into a panic. He clamps his hands over his ears and shuts his eyes, quieting his mind with the numbers and figures. Somewhere the Mastermind has seen a statistic reporting that, on average, women are likely to speak almost twice as much as men do. It should come as no surprise, then, that a woman's voice was responsible for depositing into the Mastermind's ear the word *emergency* just as he was reading it on the back of a passing bus. There's an explanation for this, just as there is for everything.

Other statistics on the Mastermind's radar: While women are more likely than men to attempt suicide, men are more likely to succeed. Also, each year, fewer teenage lives are claimed by car crashes than by suicide, cases of which tend to increase during the month of April and peak in May. The Mastermind knows all of this, just as he knows that his psychologist father could no doubt confirm that most cases of teenage suicide arise as the result of a "same-day event," that is, something goes wrong in one moment, and in the following moment of despair, a teen will make an irrevocable decision to end his or her life.

This last bit of information is what is worrying the Mastermind as he opens his eyes and moves forward. At the beginning, the plan was all his, and the plan was clear and concise: at a prearranged and orchestrated moment, the Assassins would turn their weapons on their wrongdoers. At school, the better to make a statement that nobody could ignore. At some point, though, the plan got away from him. Things got confused and out of control. Too many of the Assassins decided they weren't out for revenge after all — what they wanted was for their own selves to disappear. *No!* the Mastermind wanted to shout through the screen. That's *my* part in this story, the part where the story ends. That's *mine*.

Nobody ever listens to the Mastermind. Not his mother, not his doctors, not Wendy Neely, not even the Assassins. Nobody ever pays attention to him. Nobody ever does what they say they're going to do. Nobody in this world knows how to keep a promise, to follow through, to finish what they start. The plan, it has fallen apart. It is in shambles. Let them do what they want, those stupid Assassins. Let them kill their adversaries; let them kill themselves. Does it even matter? His computer, where all of them live, is destroyed now anyway, so there. The problems of those strangers are no longer his. Those problems have disappeared forever, and soon he too will fly away.

As he moves forward toward his goal—toward finishing what he started—the Mastermind can feel his fury mounting. He can feel it even in the soles of his feet, one deliberate step after another. Step after step after *step on a crack*. He always avoids the cracks, but today, as of right now—there is still time—he decides to walk the rest of the way on the cracks only. Follow the cracks.

The Mastermind follows the cracks all the way into campus, where he finds himself surrounded by people who look marvelously happy. What's the secret? the Mastermind wants to know. Just whisper it in my ear. I won't tell anybody, I swear.

The Mastermind is following cracks, head down, wings reflecting the hot, white light of the California sun, when a voice threads through the fog of all the other cacophonous, anonymous voices and filters into his ear. This singular voice, it travels as pressure waves into the Mastermind's cochlea, where the mechanical vibrations change to nerve impulses that are then transmitted to the Mastermind's brain, which immediately, startlingly, such that the Mastermind is thrown off balance (the vestibular system of the inner ear, it's where balance happens), makes the connection: this voice belongs to nobody else in the world but Wendy Neely.

What are the chances? The statistical probability?

The Mastermind spins around in search of the voice, which has spoken his first name. There, directly behind him, wearing orange sunglasses that he immediately recognizes, is Wendy Neely. She is laughing. Wendy Neely, she is always happy. It was Wendy's perma-contentedness, coupled with the Mastermind's preoccupation with human psychology (which has, of course, everything to do with his preoccupation with his father), that first led him to his obsession with happiness thresholds. Everybody's got a happiness threshold — it's a thing you're born with, like an arm or a knee. Just imagine that for a second.

"What's with the wings?" Wendy asks. Smiling. Happy. "What are you doing here?"

Wendy moves to hug the Mastermind, but it's awkward with the wings, and besides, he doesn't want her to touch him. If she touches him, even for a second, all will be lost. Maybe it's lost already, the Mastermind thinks with a fresh wave of panic. Her voice has touched his cochlea, and already he feels himself starting to reel. He takes a step back.

Wendy says his name again. Her smile is fading.

"What are you doing here?" she asks again. When the Mastermind just stares, she keeps talking. Talk talk talk. It's been five seconds and already she has said so many words that the Mastermind can't count them fast enough, onetwothreefourfivesixteenseventeentwentythreetwentyfourforty.

"Oh my God, I think I've got your dad for Social Psych! I mean, how many Angels are there around here, right?"

Angels are everywhere, thinks the Mastermind. Emergency angels, highly improbable coincidences: they're all over the place.

"And, oh, hey, I'm in a play this semester, and you'll never guess what it is. *The Glass Menagerie*! Remember when you helped me run those lines? I swear this play must be having some kind of revival or something. Seventy freaking years old and all of a sudden it's everywhere, all over the place. I'm Amanda again! I mean, what does that even say about me, right?"

Talk talk talk talk talk. Talkity talk talk taaaaaaaaalllllk.

The Mastermind is amazed that Wendy has so much to say, even more amazed that she is saying absolutely nothing. There are words between them that he feels should be said, and she is picking any and all other words than those. His heartbeat rises into his ears, two cymbals clanging, *crash bang!*

The Mastermind can feel beads of sweat appearing one by one on his forehead. This is the exact opposite of the way this plan was supposed to unfold. Nothing ever goes the way it's supposed to go. Nothing.

"Are you okay?" Wendy asks, suddenly concerned. "You look really pale."

Yes, the Mastermind can sense that he must look very pale. *Peaked,* his mother might say. His heartbeat is still there (thrumming now on his tympanic membranes), but his voice is suddenly gone, trapped like an animal in his throat. Throw open that cage and there will be so much screaming, and it will be loud, loud, it will shatter things, and this is not at all the way this scenario should be playing out. Who put Wendy Neely here? She needs to go. She needs to exit stage left and run for her life.

Wendy doesn't go, though. She takes the Mastermind by his wrists and says, "Why don't we sit down. Let's just slowly sit down, right here. This lawn is a perfect place to sit down. See? Sit with me."

The Mastermind's mind is all over the place. First it's on his arms, which are being held in Wendy Neely's grip. What makes her think she's allowed to touch him like that? You can't just go around *touching* people that way. His mind is also on his backpack, which Wendy has somehow disentangled from his wings and eased from his shoulders. It's now lying beside her on the lawn, the letters within throbbing with an urgency to match his own heart, *clang bang clang*. Can Wendy hear that? Her letter's in there, in the pack, and it's loud.

"Is that a little better?" Wendy asks.

The Mastermind can't quite look at her. Don't look right at the sun; that'll burn your retinas, fool. That'll melt your wings and send you crashing to the ground.

She says his name again. And then she says softly, "I don't have to be anywhere. I'll sit right here with you until you're better."

The Mastermind's mind is also in Maine. New Hampshire, Vermont, Texas, Idaho. Racing all over his map of destruction. He dares to look at Wendy. Just for a second; he'll just look for a second. Just a second won't burn anything.

So he looks.

There's Wendy Neely, smiling. Not smiling like she's in love with him, but smiling like she knows him. Like she remembers him and cares about him and is worried. So far nothing is in flames, so he risks looking closer: at her eyes, her lashes, a faint blemish on her chin. She has pushed her orange sunglasses onto the top of her head; they glint in the sunlight, but still—miraculously—nothing catches fire. The Mastermind dares to consider the curve of her jaw, the outline of her ears. And here is the thing, here is the shocking thing: Wendy Neely is just a girl. Just an ordinary person. So different from the image he has conjured in his imagination all this long while.

"You hurt me," he says. The words just tumble out, stupid and dull as stones.

Wendy looks genuinely surprised. Despite what people say about him, the Mastermind is able to look at another person's face and make sense of what is happening there. He knows how to recognize hate, fear, surprise.

"What?" Wendy says, quiet.

The effort of speaking has overwhelmed the Mastermind. He can't do it again—just those three words have emptied him out. He is suddenly lightheaded, a sky-bound balloon, slowly leaking air.

"I'm sorry," Wendy says, confused. "I never meant to hurt you."

I'm sorry. I'm sorry. I'm sorry. The Mastermind has long imagined Wendy Neely telling him that she's sorry, but now that she's here, right in front of him, saying it like she means it, he makes a horrible discovery, one that makes him feel sick with shame: Wendy Neely does not owe him this apology. She doesn't owe it, but the gift of it, the way it sounds when she says it, the relief it gives him, the everything, the whatever it is, steals the air from his balloon, or from his lungs, or from beneath his awful wings.

Contrary to what people might say or think about him, the Mastermind knows what shame is. He knows about remorse and regret, knows that if he gets up right now this second, runs as fast as he can away from Wendy Neely and toward his father's building and in the direction of his mission, his plan, then he can outrun the remorse and regret and the inevitable consequences of his actions. He can fly straight away from all of it, he can be done with it, he can soar on a wave of blameless peace into another world where none of it will matter, where nobody will remember a thing, where he will be free.

Free.

Happy.

"Did my father teach you about happiness thresholds?" the Mastermind blurts. He didn't mean to talk, but now he has. He wants the words back, but now they're gone. There's not much air left in the Mastermind; his vision looms and swims, starry. That granola bar was ages ago. He should've brought his insulin pen, but he didn't plan on needing it. He didn't plan on needing anything or anyone ever again.

"Happiness what?" Wendy says, frantic. She tightens her grip on the Mastermind's arms and shakes, gently.

"Happiness thresholds," the Mastermind repeats. Dizzy, dizzy. Maybe the stars before his eyes are really there, or maybe this is just the Wendy Neely effect: she emanates glitter and light. Her happiness threshold is off the charts. The Mastermind's tongue thickens in his mouth as he tries to explain: "You're born with a certain amount of happy, see. You can win the lottery, or everyone around you can die in a fire, whatever, doesn't matter, your body and mind will eventually return to the same level of happy that you started with."

Wendy's eyes sweep the Mastermind's face. She's not getting it. She doesn't get it. So hard to explain.

"Do you know the Fates?" the Mastermind asks. His tongue is now wrapped in gauze, dense and dry and sticky. He needs to get this out. "They were called the Moirai."

What Wendy Neely hears: "Theyvu coulda bore eye."

But see, the Mastermind thinks she can understand him, so he keeps going: "Clotho, Lachesis, and Atropos. One was the spinner of the thread, one was the measurer, and the third one, Atropos, she was the cutter." The Mastermind makes an awkward scissors motion with his fingers. In front of him, Wendy's eyes are filling with tears. Carefully, she removes her right hand from the Mastermind's wrist and reaches in her pocket for her phone.

"And that's how long your life is," the Mastermind says around his mouthful of gauze. He feels warmth in his ears, as of bells ringing, or alarms. It is an effort to speak above the roar, but he keeps going. "It's up to these three women, these Fates, who know nothing about you at all. So let's say you get only this much thread"—the Mastermind holds his hands apart, a short distance, horribly short—"then whose fault is it? The one with the scissors? The one who measures out the thread? Or the one who spins the thread in the first place?"

Wendy keeps her eyes on the Mastermind's eyes. Careful, careful.

"Personally, I think it's the thread-maker's fault."

"You're right," Wendy says, nodding at what has sounded to her like gibberish. Blinking away tears but still looking right at the Mastermind. Her fingers are on the phone now, doing something apart from what her eyes are doing. "You're right, you're right."

Stars and stars and stars. Has the Mastermind already fallen? Did he fall upward, into the sky, and is it dark now? He might as well keep on talking, then.

"The happiness thresholds, they're like that," the Mastermind says, addressing the stars. "Some people's are like this"—he throws his arms wide; blood needles through his body, thin and high and cool—"and some people just get a little bit. Such a little tiny bit of happy that you can barely see it at all. They can have the whole world, these people. Everything they've ever dreamed of having, but their happy — it will never be bigger than this." The Mastermind makes of his thumb and forefinger a small circle, not even big enough for a pencil to slide through, and holds it to his eye, peering at the stars as one by one they flicker and fade, the light fantastic winking out, goodnight goodnight goodnight goodnight goodnight.

SANDRA HESLIP,
TOO LATE

(11:08 AM CDT)

The deserted teachers' lounge smells the way it always does: burnt coffee, disinfectant, the remnants of someone's cheesy, greasy, microwaved lunch. My stomach does a Pavlovian lurch. I turn my phone on, and as it slowly comes to life I become aware of a change in energy outside the door, in the hall. Something is happening.

"You can pack up your desk," Dennis says, appearing from nowhere, "but first I need a list." His arms are stretched across the expanse of the entryway, hands pressed to the opposing walls; dark circles of sweat stain the armpits of his shirt. He slaps both sides of the cinder-block door frame in emphasis.

"Now," he says. "Right now, I need a list of every single one of your seniors not accounted for. Talk to their friends, get their phone numbers, do whatever you have to do. And do it *now*."

» » »

Before he disappears down the hall, he jabs a thick finger in my direction, like *You did this. This is all your fault.* Immediately my heart clogs with panic and shame. It was a stupid thing to do, dismissing my class like that, casting them off into a world lit by lightning. I knew—surely I must have known?—in that moment that it would cost me my job. Now I know it for sure, and the undertow of that knowledge pulls me down onto the couch, which sighs and releases its familiar, sickening smell of mothballs. Where did this awful couch come from? It smells like somebody's dying grandmother's house; it smells like misery and giving up. On one of the cushions there is—there always has been—a faint, boot-shaped stain that looks like coffee but might be vomit. Probably it's vomit. Bile rises sour and sharp to my throat, and I swallow it hard, will myself to keep it down.

The phone stirs in my palm, a living thing, cheerfully jangling. Twenty-seven new text messages, all received in the last few minutes. I know there's no time to waste. I know I need to be following Dennis's orders and accounting for every senior in my honors English class, but for some reason the phone—this fetter, this weird lifeline that has in this moment replaced the truth outside the door with its own compact, handheld version of the facts—takes precedence. My sister, my mother, *Call me, call me as soon as you can,* and—I skip to this one, and see that it's one of several—Eric. Eric. He has remembered. *Please be safe,* one says. *I think of you every day,* says another, and although my mind goes straight to our lost boy, his and mine, the next message confirms something else: *And on the rare days when I don't think of you, I think to myself, Ha! I didn't think of her once! Which amounts to thinking about you, so, yes, every day. Just so you know.*

I smile at this. I even laugh as the tears start. Not because I want another beginning with Eric — he doesn't want that, either, and we're both smart for understanding the truth — but because, just for a second, things feel new. We think we want and need so many things in this life, but this, I realize, is the key: just, every once in a while, to feel new again.

The stack of yearbooks is still on the table. I flip one open to the seniors section and look again at their faces: new, new, new. This is just the beginning, and they are all so beautiful, and I'm praying — or silently pleading, whatever it is you want to call it — that if one of them is broken, or is planning to break something, that it's not too late. I want what I said to Adrian George to be true: it's not too late.

Then, even though I've promised myself never to let him enter my thoughts, never to say his name in my mind's ear, I think of him. That boy in Connecticut, the ultimate Lost Boy. How long was his drive from the scene of one unspeakable crime to the next? How do you even operate a motor vehicle? Do you wear a seat belt, or is that beside the point? Do you observe the speed limit? Do the rules even apply? Let's say the drive was twelve minutes. Let's say it was ten, or even eight. Let's say he had to stop at a red light and in the adjacent car there's a tiny baby asleep in a car seat in the back. Let's say there's Christmas garland encircling the lampposts, wreaths on windows and doors, the most wonderful goddamn time of the year, not that it ever will be again. Let's say there's a couple walking hand in hand in the crosswalk—they're wrapped in scarves, wrapped in the pleasure of each other, steam rising from their coffee cups. Let's say someone else on the sidewalk trips and falls and a passing stranger helps her rise to her feet. Let's say there's a piece of paper, torn loose from a nearby telephone pole, floating aloft on the winter wind, and this piece of paper gets trapped on the Lost Boy's windshield as he's stopped at that light. Maybe the paper says MISSING and has a picture of a calico cat. Maybe it says GARAGE SALE SATURDAY (Saturday is coming! It comes once a week! It's a promise you can count on! Tomorrow and tomorrow and tomorrow!), or maybe it just randomly says FUCK YOU, ASSHOLE. How about that? Let's say there's another human being on the scene (another driver, a hurried pedestrian, doesn't matter) and this one is a man who reminds the Lost Boy of his brother or his dad, or someone he has loved or been loved by (because I believe this: I believe there was love in the life of the Lost Boy), and for a second he gets this glimmer. This moment of tenderness, this blink of grace. Let's just say that happens. I can think right now of any number of different things that the Lost Boy might have encountered on that twelve-minute (ten-minute? eight-minute?) drive that could have made him stop. Turn around. Change his mind. Change the horrible way the story ends and start new.

I am scanning the yearbook faces.

This could be my daughter; this could be my son.

I'm out the door and on my way to find them, each and every one.

LINCOLN TO THE MOON

(12:28 PM CDT)

Back there on the singing bridge, Laura Echols told me the whole story. Now it's gone, carried away on the wind that whipped our hair around, made us shiver, made that impossible spiderweb sway. I guess it's not all the way gone, because I've got the story now. It hasn't yet become a part of me, though, because I'm not sure I believe it. It's like when we stopped to get gas and I saw that little TV screen above the gas pump. On the screen, the news feed showed a picture of downtown Boston, empty as a ghost town, halted in its tracks. I mean, how do you believe a thing like that? How do you look at that eerie stillness and convince yourself to believe that one person, one single solitary guy, is the reason an entire gorgeous major U.S. city is on lockdown? It looked made up. It looked like a movie, like any

« « «

minute the zombies would arrive. And you know what? I'll take the zombies, man. Give me the zombie apocalypse any day over one living, breathing human's willingness to hurt another. You know what I'd be doing if I lived in Boston right now? I'd be running down the middle of Boylston Street screaming my head off. I'd be going, *Come and get me! I dare you!*

You know what, though? No, I wouldn't. I'd be doing what everybody else is doing: shutting up, shutting in, keeping quiet so the police can do their job. I'm amazed, though, that there's nobody out there running and screaming in those empty streets. It's proof, isn't it, that people are capable of listening and following the rules. That there is more good than bad in the world, that people, on the whole, are more kind than evil. *Find the helpers* is what everybody said after the bombs went off four days ago. People were trying to figure out how to talk to kids who were damaged by what they saw at the marathon, or to kids who might not have been there but saw it happen on TV, just like a video game only this is for real. *Find the helpers. There is more good than bad, more light than dark, more hope than despair.*

This crazy plan Laura has just revealed to me, it can't happen, man. It cannot. Bad things happen in threes, and if this goes down while the whole country's holding its breath, waiting for the boogeyman to be caught, waiting for the zombie apocalypse — that's like three multiplied by three million. No way. Not happening.

We're back in the Lexus now, headed back where we came from, and the more I think about this horrible mess Laura's got herself into — has now dragged me into whether I like it or not — the more I realize I'm pissed off about it. Shoving the accelerator a little too hard with my foot.

"Slow down," Laura says.

What? Laura Echols wants me to slow down? That's hilarious. I gun it a little harder, watch as the speedometer glides to eighty, eighty-five. This Lexus, man. This deluxe luxury vehicle! It's like a spaceship. Watch, Laura Echols, as I zoom us to the moon!

Ninety, ninety-five. This machine is completely unreal, and really, it might as well be a toy. A thing Laura Echols plays with when she gets bored, just because she can. Why not play with a few thousand pounds of machinery, or a boy's heart, or your future, or your very life? Because it's all just a funny, funny game, right? Ha! Ha! Ha! Ha! Ha!

"Lincoln, slow down," Laura says again, and I hear it in her voice: fear. Panic. Lo and behold, the siren herself is choking on her own seductive song.

One hundred miles an hour. One hundred five, one hundred ten. Zoom zoom zoom zoom zoom, straight up into the blue blue sky. Yes, 9/11 blue, that's exactly what the sky is. I've thought it a million times today, just as I've thought of my winged father and of first-grade April Donovan, soaring way up into that sky on the swing. Man, listen, you could have asked anybody anywhere in the country what the sky looked like on that terrible morning in 2001, and from sea to shining sea the sky was heartbreak blue. How often does meteorology conspire to make that happen, I wonder? Is it like that today: is the whole country awash in a perfect blue sky, the better to break everybody's hearts as we sit in front of the television—or in front of the gas pump or even just in front of a phone the size of a deck of cards—and watch and wait for the Boston Police Department to catch their guy? As Laura Echols's stupid game unfolds on the Internet all across the nation? It's like watching *CSI,* but better—better meaning worse. I bet people are eating fucking popcorn, because that's apparently what life is now: a televised drama, where everybody wants to play God.

Zoom in, zoom out. The highway itself is a game, an elaborate obstacle course designed for the amusement of thrill-seeking Americans. See Lincoln go. Go, go, go!

"Lincoln, *stop!*"

Laura grabs my arm and horns are blaring and dust and gravel are flying and the rear of the Lexus flies wildly to the side in a half spin as we swerve, rubber burning, to a stop on the shoulder. Cars pass us fast as lasers, *swoosh whoosh whoosh,* each a shiny bullet we just dodged. The Lexus shudders as they pass; my hands shudder on the wheel. Never in my life have I felt anger like that, ever. It is gone now as quickly as it came, but the ghost of it shivers in my veins, in the stillness that fills the car. Everything, everything, comes down to just one moment. It is or it isn't, it happens or doesn't.

Next to me, Laura Echols has a hand pressed to her chest, and her face is the face of someone who is stunned and relieved and glad to be alive.

Someone who does not, under any circumstances whatsoever, want to die.

MONDAY, MAY 2, 2011

(APRIL'S MENTAL MOVIE REEL, FRAME THREE)

It's sophomore year, and I'm in the hospital for the first time since I was born. Yesterday in the pool I thought it was just bad cramps, like killer cramps, but it turns out my appendix had burst, so here I am, and apparently Osama bin Laden was killed sometime during the night. This news has drifted to me in broken, foggy bits and filtered somehow into my in-and-out consciousness: slices of hushed conversation between my parents and the nurses, the clipped monotone of a reporter's voice coming from a TV down the hall. Also just the change in the air; even under the weight of this fog, I can feel its unmistakable buzz. Something has happened.

But maybe this is all just a fever dream, courtesy of the pain meds. You could tell me right now that Osama bin

» » »

Laden was in my hospital room bearing get-well gifts and flowers and I would probably believe you.

My room is quiet and I am, for the moment, alone. I shift my eyes—God, my eyelids weigh a ton—to the TV mounted to the ceiling in the corner. It's on but silenced, and the muted images of a dark compound in Pakistan look for all the world like something out of a video game, only not as high def. The video games look realer than the real thing. Noise drifts from a room across the hall: the soundtrack, I realize, to this thing I'm watching. There are cheers. Cheers. I don't know whose—do they belong to people inside the television? people inside this building?— but they explode in my ears. *Wrong,* goes my brain. It's one thing when the wicked witch is dead, but it's a whole other thing when everybody rises up to sing and dance. *Ding, dong. Sad, wrong.* I fumble for the remote and turn the TV off, but still the sound comes at me, keeps coming at me. What am I crying for now?

So now I'm April Donovan, sans appendix, which is weird but sort of cool—like it's cool that human bodies have evolved in such a way that an entire organ can be rendered useless, like, oh, hey, you don't really need your appendix. It's just there to screw things up so you have to miss a swim meet against Central. I'm all medicated and woozy, thinking woozy, deep, irrelevant-body-parts thoughts like that as I'm hanging out in my hospital bed while the machines beep and the nurses squeak down the hall in their soft white shoes. The nurses are all super-nice, and I'm thinking maybe I could be a nurse when my future happens, but don't you need math for that? You need math for everything. I'd rather be in the pool. All I want to do right now is get back in the pool.

Here's what's cool about being in the hospital, though: you get visitors. My sister, Monica, has been hanging out here a lot, which is really nice and all, but she keeps bringing stuff with her that she knows I can't eat right now. Thanks a bunch for bringing french fries and a milk shake in here, Mon, and eating them right in front of my face. That's super-thoughtful. She did bring a book, though, and earlier? When I was all out of it and sleepy? She sat in the chair next to my bed and read out loud to me from *Anne of Green Gables,* which she knows I always return to, womb-like, when I'm sick or sad. It was really nice, the reading out loud. It makes me think that people should read to each other all the time, that it shouldn't just happen when you're a little kid.

But I must have fallen asleep while Monica was reading, because I wake up to find a bookmarked *Anne* on the table next to a vase of daisies. Tied to the vase is this black Mylar balloon that says OVER THE HILL, which makes me laugh, and oh my God, it hurts to laugh. Gavin and Gina should know better than to be making me laugh like that when my freaking appendix just burst. I'm sad that I missed them and hope they'll come back soon.

Then I'm thinking maybe I do hear them, that maybe Gina and Gavin are coming down the hall right now, but weird and hello, random: the person who enters my hospital room is Pal Gakhar. What's he doing here? I mean, Pal and I have always gotten along or whatever, and one time in ninth grade I had a crush on him for, like, thirty seconds under a weeping cherry tree, but we're not *friend*-friends. Not visit-in-the-hospital friends.

"My dad told me you were here," Pal says.

Oh yeah, Dr. Gakhar. Pal's dad is my anesthesiologist. I remember our foggy conversation, the slim band of gold on his finger, the soothing music of his voice as he helped ease me, soft and safe and sure, into dreamland: where I go to school, what grade I'm in, how he has a son at that same school, then out like a light, gone.

Pal is carrying a flat box under one arm. With his other hand he gently tugs on my balloon. "Since when are you forty?"

Yikes, it hurts to laugh. "No, that's from Gavin and Gina. It's this dumb joke we have, like we'll give each other graduation cards on birthdays, condolence cards when we mean congratulations. That sort of thing."

Pal smiles. "You guys are crazy."

"I know."

"Hey, I brought a copy of my biology notes, plus the homework," Pal says. "You didn't miss much. Oh, and this, too. New issue, hot off the press." He's waving around a copy of *Kafka's Thorax*. "Behold the last-ever hard-copy edition. You know we've moved the whole operation online, right? We've already got, like, two thousand followers.

People in other states, other countries—it's wild, man. Ben thinks we could be the next *Onion.*"

"Thanks," I say, feeling strangely moved at this array of unexpected gifts. The medicine is so weird. "What's in the box?"

Pal holds it up: Scrabble. "Wanna play?"

A nurse floats in to check on me. Her scrubs are covered in a pattern of lizards, and this makes me like her. I also like the cool of her hands, the ease of her smile, the way she performs her tasks swiftly and surely, like everything is going to be okay. On a whiteboard she has written the date—today is Monday? for real?—and the hours of her shift and also her name, Ann.

"I love that story," Ann-the-nurse says when she catches sight of my book. "I always wished I had an *e* like my bosom friend, Anne Shirley."

I officially love Ann-the-nurse. She knows Pal—must know his dad—and together they laugh about something before she makes a few notes on the clipboard at the foot of my bed and disappears from the room.

When Pal sits down, it's not in the chair but right on my bed. I have this urge to sit up straight and yoga-cross my legs, but I'm too tired. I worry for a second that I probably look awful. My legs beneath the blanket are weird, too; they look like somebody else's legs. Too skinny. I want my strong legs back. I want back all my strength, from the inside out—without it, I realize, I'm not me at all.

Pal unfolds the board and places it carefully across my blanketed shins.

"This okay?" Pal asks.

I nod.

Pal shakes the little canvas bag full of tiles and offers it to me first. Pretty soon we've got a good game going; we're matching each other evenly, and I watch Pal's lashes as he concentrates, as he scratches our scores onto a pad of paper with a stub of Scrabble-issue pencil. I notice that there's a bunch of used score sheets in the box, and it makes me happy for some reason, to think of this box as being a part of Pal's family's life. My score sheet will go in there with all the others and be part of the Gakhar family Scrabble story.

At one point Pal goes for a triple word score with a word I don't know.

"That is so not a word," I balk. I pronounce it "tee-tee," like the word my Alabaman grandmother uses for *urinate* because she thinks *pee* is impolite. I'm trying not to laugh because it hurts. The sitting up is making me hurt a little worse, but I don't want to stop playing because I can't remember the last time I played Scrabble. This is random and fun and not at all what I expected as far as hospital visits go.

"It is so a word," Pal says, grinning. He pronounces it "*tie*-tee," accent on the first syllable. "*Titi*: any of a genus of South American monkeys with small round heads."

This is so funny I think I am going to ruin all the good

work that has been performed by the doctors who removed my appendix and put me back together again. I'm trying so hard not to laugh that I'm silently weeping.

"Could you use it in a sentence?" I manage to ask Pal.

"*Titi*," Pal says evenly. "Noun. From the Spanish. As in, 'On Sundays, or *los domingos,* I enjoy taking long walks and performing various antics alongside my pet titi.'"

This cracks me up.

We finish the game and along the way exchange the sort of hilarious repartee (from the French *repartir,* to retort) that can be shared only by two former middle-school spelling bee whizzes who at one point in their lives devoted an unhealthful amount of time to memorizing the pages of *Webster's Third New International Dictionary.* This time, Pal lets me win. I'm holding open the little drawstring bag and Pal is pouring in the tiles when I call him on it.

"Why'd you do that?" I ask. Looking right at him.

Pal looks right back. "Why'd *you* do it?"

I try to give him a look like I don't know what he means, but of course I do. Half of my mind has been back in that sixth-grade classroom this whole time, after all. The carpet pattern, Pal's khaki pants, Leona's eyes refusing to find mine: they're all right there. The images of those things are so bright — so alight with shame — that I think they must be playing across my face, which is suddenly burning.

"I don't know," I say, choking on my own lame voice. I will not cry.

Pal stares at me—not mean. Not what I think I deserve.

"April," Pal says evenly, "do you know that sometimes patients won't allow my dad to work on them?"

Echoes of those cheers, floating across the hall. *Ding, dong.* I dare myself to speak, but all I can do is shake my head. Maybe if I shake it hard enough, I can make this conversation go away.

On the Scrabble board, our tiles tremble. I steady my legs, willing myself still, grateful for something to stare at: ARTIFACE, a word Pal built onto my FACE.

"These patients," Pal continues, "are not interested in any explanations I—or you, or my father, or anyone—might have about the finer points separating, say, Hinduism from Islam. Or, you know, freaking insane radical extremism from Islam, or Christianity, or —" Pal stops. Shakes his head. "One thing. One face. That's all they see."

I manage to tell Pal that I know. I know. But what the hell do I know? What exactly do I know?

"People aren't always what you think they are," he says evenly. Then he puts the Scrabble things back in the box, slides the homework and newspaper neatly under Gina and Gavin's vase of daisies, and—one last smile before he goes, one last surprise kindness—disappears down the hall.

Pal visits me in the hospital just the one time, just for the length of that one game of Scrabble. I get well and return to swim practice and go back to school, where Pal is once again more acquaintance than friend, though we always smile and wave at each other in the halls. Spring is in full bloom, and

Osama bin Laden is gone, and Pal Gakhar is one of twenty-eight students in my sophomore biology class.

I keep Pal's biology notes, though, from the days I missed school. They are so pretty that I can't throw them away, so I pin them to the corkboard in my room. Precise drawings of the parts of a fetal pig are neatly labeled in perfect block capitals, the handwriting of a future architect, maybe. Somebody smart and careful, as good at art as he is at math and science.

Somebody with a marvelous future ahead of him.

GAVIN'S EIGHT MILLION STARS AT MIDNIGHT

(12:07 PM EDT)

Holy sweet miracle in a pair of silk pajamas, I can hear the sirens. The reinforcements. Let me tell you what, it is #musictomyears. I've never heard anything so beautiful in my entire life. Messiah in a cop car, hurry your ass on up. Let's get this place surrounded and get on up out of here, starting now.

Gina makes this sound — this sort of half cry, half laugh yelp.

Mr. Goodrich shushes her and holds his hands up to all of us, like be still, be still. I swear it looks in the dim light like he's about to cry, like he's finally going to lose it, and I'm thinking, no, way, bruh, don't you dare lose your shit. Don't you dare do that right now.

Let me tell you about this one time when Valentino didn't run fast enough and when I didn't, either. I saw it

« « «

happen, too, like it was this terrible slow-motion agony, like those dreams where whatever you're running from is coming at you at turbo-nightmare speed and there you are: stuck. Frozen. Can't move.

Valentino had gotten out, but nobody knew it. When I came out the door to go to school, there he was, standing in the yard across the street, sniffing at something. He perked up when he saw me, one ear all flopped over but the other raised and alert, like, hey, I know you. In the morning light, his pale gray fur looked almost translucent, my gorgeous angel dog.

Valentino, you silly bitch! Get back over here!

He stared at me for a second and then—staring right at me!—decided he was sleepy or bored or something, so he just plopped right down on the lawn, just stretched his front legs out in front of him, all looking like a sphinx with a funny riddle in his head.

So then this car comes flying down the street and I'm watching it, I'm watching to see if Valentino sees it and knows, but he's getting up then and he's watching me and looking all happy and leaps up fast as anything to try to make it across and too much is happening at once, I'm screaming at the car and at Valentino, but I'm stuck, I'm not going anywhere, and when this car hits my dog, that moment—that moment is the worst thing I've ever felt in all the world. My moms come screaming out the door, and this guy in the car, he's super-nice, he stops and gets out and we all go for Valentino—who isn't even bleeding, Jesus

Christ, but is heaving in this way that breaks my heart, like he is broken and he can't be fixed.

The guy rides with us to the vet. Mom Resa and I are in the back, holding Valentino across our laps. His chest keeps heaving and heaving, but I've got his eyes locked with mine, and I am sending him messages. *Valentino, don't you die. Don't do it, Mr. Beautiful.* Valentino's eyes, man, they go on and on and on. It's like looking directly at a soul, like this right here, this innocence and grace, this will to live — this is what a soul looks like.

Greyhounds, man. Do you ever think about how fragile they really are? All that speed, held up by these spindly little legs, these tendons that look like effing dental floss. Who's not fragile, though? Who's not? You tell me, bitches.

What I'm trying to say is that Valentino lived. He had a break in his hind leg, but he healed, and he lived, and every night of the world he sleeps curled at the foot of my bed on his red blanket. And he looks at me with these eyes that make me sure as anything that there is such thing as a soul. When he got hit, when he got hurt, I did not cry. All the way to the vet, me and Resa holding on to that beautiful creature, I did not cry one single tear. It was not until they had Valentino up on that cold silver table, his nails scrabbling all desperate against that slippery surface, the silk of his ears folded back and his chest going in and out so hard I worried he would burst, and the vet told us, the vet said, *He is going to be okay, we're going to take care of him —* then. Then, when I knew he would live, is when I cried for

Valentino and for my own terrible mistake, the mistake of not getting there faster, of letting him get loose in the first place. I cried and cried. I cried so hard I puked.

"Mr. Goodrich," I whisper. The sirens are coming from everywhere now, in glorious #surroundsound. "Don't cry."

While we're listening to that beautiful song of the sirens, Nate Salisbury gets up and starts stepping over people's legs and arms and knees until he gets to Gina. He kneels in front of her and does this thing where he sort of lifts her hair and smooths it away from her face, gathers it behind her shoulders. Then—you will not believe this! you will not believe what he does!—he sort of curls his hand behind Gina's ear, and when he opens his palm he's got a quarter in it. Nate Salisbury! Doing #effingmagic! In the Lockdown Closet! Then Nate, he leans his forehead against Gina's forehead, and for a second—I'm this close to them—it looks like they're passing a thought back and forth through their skin, through their skulls. I look away as Nate kisses her, because whose business is that? Not my business. Gina shifts so Nate can sit next to her, and he does. Then he leans over Gina to talk, to say something to me, and you know what he says? He says, all quiet and on the sly: *Hey, Gavin, it'd be cool if you maybe didn't mention to anybody that little transaction you saw happening under the bleachers this morning, okay?*

Because you know what? It turns out that was *Nate* under the bleachers this morning, all incognito under a hood. Nate Salisbury, purchasing a little bit of recreational bud from his top-secret supplier. Ahead of the 4/20 holiday and all.

Holy heart attack, Nate. Way to scare my ass to death.

So but then, wait. What is happening outside this Lockdown Closet?

"Where'd you learn magic?" Gina asks. Nate just grins, and I hope that for real and for true, Gina will finally get that Nate Salisbury is about a thousand times cooler than that famous magician she's all obsessed with. Here's a secret, bitches, listen up: the real thing is always way better than the made-up thing in your head. You can't hold the made-up thing by the hand, the way Gina's holding Nate's hand right now. She's got him by one hand and me by the other, and the sirens are screaming.

In my head, I'm going through my list, and it looks like this:

- Valentino's ears
- Mom Leslie's garden
- Mom Resa's laugh
- Gerbil at April's house
- Otis Redding
- Heartbreak Hill, bitches
- Poe's room on the lawn at UVA, #completewithraven
- Mr. Goodrich's grandkid on the way
- Nate Salisbury's voice, and his quarter trick
- Gina's birthday presents
- Thunderstorms on the porch

- Eight million stars at midnight
- The dizzy you get with a kiss
- Previews before the movie
- Photo booths, acting stupid
- Driving with the windows down
- Friday afternoon, right after the bell rings, that freedom
- Any freedom, any at all
- The snooze button
- Snow
- The ocean, where whales live, and miraculous-ass jellyfishes and whatnot
- A bonfire and a guitar and blackened marshmallows and a tent
- The world outside this room
- The class of 2013
- Love
- Love
- Love
- Love
- Love
- Love
- Love

ALL THE PHOEBES

(7:02 AM MDT)

Phoebe has kept running and breathing through the pain in her lungs and calves and she is okay now, she knows that her legs will now carry her for as long and as far as she wants. What she wants is to run all the way to Nebraska. Her thoughts are all mixed up — how long will it take until they find out, until they find her, until she goes to jail? — the thoughts are coming fast, they are snowballing past the parameters of her own understanding of how these things go, she doesn't know how these things go, she is new at this, all she wants is to carry on, to keep running, she thinks she can be in Nebraska within the hour if she just keeps up this pace, if she just keeps going, go go go go go.

"Listen," Angela is saying. "Phoebe, whoever this Dylan person is, just, you know what? Fuck him. Fuck her. It's

« « «

nothing. It's stupid! Not even real. You don't throw your life away for that."

Phoebe nods hard, too winded to open her mouth to speak. She has told her sister everything, and just as she knew would happen, the fierce need, the angry desire, the desperate immediacy of the whole plan now seem considerably less. She feels the lessening as if the weight of something heavy—a cinder block, a Buick—were being lifted from her chest.

"Dr. Fannin says—" Phoebe begins.

"You know what? Fuck her, too. We're not talking about her right now."

Angela flaps her hand in the air as if the thought of Dr. Fannin is a bothersome insect. Dr. Fannin is Phoebe's therapist, and she is perfectly nice, perfectly kind, even if she does have this annoying habit of silently mouthing the words that Phoebe is speaking even as she—Phoebe herself—is in the act of speaking them.

For months, Phoebe's mother has paid eighty-five dollars an hour for Dr. Fannin to mouth words that Phoebe hasn't yet fully even voiced. It has gotten to where Phoebe won't even talk, such is the extent to which she dreads watching Dr. Fannin's mouth open and close guppy-like around these things that are supposed to be her deepest thoughts and feelings. Sometimes she'll sit there for the full fifty minutes and stare at the wall, or the orchid on Dr. Fannin's desk, or at Dr. Fannin's steepled fingers and serene gaze. Dr. Fannin knows her stuff and always says the right things, but it occurs to Phoebe that what she has needed all this long while is not the carefully measured nods and thoughtful assessments of a licensed professional, but the outrage and impatience of her own sister, someone with whom she shares blood and history and also a bathroom, someone who will reach out and grab her hand and yank her around and look her straight in the eye and say,

"Look. Look at me. I love you. Do you hear me? I love you, and I am having no more of this. No more of it. Starting now this nightmare is done. This minute."

They run all the way to the school, which is still asleep in the pink light.

Clarity is slowly coming to Phoebe, and she feels it as a fissure, a tiny hairline crack through which light—*her* light, the thing that makes her Phoebe—is straining to shine through.

The run has been good. It is a thing she has started, and if she finishes, it will be this wondrous miracle, the first thing she has started and finished in she doesn't know how long. Usually when she starts a thing, anything, it is four thousand distractions and diversions and heartaches and worries and compulsions before she can get through that one single thing. It can be a thing as insignificant as brushing her teeth, during which she will remember a piece of paper in her backpack, which will make her think to check something in her e-mail, which will then suck her in, toothbrush still in mouth, with its own pull of dread mixed with anticipation, always feeling at least four things at once, this tangled collision of feelings, and she'll accidentally swallow the toothpaste but keep gnawing on the brush, absentmindedly, because her mind is absent now, it almost always is. Her mind is in Nebraska, or New Orleans, or someplace, anyplace, where she doesn't despise herself so much. When (an hour later) she finally gets around to returning her toothbrush to the bathroom, she will stare at her face in the mirror, will find some imperfection and pick at it until it bleeds, and then she'll look for her astringent but won't be able to find it, and then her phone will alert her to an incoming text message that needs answering now, even though her face is still sort of bleeding, but *ping*

> *the message*
> *and her thoughts*
> *but her face*
> *and she didn't floss*
> *and what was she looking for again, in the backpack?*
> *but someone linked to this video and there goes eight*
> *minutes of her life*
> *and it's too late now to even start her homework*
> *so fuck it until tomorrow*
> *and tomorrow*
> *and tomorrow*

Phoebe can feel the spreading warmth of the sun at her back. The soccer field is spangled with dew. Angela's ponytail swings back and forth and brushes Phoebe's shoulder.

On the telephone wire is a procession of black birds, sleek and perfect as anything.

"Watch this," Angela says, picking up speed. Phoebe watches as she sprints beneath the wire, swings her arms into the air, and lets out a long, clear *whooooooop!* The birds rise all at once, soaring skyward in a formation that somebody must have taught them, only nobody taught them that. Nobody taught them, but still they know. Phoebe has heard that birds will stay in formation like this, even if one of their members gets lost. Like geese in a *V*—say one of them gets shot and killed and falls to the ground, where the hunter will rush to inspect his quarry. The rest of the geese will keep going, even if there's a hole in their *V*.

They keep going because they have to. Maybe they're better off. Maybe that goose was weighing them down to begin with. Maybe that goose didn't have what it takes to be part of the *V*—maybe something was wrong, really wrong, with that stupid goose.

Or maybe—maybe—the hole means something else: the geese are mourning and honoring their loss. Here is our broken *V*.

I'll meet you at
I'll be there
I can't wait to see you touch you hear you hold you

Phoebe sprints as hard as she can—feet pounding out the words in her mind—to catch up with her sister. And that's when she sees them: the old couple, he in his Irish cap, she in her heavy skirt. They are just entering the field, making their way toward the track.

"Come on," Phoebe says, touching Angela's arm. "I want to talk to them."

The sisters jog across the grass, green and slippery and sparkling.

"Hello," Phoebe says when she reaches the couple. She's marveling at how peaceful they seem to her, how not in a hurry. Phoebe herself is dying of urgency. The couple's calm is something she wants to climb into, like a skin.

"Good morning," the man says. He removes his hat, pressing it to his chest, and dips his head. The ceremony of this gesture so moves Phoebe that once again her voice is lost to her. She looks with anguish at her sister, willing her to return the man's greeting.

"Hi there," Angela says. "My name's Angela, and this is my sister, Phoebe."

Phoebe shakes the man's hand—dry, cool, *real*—and then the woman's. The man introduces himself and his wife, but their names are gone from Phoebe's mind almost as soon as they enter it. She wants the names back but is too overcome to ask. Why can't she hang on to anything? What wire in her brain is broken? The couple is smiling, smiling. Then the man says something that Phoebe would not have expected, not in a million years.

"Look at that," he says, gesturing at the wide expanse of

green, that field of diamonds. "It looks like a benediction, doesn't it?"

Benediction. It's a word that Phoebe has encountered countless times in books but cannot recall ever having heard spoken aloud. She wants to ask how long they've been married. She wants to ask the man how old he is, what's the worst thing he's ever seen, what he thinks of geese in a *V,* what the saddest day of his life has been so far, how he got past it, how it is that he has remained on the planet for so long and still manages to walk around the track every day, taking his patient, sweet time. She wants to ask the woman if she is a mother, if she has children or grandchildren and if so where they are now, how old are they, are they happy, do their lives have meaning. She wants to ask all these things, but instead she smiles. A silent agreement. An acknowledgment.

"It's nice to meet you," Angela says, reaching for Phoebe's hand. It's time to go.

As the sisters are making their way back across the field, Phoebe hears the woman say to the man, "What I wouldn't give to feel that good."

Phoebe can't remember the last time she felt good, but as she ascends the hill with her sister, as she feels the heat in her calves, pushing her up that hill, as she fills her lungs with air and blinks against the startling brightness of the risen sun, she promises herself that she will feel good again soon. Good. Goodness. Soon.

She finishes the run.

She finishes the thing she began.

Back at the house, the girls' mother is waiting for them. Her eyes are rimmed with red, and in her fist she is clutching a phone.

"I've been calling and calling," she says, fist now pressed to her chest. "Where were you? Angela, why didn't you answer? Phoebe, I thought you were sick! Where have you girls been?"

Phoebe can see it, the worry on her mother's face. The love. Just for a second, she sees her mother's lined face, her weary body, as a casement for all the women she— Christina, their mother—has been in her life. All the girls. They're wrapped around one another like dolls within dolls: the five-year-old who burned her left hand on the stove folded into the girl who soared down the sidewalk on a red Schwinn with a banana seat, this one tucked into the outline of the teenager in her concert T-shirt (REM GREEN), eyes shining and wild with secrets. The teenager is curled into the Gonzaga student, bookish and sweater-clad and filled with dreaming, who married a man who became their father, who was responsible for turning her into a mother— *their* mother—and this mother-doll has the thickest outer covering yet, hard and solid as a sarcophagus, this shell of parenthood. Impenetrable, as in, *World, with all of your darknesses, do not, under any circumstances whatsoever, bring harm to my daughters.*

How many girls live inside Phoebe? How many women are waiting to wrap their skin around her? Phoebe can see them, holding out their arms. She can hear them whispering.

Phoebe rushes to her mother and embraces her. Their hearts are pressed together, two frantic birds. Phoebe holds her ear against her mother's ear — that perfect shell, echo of Phoebe's own — and listens for the primal, oceanic sounds of all those women and girls, all those Christinas, their promises and secrets and plans.

"I'm sorry, Mom," Phoebe says, pulling away so that she can hold her mother by the shoulders and look her in the eye. She is heartbroken to see doubt there. Fear. Sorrow.

"I'm back now," Phoebe says. "I'm not going anywhere. I'm back."

APRIL SKY

(12:01 PM EDT)

Shining pieces of sky are filtering through the water, glint-ing as they swirl, slow-motion, to the bottom of the pool. It is a strange and beautiful thing to see. My body floats upward toward the light, and as I break the surface, a tiny shard of sky catches in my lashes, in my eye.

» » »

THE MASTERMIND, SWAYING

(9:04 AM PDT)

The Mastermind is being carried away.

Is he in a cop car? Is this his arrest? Is this real?

Wait. No. He's still falling. Still on his way down. Dizzy, dizzy. Everything a wild unraveling. Behind his eyes he can see bright pinpricks of light: *the light fantastic,* those words ignite in his brain.

"The light fantastic," the Mastermind mutters, muffled.

"What?" Wendy says. "What'd you say?"

Wendy is leaning over him, gripping his hand. They wobble and sway; things he can't identify wobble and sway above their heads. His vision is coming back to him in wavy slivers. On his other side, a sickly slice of light reveals a face he doesn't recognize. The face says (blurry dream, medicine-thick), *You're going to be fine.*

« « «

The Mastermind's arm is covered in a white bandage, underneath which snakes a tube connected to a bag of strange fluid. The bag, it sways slowly. Strange movement, like they're on a boat. It's a boat — no, wait, a pirate ship — and they're out on the water, playing make-believe. Playing walk-the-plank with the other Lost Boys. Hiding from Captain Hook.

The Mastermind peers at Wendy, piecing together the slivers that make up her face.

"I'm riding with you to the hospital," Wendy says. "We're almost there, okay?"

The Mastermind considers this and how it fits into his midfall dream. So where are the sirens, then? What's he doing in an ambulance when somebody could have just wheeled him across campus to the university hospital? It's all wrong. Not adding up. But the face of the paramedic has come fully into focus now: a woman whose expression is still. She appears unaware of the Mastermind's secrets. She appears uninterested in arresting him. The ambulance is just another vehicle moving through traffic. No lights, no sirens, no emergency — just a strange, medicinal calm.

"The light fantastic," the Mastermind repeats. His voice doesn't sound like his own. Slowly, he turns his head and gazes at Wendy. "Those words. From your play. What do you think they even mean?"

Wendy is searching the Mastermind's face. She is searching for the right words. She starts to say something but stops herself, switches gears. In her lap are the

Mastermind's wings, and she fans her fingers across them. "These make me think of Icarus," she says. Then, switching gears again, "I didn't know you were diabetic. Why didn't you tell me?"

The Icarus thing confuses the Mastermind. He would not have guessed that Wendy Neely would be familiar with the story of Icarus and Daedalus. Her recognition of it feels like an invasion, an intrusion. He doesn't want to lose the thread of the other thing, either. The light fantastic. That thing. He closes his eyes, wanting to go back. Sway, sway, sway.

"No," he says, letting go of Wendy's hand. "What do you think it means? 'The light fantastic'?" He feels strangely desperate to know Wendy's thoughts on this.

Wendy shrinks back. A flicker of fear across her face. "Well, in the play, when Tom Wingfield says his father skips the light fantastic, he's saying that the father left. Right?"

The Mastermind shakes his head again, hard. He'll shake his brain right out, right out here in this ambulance, that's how much he sometimes wants to be rid of its heavy burden. "No," he says. He doesn't want the obvious answer. Speaking feels like swallowing the whole of the ocean, but he carries on. "I know that part. What I mean is, what do the words mean to *you*?"

"Quiet now," says the paramedic, briefly placing her palm on the Mastermind's chest. This touch — this small thing — sends the Mastermind into a momentary flail of heartbreak, during which he finds himself hoping, just for a split second, that somebody will catch him before he hits the ground.

Wendy is silent for a moment, and then finally, as if daring herself to speak, she says—he can barely hear: "It's such a weird coincidence. Just last week, in my art history class, we were talking about that painting. Sixteenth-century Dutch guy? Do you know who I mean?"

The Mastermind regards her blankly. What is Wendy even talking about? She doesn't know what she's talking about. She has always been a little bit on the stupid side, Wendy Neely, prone to parties and talking too loud.

"Broiler," she says. "No! Bruegel. Pieter Bruegel. *The Fall of Icarus.* It's this picture of, like, a peasant guy. Ships at sea, a flock of sheep, some shepherd who hasn't got a clue. Do you know the picture? Have you seen it?" Wendy's babbling the way people do when they're trying and failing to lighten moments of bewilderment and fear.

Slowly, the Mastermind shakes his head no. He doesn't know this Bruegel painting, and his skin is crawling with the not knowing. He does not wish to further discuss Icarus, or Dutch paintings, or coincidences and whether or not they constitute proof of God's anonymity. He feels suddenly nauseated, the Mastermind. Dizzy all over again. The liquid in the bag, it's filling him up with sleep and lies, delaying his meeting with the ground. He'll just close his eyes, and this will be the last part. God, Wendy Neely, stop talking. Just shut up.

But Wendy, she can't stop. "Yeah, so the whole point of the painting is that life is going on all around, right? People are just doing their thing, but if you look really close—like *really* close, like you can imagine that nobody even saw him fall—there are Icarus's legs, kicking around in the sea. You just see his legs! That's the only part of him you can even see!" Wendy knots her fingers in the feathers of the Mastermind's wings and barks a nervous laugh.

The Mastermind, gaining clarity and dread, absorbs this. Despite everything—his vision in slivers, his body prostrate in an ambulance, his bloodstream and weakened nervous system drunk on these fluids—he gets it; don't think for a second that any of this is lost on him. Behind his closed eyes he's picturing a different painting of Icarus: in this one, the fallen boy is surrounded by beautiful water nymphs, who, cradling his splendid wings, lament his untimely death. One of the nymphs has—what do you call those things?—a lyre. Some kind of harp. One of the nymphs has a huge bare bottom, pale and round as the moon.

"Anyway, it's a coincidence," Wendy says. Her voice is too loud, edged in bright shards of reality. "Like seeing you at all is a coincidence, right? I still can't believe it."

Coincidence, coincidence. *Blah, blah, blah!* He wants the world rid of this word, which does not leave room for cause and effect. Doing. Deciding.

The Mastermind's throat and mouth are so dry, he has

to lick his lips before he can speak. "Skipping the light," he says. "It's when you make your decision. That moment."

Wendy considers this. "Yeah," she says. "I can see that. And the moment can go either way."

Which way has the moment gone? the Mastermind wonders, mind swaying once again toward the delicious realm of sleep and nothingness.

He doesn't know.

TRENDING NOW

1. Kim Kardashian Pregnant
2. Pabst Blue Ribbon
3. Boston Manhunt
4. Marathon Bombings
5. Royal Baby
6. Kanye West
7. Musharraf Arrest
8. West Texas Explosion
9. Rush Hall of Fame
10. Quinoa Recipes
11. Gwyneth Paltrow Workout
12. Botox
13. Maine School Lockdown

« « «

LINCOLN AND THE LABYRINTH

(12:32 PM CDT)

"We're going home," I say to Laura, easing the Lexus back onto the road. I'm calm now. Over there in the passenger seat, the siren has lost her voice, but she's alive. She's still alive. Odysseus's men — man, how stupid were they? So stupid. All those Greek heroes, there they were, all strong and capable and sculpted and warrior-like, and what was always killing them? Some stupid small thing, like their ego or their balls or their pride. That guy Icarus, flying too close to the sun. I mean, what'd you think was going to happen, idiot? Who do you think you are?

Laura Echols's phone chimes, and — I can't believe this — she starts pawing through her bag to find it. Her braid sways forward while she leans over; if you caught a glimpse of her like this, you'd think she was any ordinary

» » »

girl, that this was just an ordinary day, the two of us out for a joyride, cruising along on a buzz of sunshine and freedom. There is nothing life-or-death about the way Laura leans back casually, checking to see who's calling. In fact, it is almost as if this ringing phone is what has brought Laura back to life; the color has returned to her cheeks, and her face is animated, expectant.

"Who is it?" I ask. It had better be God or somebody like that.

"I don't know this number," Laura answers. Her nonchalance infuriates me. I mean is this even happening? Is Laura Echols receiving random phone calls in the middle of what feels like the end of the world? Is that where we are now? I reach over and grab the phone from her hand. I make a move to throw it out the window, but I hit the wrong button on the door panel: the lock, not the window. The phone hits the glass and falls against my thigh, still chiming merrily. Laura reaches for it, but I elbow her arm away.

"Hello?" I say into Laura's phone, ready to speak directly to God. *God,* I would say, *get with it! You've got an endlessly fucked-up flock down here! Send shepherds who know what's going on! Send angels! It's an emergency!*

"Hello, Laura?" says this shaky, confused-sounding voice. The voice sounds alarmingly like somebody's mom. Somebody's mom who has mistaken my voice for Laura's, thanks a lot.

"No," I say stupidly. "This is Lincoln Evans. Who is this?"

"Lincoln," the voice says in a rush of breath. "Where are you? Are you with Laura?"

I know this voice. This voice belongs to my English teacher, only she doesn't usually sound like this. Right now she sounds like she's forcing calm on top of hysteria. She knows.

"Lincoln," Ms. Heslip says. "I need to know where you are."

Laura is flailing wildly for her phone. The Lexus veers, a dangerous surge and teeter, as I shake her off.

"We're on our way home," I say, scanning signs. My teeth chatter as I read the signs aloud to Ms. Heslip, a nonsensical list that tells her nothing. There's a sign for McDonald's. There's mile marker eighty. Now that I've got her on the phone, this voice that sounds Mom-ish, I'm near to tears. I want her to come get us. I want her to make soup.

"I'm on my way," Ms. Heslip says. "You drive and I'll drive. We'll meet in the middle. Keep going."

Laura has buried her face in her arms. I have no idea what's happening with her. What if she tries to open the door and get out? The lock. The lock. I can't drive and hold the phone and keep the doors locked all at once.

"I should hang up," I say to Ms. Heslip. "This isn't safe."

"Just this once it's safe," she says, and her voice is bobbing around, like she's running. Lots of unidentifiable noises in the background. I want to be able to picture her background, the familiar landscape of anything I might know and recognize. The school parking lot, for instance, in all of its commonplace glory.

And that's the scariest thing about all of this: how *ordinary* this whole happening seems, in its weird way. I feel outside of it, looking in, and Ms. Heslip's voice is the thing pulling me back. Who's that other Greek guy? The labyrinth guy. Theseus. Ariadne's ball of thread is what gets him through that labyrinth. Ms. Heslip's voice — that's the ball of thread.

"I'll keep talking to you," Ms. Heslip says. "I'll talk you home."

Home. Home. Home. I want it so bad. It is so many things: My mom, buttering a piece of toast in the morning before work. The way the smell of the toast wakes me up and makes me feel safe, just this private moment I have to myself before I climb out of bed and get dressed, the way that safe-toast smell feels — I can't really say what it is. There's so much I can't say; it's *stuff*, but it's also a feeling. My mom's keys and her purse on a hook by the back door. The detergent she uses to make our clothes and our towels smell good. The way the pantry door always sticks, and the stuff in there: lots of Campbell's tomato soup, waiting to be eaten with grilled cheese and oyster crackers. The pots of herbs on the windowsill, most of the stuff dead, but the lavender keeps going and if you rub it between your fingers, it smells like sleeping, dreaming. Sometimes my mother puts a sprig of it beneath her pillow, and sometimes, when she works the all-night shift and the house starts to feel like it's folding in on itself and I'm too awake, like heart-racingly awake, I will go to her room and breathe into her pillow until I fall asleep.

There have been lots of homes, but the feeling is what stays the same. There's not a name for it. There's also not a name for this thing that lives inside me — this happiness, I guess. This weird capacity for joy in spite of everything. I've always been able to get to it. I may not have been born beautiful or brilliant or lucky, but I've been happy. If I've made a mistake, it's been in thinking that everyone's happy is the same. If I make a mistake now, it will be in letting somebody touch it, letting somebody take it away.

"Lincoln, you okay?" Ms. Heslip asks.

"I'm awesome," I say. The word just tumbles out, sarcastic and mean, an accident. I've sworn off this word, starting now. It has lost its charm with me. *Be awesome,* the whole wide world seems always to be telling us. *Do something awesome!* Laura Echols, go forth with your cello and your awesome scholarship to Vassar and bring upon yourself heaps and heaps of awesome. Be the most awesome you can awesomely be. Don't settle for anything less. It's a huge lot of pressure, the constant expectation of awesomeness. What if you don't feel awesome? What if awesome is the opposite of the way you feel? How about this, assholes: be *kind.*

"Lincoln, where are you now?" Ms. Heslip asks, and I start up again, reading the signs as they blink past. They are comforting in their ordinariness, as if the world can't possibly be broken if there are twenty-four-hour diners serving stacks of pancakes ladled with syrup. I'm starving. I want to go to that place and get the pancakes. I want to go to so many places.

"Can you put the phone on speaker?" Ms. Heslip asks, and I do. Laura lifts her head from her knees at the sound of Ms. Heslip's voice. She doesn't say anything, but her breath catches. I put Ms. Heslip in the cup holder, where the thread of her voice can reach us both. I can see that Laura feels it, too, the pull of that voice. I can see that she, too, wants to go back to where it is leading us, and I cannot wait to get us there.

THE FORUM,
AN INTRODUCTION

Delaware Wednesday, April 17, 2013, at 11:52 pm

VERMONT LIKES THIS

Hello. Am I too late?

Mastermind Wednesday, April 17, 2013, at 11:59 pm

VERMONT LIKES THIS

Right on time. We have a new Delaware, everyone.
Delaware 2.0.

Texas Thursday, April 18, 2013, at 12:01 am   VERMONT LIKES THIS

delaware II! two more sleeps. tell me a bedtime story.
yours.

» » »

Delaware Thursday, April 18, 2013, at 12:07 am

VERMONT AND 6 OTHERS LIKE THIS

It's an old story. Old as Salem and witches.

Vermont Thursday, April 18, 2013, at 12:08 am

Oh god not another one. Fucking spare me OK? Not why we're here, not what this is about

Idaho Thursday, April 18, 2013, at 12:10 am

NEBRASKA AND 8 OTHERS LIKE THIS

Story of my life. Salem! The Crucible, yo.

Texas Thursday, April 18, 2013, at 12:10 am

IDAHO AND 4 OTHERS LIKE THIS

wait hold on a sec is a crucible the same as a bell jar????????????

Nebraska Thursday, April 18, 2013, at 12:11 am

IDAHO AND 6 OTHERS LIKE THIS

It's all the fucking same.

Vermont Thursday, April 18, 2013, at 12:11 am

DELAWARE LIKES THIS

Says another special snowflake UGH Im so fucking tired of all of you

THE CEILING FLIES AWAY

(12:02 PM EDT)

My eyes are kaleidoscopic with glass. Back under, back under to wash out the shards. Through those shards, all broken with light, there was a shape at the edge of the pool. A shape with a menacing shape in its hands. I knew the shape before I saw it, have known it all along, the knee that touched mine on that hospital bed, the V of hair above a little kid's swim trunks.

Sirens. Thin, high wail, growing closer. A cramp twists the arch of my foot and climbs up my calf, a fiery bloom. I try to kick it away, kick all the way to the bottom. Down here on the floor of the pool, everything is peaceful and still. I'm gliding along the surface, quiet quiet quiet. The spelling bee words go floating past me, beautiful silken ripples of light: *Aquiline. Pirouette. Flambeau.*

» » »

Pal Gakhar's mom's hair in the pool, a dark swirl entwined with the swirl of my own mother's hair, our two mothers, laughing with straight, white teeth. Afterward they would wrap us in thick hooded towels; mine was a duck to match my yellow suit, and Pal's was a dragon, little orange triangles ridged along the top of his head. The towels were warm and dry and safe; our mothers were open-armed, beautiful, ours.

Peregrination. Vicissitude. Antediluvian.

Pal's white teeth, gleaming in the pink shadows of the weeping cherry. Pal's slim fingers on the Scrabble tiles. Pal with his friends on the lawn, the neat arc of the Frisbee, the grace of arms flung out wide, the infectious song of laughter, the invisible thread linking Pallav Gakhar to his friends, the way they seem like brothers, every bit as blood-bound as that.

Pallav Gakhar, National Merit Scholar.

Pallav Gakhar, Salutatorian.

Once—a Thursday in January—I watched Leona Reece open her locker to find a purple iris, one single graceful stem. I happened to be standing there and saw her face, more worried than touched, as if she thought the flower might explode. I wondered then about Leona, if after someone has been cruel to you—even if years have passed; even if now you are altogether marvelous and really always have been—you are always waiting for the cruelty to return. Expecting it. Gavin's dog, Valentino? Once—this was years ago—a plant hanging from the ceiling came crashing down near the bright spot in the sunroom where Valentino was sleeping. Now, all this time later, whenever Valentino goes in the sunroom, he cuts a wide path around the spot where the plant fell. He won't go near that spot, even if you try to drag him by his collar. It's like the memory of that falling plant is part of Valentino's body now.

On that January Thursday, I crossed the hall to where Leona stood and smiled at her. *Pretty,* I said, and reached out to touch the iris. *Is it a present?*

Leona shook her head, confused, and that's when a white card tumbled from the clutter in her locker and landed on the floor, softly skating. I bent to pick it up, and on the front I recognized Pal's handwriting, the same swift block letters I'd seen written on biology notes and years' worth of blackboards and whiteboards. *Please write the problem on the board. Be sure to show your work!*

So Leona Reece had received a gift from Pal Gakhar. It was none of my business, so I stood up and handed the card to her. It was then, just as I was turning to go—years too late—that I finally thought to apologize to her.

"Leona," I said. "I'm sorry."

Leona studied my face and said nothing.

I said it again: "I'm sorry. I apologize."

What did I think was going to happen? That her face would dissolve into a smile? That she would hug me? That we would be friends forevermore?

What happened is that Leona tilted her head and shook it, very slowly. What came out of her mouth came slowly, too. Quiet, deliberate. "Wow," she said, mock-fascinated. "Isn't that beautiful." She stared at me some more—seconds like hours, the weight of that shame—before continuing: "So are you twelve-stepping it or something? Is that what this is?"

I had no idea what Leona was talking about.

"Do you feel better now?" Leona asked. Her voice was steady and low. "Because any apology coming out of your mouth is not about me, it's about you. You know that, right?"

Shame, shame, shame. My face was on fire with it.

"Do me a favor," Leona said. Quiet, slow, deliberate. Then she raised her arm, and for a wild second I thought she was going to slap me. Instead she touched the tip of the iris to my face. "Don't insult my intelligence with your *apology*. Okay?"

And then she smiled at me sweetly and walked away, leaving me there with my mind, telescoping in and out of the jewel-colored sleeping bags, the horrible cruel purgatory that was middle school, and Pallav Gakhar, bestower of irises, admirer of Leona Reece, winner of the district spelling bee in grades six through eight.

Pal's mother worked at the library, and that's where Pal would go after school, doing homework in the carrels or reading on an overstuffed beanbag chair until her shift ended. This was in middle school, before anybody could drive. You could walk to the library from school. I spent afternoons there, too, and Pal's mom always knew which books I would like. Try this one, she would say, slipping a book into my hands, and always I would love the choices she made. I loved, too, her beauty. How everything she wore was drenched in colors of flame and celebration. It must always be a celebration at Pal Gakhar's house, I thought then, jealously. A house no doubt filled with rows and rows and stacks and stacks and shelves and shelves of books.

Puerile. Contretemps. Prospicience.

Prospicience. Noun. From the Latin *prospicere.* To look forward. Foresight. The act of looking forward.

THE LAST MOMENTS
OF THE FORUM

Nebraska Thursday, April 18, 2013, at 2:17 am
Delaware: you still awake? Tell me the real story.

Delaware Thursday, April 18, 2013, at 2:17 am
I'm tired, and the story is long. It starts here:

http://kafkasrevenge/mondayapril152013/
WhatTaxesYou/letstalkmicroaggressions/

Nebraska Thursday, April 18, 2013, at 2:19 am
Wait. I don't understand. Also I just tried the link
again and it's disabled. Two minutes ago it was there.
Was that your real name?

« « «

Delaware Thursday, April 18, 2013, at 2:29 am

It must have taken the Mastermind all of about
5 seconds to spot that. Sorry, Mastermind: My bad.
Does it really matter at this point? Nebraska: What
part do you not understand? They came after me. From
all directions. They came at my mom, man.

Nebraska Thursday, April 18, 2013, at 2:23 am

They. They. We all have a different they. Who is they?

Delaware Thursday, April 18, 2013, at 2:23 am

All of us? Just a guess

Nebraska Thursday, April 18, 2013, at 2:25 am

It makes me tired to think about it

Delaware Thursday, April 18, 2013, at 2:29 am

That's just it. Nothing will ever be the same. There's
before and there is after and I just want it to go away. I
just want to go to sleep. And sleep and sleep and wake
up in a place where the punishment fits the crime.

P.S. "I do not agree with what you have to say, but I'll
defend to the death your right to say it."

Nebraska Thursday, April 18, 2013, at 2:30 am

Who said that? You sound like a lying politician fyi

Delaware Thursday, April 18, 2013, at 2:31 am
Ha ha, no. Me. Delaware. I said it. And also Voltaire.
Make sure they put it on my tombstone.

Nebraska Thursday, April 18, 2013, at 2:33 am
Ha ha but I'll be gone too, remember? (Candide . . . all
I remember is someone loses a chunk of their ass?)

Delaware Thursday, April 18, 2013, at 2:35 am
Right. You'll be gone too. My bad. What, so I think
I'm the only one around here who wants to go to sleep
forever? I better check my fucking privilege. Also, Dear
Voltaire: Sorry, sir. 2013 is no place for your Age of
Enlightenment satiric polemicist fuckery. Please take a
number and line up at the stake.

Nebraska Thursday, April 18, 2013, at 2:39 am
I'm the most privileged person you've never met.
Wasn't Voltaire supposed to be kind of a dick?

Delaware Thursday, April 18, 2013, at 2:40 am
Ha ha doubt it I'M MORE PRIVILEGED THAN
YOU BUT MY MISFORTUNE IS STILL BIGGER
THAN YOURS STEP ASIDE MAKE WAY

Thanks for staying up with me, Nebraska. I wish this
were really all as funny as I'm pretending it is. See you
on the other side.

Nebraska Thursday, April 18, 2013, at 2:48 am

Wait. Don't go. Are you still there? First I want to play
a little game . . . it's called Things I've Lost. You go
first.

Delaware Thursday, April 18, 2013, at 2:51 am

In the space of 72 hours, I have lost the following
things:

My self-respect
My scholarship
My future
My chance
My girlfriend
My peace of mind
My mind in general
Sleep
Sleep
Sleep
My voice. Which feels like losing freedom. Which feels
like losing everything that has ever mattered to me.

My parents' respect. That's the worst part. There are no
words for this shame.

Your turn. Go.

Nebraska Thursday, April 18, 2013, at 2:55 am
Dignity. Body. Privacy. Self-worth. Grace. Seventeen pounds. My parents. The friends I thought were my friends. Stillness. Peace . . . I could go on and on and on.

There's no getting these things back, Delaware. I've tried and they're gone. Gone. I can't get them back.

Delaware Thursday, April 18, 2013, at 2:56 am
I'm sorry.

Nebraska Thursday, April 18, 2013, at 2:57 am
I'm sorry too.

Delaware Thursday, April 18, 2013, at 2:57 am
Hey can I ask you something?

Nebraska Thursday, April 18, 2013, at 2:57 am
What.

Delaware Thursday, April 18, 2013, at 2:59 am
Do you have any brothers or sisters?

Nebraska Thursday, April 18, 2013, at 3:06 am
You're not supposed to ask that kind of question, you know.

But no. The answer is no. It's just me.

Delaware Thursday, April 18, 2013, at 3:07 am

Wait, you're worried about rules? Grand scheme, Nebraska. Anyway, sorry. For asking, I mean. Not because you don't have a sibling.

Nebraska Thursday, April 18, 2013, at 3:08 am

Haha once a rule follower, always a rule follower. Not much could offend me at this point.

Delaware Thursday, April 18, 2013, at 3:08 am

Go to sleep, Nebraska. I'll meet you there.

PHOEBE, HALFWAY

(9:25 AM MDT)

Dear Nebraska,

I guess you already know that the forum is gone. Not a trace of it anywhere. It is almost like it never existed at all. All those hours, all those plans, those things everybody said. If a tree falls in the forest, right? That stupid cliché.

Cliché: Do you know that when I was a little girl that's what I named my favorite doll? I didn't know what it meant. I guess I had heard it somewhere and liked the sound of the word. And really, it's a beautiful-sounding word. This is a secret I'm telling you, Nebraska. Funny how you know all of my secrets but not my name. Did I mention? My name isn't Idaho. It's Phoebe. Phoebe Ringling, like the circus. Phoebe the freakshow, at your service.

« « «

I don't know why I'm writing. I don't know what to say, or how else to get this letter to you. Did you ever do the balloon project at your elementary school? We did it in third grade with our wishes and hopes for the world. One girl's wish made it all the way to California and nobody knows how.

Nebraska, I'm going to try to explain how it is, and I hope you will understand what I'm trying to say. It's like there are two worlds: the one I carry my body through (school, home, one foot in front of the other, again and again, over and over) and the one out there — the one in the screen, where everything is possible, where there is never not a million surprises waiting to happen, where things are always new, where I myself, me, Phoebe Ringling, can always hit refresh and always be brand new. I can tell you my hair is long and straight. I can tell you that my eyes are almond-shaped. I can tell you that the world I live in is perfect.

I am telling the truth when I tell you my name, but Nebraska, I have told you so many lies, and I'm sorry. The worst part is that half of the lies are things I believed to be true at the time. If a tree falls in the forest, can't see the forest for the trees . . . which cliché do you like better, Nebraska? I think I like them both. I think they both apply.

Vermont went through with it, I'm sure you've heard by now. And Maine is in custody. But that kid in New Hampshire — he wasn't even one of us! Can you even imagine, a coincidence as weird as that? It makes me laugh. It makes me laugh until I cry.

Listen. Nebraska. I am writing because some part of me—you know, the part of me that is a tree that falls in the forest with nobody around to hear it fall?—is in love with you. Which is funny, because I have also lately been in love with a boy named Dylan Fisher. Do you know him? Dylan? Nah, neither do I. Neither does anybody anywhere, ever.

My balloon is never going to reach you in time, but maybe it will reach somebody, somewhere. Somebody living like I have been living in that bright, blinding, everything's-possible world. Somebody who can't see the forest for the trees (ha ha ha ha ha!). Here's what I've got to say to that person, or to you, Nebraska, if my balloon somehow magically makes it that far, if by the magic of coincidence this bright blue balloon drifts down from the sky right to you. (I can see it! You on your back porch, reading a book maybe, thinking to yourself, this is the last book I will ever read on this earth, but then you look up and see it! A pinprick of a spot against the sun is what it will look like at first, but no: It's a balloon! With a message tied to it! Just for you! Like a message from God!)

Only that's just it, that's the thing I want to say to you or whoever: I'm not God. None of us is. Not even close. I don't know if I believe in God, but I believe in something, and not a single one of us is that thing.

Also: You might not think it now, but there is love in

your life. Even if it's only my own weird love for you, a thing you can't really touch or believe to be true. Do you have a sister? Check there first. Check with whoever's holding you to that other world, the real one, where you do your actual breathing and where you hang your heart.

Nebraska, you should see my mother in her green bathrobe. You should see this old man who walks with his wife near my school. Your heart would break and break and break.

One more thing: I've been staring at your state on the map, Nebraska. It's really not that far. If we started driving now and didn't stop, we could be in New Orleans by tomorrow night. We could be drinking Hurricanes on Bourbon Street. We could be getting our palms read.

I can hear her now, the fortune-teller who will trace the lines on your palm and reveal the secrets of your future: This lifeline is long, she'll say. It goes on and on and on.

Maybe you don't have a car. So get on a bus, Nebraska! I love you. I'll meet you halfway.

Love,
Phoebe Ringling (Idaho)

P.S. Please hurry.

APRIL, SPINNING

The underwater movie reel is spinning so fast I can't keep up. It's like stop-motion—like it takes a thousand frames to fill a single second of film. The years and days and images are a whir, a blur: Pal's dragon towel his straight white teeth the library pink tree hip bones Leona Reece *don't insult my intelligence* purple iris triple word score and the compound in Pakistan and Pal and his boys and the Frisbee and the bio notes here are the parts of a fetal pig *epididymis caudal vena cava thorax*—no wait, *thorax,* that can't be right, that's a bug, *Kafka's Thorax,* Tax Day Edition ("What Taxes You? Let's Talk Microaggressions" by Pallav Gakhar, Salutatorian and National Merit Scholar), hot off the virtual press. Tuesday April 16 2013 Pal's locker slashed with a bright red X: GET THE FUCK OUT.

« « «

MICAH ENNIS ANGEL

The Mastermind, his name is Micah. Micah Ennis Angel. He is fourteen years old, weighs ninety-one pounds, and is five feet, four inches tall.

Right now, all ninety-one pounds and five feet, four inches of Micah Ennis Angel are spread out on a gurney in an ambulance, and he has not yet determined that this is real. That this is happening in real time. That he is not dreaming; that he is not already dead, or suspended dream-like in the midst of his flight down from the roof of the building where his father has an office. Dead, half-dead; surely he is one or the other and the wash of peaceful, blameless darkness will envelop him soon.

Half-dead. As in a math teacher at a high school in Maine, whose body, fast fading, a gunshot to the chest and another to the outer part of his skull, has lately — in real time, mere minutes ago — been transported via an

» » »

ambulance not unlike this one to a hospital in Bangor, where the math teacher will not last long enough to see or touch the hands of his wife and young daughter, who just last week learned how to walk.

Who is responsible for this? The Mastermind. His name is Micah Ennis Angel.

My name is Micah Ennis Angel.

My father's name is Ennis. Ennis Angel. He is a licensed psychologist and a renowned professor at a California university where fifteen years ago he had an affair with a student. The student was my mother, and she was part of a sleep experiment being conducted by Professor Angel. I, Micah Angel, am the product of a sleep experiment that led to an ill-advised marriage that was eventually shattered by subsequent "experiments" involving female undergraduates and sleeping. My father, Ennis Angel: he is a brilliant man, an expert on (among other things) sleep, female undergraduates, and human memory.

Here is a memory belonging to me, Micah Ennis Angel:

I am little. Maybe three years old, but probably even younger. Human memory is an unreliable thing; it could be that what I'm really remembering is the video of this moment. Which one is real? In the memory—or on the screen—I'm sitting crisscross-applesauce on a rug in my room. The rug has alphabet letters on it, and I'm sitting on the *T,* where there is a picture of a tiger. Across from me my father is also sitting cross-legged on the rug, and in his hand he holds a bunch of cards.

"Pick one," he says, and spreads the cards facedown on the floor.

I point to the one farthest away from me, and he reads aloud from it: *happy.*

"Okay," my father says. "Can you show me what happy looks like?"

I'm supposed to make happy with my face. My father is waiting, squinting into his video camera. Later I will understand that this is all some sort of project he's doing for work. What does a happy face look like? What about worried? What about sad, mad, bad? When do small children start to draw these distinctions?

"Show me *happy,*" he says again, this time in a high, unnatural voice designed to hint at what my face should be doing. Only I'm not doing it. On purpose, I'm not doing it. I know what happy looks like; I just don't want to show him that I know.

"Micah. Are you feeling okay?"

In real life (is this real?), in the ambulance (when, when will I hit the ground?), Wendy Neely puts the back of her hand against my cheek. This is a thing my mother sometimes does. My mother. Her keys are in the freezer. What if she never found her keys? Wendy Darling, she was the mother of all the Lost Boys.

"Wendy," I say, my voice still foreign to my ears, faraway and gonging. I watch the magic liquid sing its way through the tube. It has a high-pitched hum, like the air inside a plane about to take off. "Do you know why there were no

Lost Girls?" My teeth are chattering. It's hot, but it's also cold, freezing cold.

"What?" Wendy asks. Her face: it's what sad looks like. It's what scared looks like. *Micah, can you show me what it means to be afraid?*

I close my eyes. I'm so ready to hit the ground. No more talking, please.

But in my head my voice is still going, still reaching out to Wendy Neely, and what it says is this: there were no Lost Girls because the only reason the boys were lost in the first place was that they were foolish enough to fall out of their prams when they were babies, and girls—even baby girls, according to Peter Pan—are too smart to fall from their prams. Do you remember the names of the Lost Boys? My favorite is Slightly Soiled.

And then Wendy Darling—I mean Wendy Neely—says my name and everything goes dark and soft and fuzzy— a Lost Boy falling from his pram, Icarus meeting the water, that moment of reckoning, the Light Fantastic, skip skip skip skip skip, the gentle descent, the peace of it, *this is what peaceful looks like*—until once more my eyes open.

Real, not real?

The walls are a new color. A crisp white sheet, another set of tubes. And here is my mother, crying.

Beep beep beep go the machines.

According to the machines, I'm still alive.

Look at that.

I, Micah Ennis Angel, am alive.

DELAWARE IN THE LOCKER ROOM

(11:57 AM EDT)

Delaware is in the locker room, head between his knees.
There's a leak in one of the sinks, and he's concentrating
hard on the sound of the steady *drip drip drip* of the faucet.
It's a maddening sound — is it getting louder? — but right
now it is anchoring Delaware to the moment. The drips are
happening in tandem with each movement of the second
hand on Delaware's watch. What a strange, coincidental
harmony that is, thinks Delaware. He is almost out of time.

Delaware's name is Pallav Gakhar, and what he's thinking, there with his head between his knees, is what a relief
it has been, these last few days, to be nobody but Delaware.
Delaware doesn't have a face or a race or a family or a past.
Delaware, blissfully anonymous, is just words on a screen,
nothing more. Delaware can be deleted just like that.

» » »

"My son," Pal's father had said (is saying still, will say forever, in Pal's head, as long as he is alive: not just son but *my* son). "What did you mean to achieve with this?"

His father wasn't mad. Plenty of times Pal had seen him get mad at Adhira, and when that happened his father would seem to fold into himself, drawing further into his own quiet while Adhira filled the room with her rage.

This was different. His father wasn't mad, he was sad.

"I was just—we were just trying to say that learning a certain set of *buzzwords* doesn't make a person—

Jaideep Gakhar, shaking his head, didn't need to speak aloud to stop his son's heated rush of words. Pal, ever obedient, fell silent—but only for a moment. He couldn't help it. He had to get it out; he had to make his father understand.

"It was supposed to be *satire*, Dad, don't you get it? A joke!"

Silence. Then—Pal could barely hear—"A joke."

Pal stared at his father. Hair graying at his temples. Tilt of his chin, proud. Pal himself sometimes held his face that way. He could feel the gesture—that mirror—now, in his molars, which were smashed together in an effort to grind out the words.

"It's just—it's just words, Dad. All anybody cares about anymore. Not about how anybody actually treats anybody else—like, in real life I mean, to each other's faces"—Pal was perspiring now, flailing at the air, trying physically to grasp at what he meant—"just *words,* and who gets to say them and who doesn't, and whose words hurt the most, and whose pain is the biggest, and whose voice counts and whose doesn't, and who gets to speak for *me,* Dad, for me—"

In his desperation, Pal was spitting—he didn't mean to; he couldn't control it—on his father's glasses. Jaideep, infuriatingly calm, as if this were just another practiced ritual he performed daily, took a handkerchief from his pocket and began to clean the lenses. Without his glasses, he looked— he looked vulnerable, Pal thought, and the thought almost brought him to his knees. He had to look away.

"Words," Jaideep repeated. Having finished polishing the left lens, he moved on to the right. Then he lifted his glasses toward the ceiling light and squinted. Pal did not even need to look at his father to see him doing these things: there he was, doing them. There he was, placing his glasses back on his face, restoring himself to the man Pal knew by heart.

"You chose wrong."

Pal, confused, looked up. Looked at his father's face.

"What?"

"Words. You chose the wrong words."

And then Pal said—

But there was nothing left to say. His fury had worn him out.

"Pallav," his father said, after a small silence. "How is it that you think of us? Your mother and me?"

The question had come as such a surprise. "What?"

"How do you see us," Pal's father said. Quiet, as if he himself were testing out the words, examining them from all the angles.

"You're my parents," Pal said, words clotting in his throat. His mind raced wildly to the day Adhira had first stolen the credit cards. At the time he could see only the gift she had brought him from the mall, bestowing it upon him with a conspirator's grin: a Newton's cradle, silver balls swaying and clicking, swing*click*, swing*click*—

Drip, drip.

Tick, tick.

Pal hadn't tried to be the good son. He just was, and it had more to do with his disposition—steady, curious, given to obedience—than any concerted effort he might have tried to make toward goodness. He was so different from Adhira, around whose moods and demands the entire family had no choice but to rearrange themselves.

Still, Pal had loved her fiercely, had coveted the moments when she placed her confidence in him.

"Don't you ever just get *furious*?" Adhira had asked him once. She had fought with their parents again, and had taken refuge in twelve-year-old Pal's room. He had thrilled at having her there: Adhira with her secrets, her high-school senior wisdom, her boyfriend and her car keys and her access to the larger world. He wanted to know everything, was hungry for the telling.

"No," Pal had answered, shrugging. His life, after all, was uncomplicated and good. He had friends who knew him and made him laugh. He genuinely loved school and was naturally given to its rhythms and challenges.

"God, I do," said Adhira, flopping backward onto Pal's

bed and kicking her legs in the air. "I get so mad I could scream for days."

"So what'd you do?"

Adhira twirled a long piece of hair around her finger. "Nothing. I didn't do *any*thing! They're just so — *agh* — fucking clueless."

Pal hadn't wanted to say so out loud — Adhira had brought her fire and energy into his room; she was telling him things; he didn't want to miss it — but it made him feel sad for his parents, and ashamed, to hear her talk that way. Pal knew what people at school probably thought about him without their ever having to say it out loud: he was Indian; he was a doctor's son; he would grow up to be a doctor, too; his parents no doubt pressured him toward a life of academic rigor and perfection; blah blah blah. But it wasn't like that. His parents, their life — it wasn't like that at all.

"Yeah," he said. And, daring himself to say it out loud, thrilling at the sound of the bad word on his tongue, "Fucking clueless."

Adhira had turned her face to him and grinned. "Hey. Wanna go get some ice cream? Mom's buying."

By which Adhira meant that she had stolen, again, from their mother's purse.

"Yeah," he said, basking in his sister's attention. "Fuck yeah, let's go."

That was years ago. Oh, Adhira! How Pal has missed her all this long while. How he will miss her most of all.

Drip, drip.

"Mom," Pal had said. This was years ago, after Adhira's secret wedding in Mumbai. "Aren't you ever furious with her? For leaving like that? For never coming back?"

What washed over Pal's mom's face — it wasn't fury. It was the opposite of that. "Don't you see?" she had said, pressing her palm to her heart, searching his face with shining eyes. "Don't you see, Pallav? Your sister — she's me. I am her and she is me."

Pal hadn't seen.

Drip, drip.

"Pal," his father had said. Three days ago. Eyes on the floor. Ever, ever gentle. "Tell me how it is that you see us."

How you see us. Us. Them. Even with Ben — his lifelong best friend, loyal to the end! — this is how it is now. Pal understands that this is how it will be, always, if he stays. Maybe luck will take him to some other college (*Where are you from? No, I mean where are you from-from?*), some other life, but always and everywhere he will have to carry the weight — the responsibility — of representing not just his own misguided self, not just his family, but the family before that and before that and before that: an entire lineage of people calling to him across oceans, swimming toward him against currents of history, watching and waiting for his next mistake.

Drip, drip.
Tick, tick.

How smart Adhira had been, to answer the call. Do her

mistakes even matter now? That freedom. God, Pal wants it, is starved for it. He knows, though, that it will never be his. Not when he has felt so much affection — so much sadness, now that the coin has flipped — for the life that is his, and here, and now.

Where did it go?

Pallav Gakhar wants it back.

It is not coming back.

Drip, tick.

No, Pal thinks as he tests the weight of the gun in his hand. It is too much to bear. Let someone else carry that.

Us. Them. Pallav Gakhar knows he cannot do this thing to himself, but he also knows he won't have to. All he has to do is summon them. He knows how they will see him; knows they'll shoot first, ask questions later.

Don't you ever just get furious? Adhira had asked.

Drip, tick, drip.

My son —

Yes, he thinks. I do.

APRIL'S FINAL GIFT

(12:03 PM EDT)

There is nothing in my underwater high-speed movie reel that might hint at what Pal Gakhar is doing at the deep end of the pool—the end near the locker rooms; he got in here through the locker rooms, it occurs to me dimly—with a gun in his hand. I have swum the entire length of the pool, skimming the bottom, and now there's no *not* coming up for air. My hands graze the edge, and I break the surface, head up and out, gulp after sweet gulp of air. I stay in the water, gripping the side of the pool, as I turn to look at Pal. Sirens: are they growing closer, or is that the fire of my own heart in my ears? It's all the same.

Pal is staring at the hole in the glass ceiling. He has a lazy smile on his face, like: oops. He is perfectly calm as he shifts his gaze from the shattered Bubble to me, and as our eyes meet, I understand immediately that Pal is going to raise his

« « «

arm and point that gun at me. Pal is going to point that gun at me and end my life.

There's no time to think—heart failure is going to come and kill me before Pal's bullets ever reach my brain—but here I am, in what could be the final moment of my life, thinking of my sister and the *passé composé*. Her smile and secret pinkie wave. Magical thinking: *Monica Susan Donovan, I love you the biggest and the very most.*

Pal stretches his silent smile out even wider. There is so much I want to say, so much I want to tell him. I want to say I *know* you, I remember this and this and this, but no sound is coming out. Panic has stolen my voice and will steal my heart from my chest if I don't get another gulp of air.

Then Pal lifts his gun-wielding arm, and I'm thinking: This is it. The dice have fallen, the coin has been flipped, and this is how it ends. *Checks and balances, April Donovan, and your time is up.*

But Pal, in a move that sends adrenaline and hot bile up the back of my throat, raises the gun and points it not toward me, but at his own temple. His face, that vacant smile—it's not him. The Pal I know is kind and funny and has this vibrancy humming beneath his skin. This Pal before me is some other Pal. I don't know this person—not his pale, perspiring face, not his eerie grin, not the voice that shakes as it whispers, "You shouldn't be here, April. You should go. Now. Hurry—they're coming."

I stare at him, too stricken to move. The world, it is upside down.

Pal's voice, still trembling, still a whisper: "'Dear Mr. Gakhar, in light of recent events, we regret to inform you that the Department of Admissions must rescind our offer of acceptance into the class of 2017.'"

"No," I say. "Pal, don't."

He hasn't heard me. The gun is still pointed at his head. The raspy monotone coming out of his mouth seems separate from him, as if it's traveling the surface of the water on some kind of delay: "'We hold our students to the highest standards, and paramount among the values to which we expect our students to adhere are fairness, equality, and respect for oneself and others. We strive to make our university a safe space for everyone. Marginalization of any person or group on the basis of gender, race, religion, identity, or creed is wholly unacceptable and will not be tolerated.'"

"Pal," I say again. "Don't. Please."

So stupid, those words. So empty and insignificant and wrong. I have memorized moments like this; I have over and over pictured myself in the dark of the movie theater and in the bloody chaos of the cafeteria; I have asked myself again and again what I would have done, what I would do, what I would say to the shooter as he stares me down along the barrel of his gun and asks the million-dollar question: *Do you believe in God?* I have practiced my final answer, I have played it on repeat in my head—but those were dress rehearsals for the scene in which I fight to save *my* stupid life. I don't know the words to make Pal save his own, and this hollowness coming out of my mouth—*no, don't, stop, please*—is all wrong. Wrong, wrong, wrong, and I am frozen in this pool. The water has gone to ice, my heart has gone to ice, and I am frozen.

The sirens roar and roar.

Pal's face is still alight with a benign smile of benediction, and I think he's going to speak again—I want him to speak to me, I realize; I want to hear the real version of his voice—but he says nothing. There is nothing.

"Pal," I gasp—I've swallowed water; I'm choking on the words, on my own vomit. My teeth are chattering so violently I think I might bite my tongue in half. "This is where we learned to swim, remember? You and me with our moms. I remember our baby goggles and our tea parties and the way our towels would be so warm after lessons."

The words are so stupid, I realize. Words can't save anybody's life. Memories can't, either, but they're all I've got—and aren't memories how we keep people, and sometimes ourselves, alive?—and so here I am with my last offering: a giving up of what I realize now is the best and truest gift I've ever been given. *Give me a good day,* Gavin said to me once. *When we were happy, from start to finish.* So I keep going, a constant stream of words to go with the scenes, moments, days that have zipped through my movie-reel mind in the space of just a few seconds. It's all there: the spelling bee words, the weeping cherry, the iris, the beautiful synchronicity of Pal and his boys and their Frisbee. Pal Gakhar, I say. You have lit up my life with your life. Please, please don't go.

Pal's face is still distant and strange, but there is a flicker, an almost imperceptible twitch in Pal's cheek, followed by the slightest movement in his elbow. Maybe the flicker is my mind's defense against my body's own rising panic, but I cling to it—will cling to it, always—as proof that Pal Gakhar does not really wish to hurt himself.

"Pal, just put it down."

What's weird is that the wail of the sirens still sounds far away. That's the weird part, because just as I think Pal might be lowering his hand, lowering the gun, the glass doors of the Bubble crash open and the cops are there and—which happens first? it's all happening at once—Pal raises his arm once again, this time at a spot well above my head, and that's when I hear the shots. That's when I watch, frozen, as Pal tips forward—just exactly as if he were a stiff cardboard cutout of a boy, pushed over by an invisible hand—into the water.

Every bone in my body wants out of this pool, but in seconds—*seconds,* this is some kind of a record—I am back in the deep end, swimming fast to where Pal is drifting to the bottom, eyes closed, a dark plume of blood trailing him through the water. He looks asleep or dead, but I know there is time. There has to be time. His jacket billows from his back like a flower, a balloon. His shirt has risen in the water to reveal a glimpse of skin on his abdomen—this stab of vulnerability, this awful ache. Pal is wearing wingtips. Pal is wearing a watch that ticks the seconds away into nothing. I've got my arms under his arms, and I'm pulling, pulling, pulling him back toward the light.

MAIL DELIVERY FAILED

SUBJECT: MAIL DELIVERY FAILED: RETURNING
MESSAGE TO SENDER

Dear A,

Thanks for sending the wedding pictures. You look beautiful as always and I guess if you married that guy he must
not be the total douchebag I've decided he is in my head.
Don't tell him I said that. Whatever, none of my business,
as long as you're happy. Congratulations. I hope you are.
Happy, I mean. Finally. I always thought I was but now
I don't know. What is it like there? What I mean is, are
you free? Do you feel free? Does your voice finally belong
to you? Are you sorry? What is Nani like? In the pictures
she looks just like Mom. Mom doesn't hate you, by the
way. She never did. I tried to hate you when you left, but

» » »

it didn't work out. I mean it when I say I want you to be happy. Have you heard? I fucked up, Adhira. All my life, no mistakes, then boom. I can't look at Dad. Can't even look at him. I just want it to go away. I want to go back, start again. Tell me how to start again. Tell me how you did it, how you gave yourself permission. I couldn't hate you if I tried but I'm still mad at you for going. I'm mad and want to go to sleep and I need you. I can't look at them. Not Mom, not Dad. Not Leona Reece. She's my girlfriend, or used to be, before she decided I'm a misogynistic dick. I'm a lot of things to a lot of people right now: a dick, a misogynist, a bigot, a liar, a traitor, a failure, a fool. A fucking terrorist, if you can believe that. It was just this stupid thing that Ben and I wrote, really no different from any of our other stupid things, but this one, it was like people saw in it what they wanted to see and all of a sudden I don't even know who I am anymore, what I even wanted to say in the first place. I'm a lot of bad things to a lot of people right now but just for a second all I want to be is your brother. Can I just be your brother?

The cat never liked anyone but you, by the way. She misses you. Not as much as I do, though.

Write back, okay? Soon as you can. Tell me what to do. Help me fix it.

P

KAFKA'S THORAX

WHAT TAXES YOU? LET'S TALK MICROAGGRESSIONS
A Conversation with Pallav Gakhar, Salutatorian and National Merit Scholar

Ben Higgins: Today at *Kafka's Thorax,* we're pleased to interview one of our own, Pal Gakhar, about what it means — excuse me, how it *feels* — to identify as "other" in today's American public-high-school society. So tell us, Pal, when's the last time you experienced a microaggression at the hands of your peers?

PG: Just now, fucker. I wasn't sitting around perceiving myself as "other" until you just called me that. I know what: How about you refrain from othering me without my consent? Who do you think you are?

》》》

BH: Whoo! Checking my privilege over here. A thousand apologies, Pal. Carrying on: microaggressions. Gimme what you got.

PG: Well. It's just really hard.

BH: I know. I see what you mean.

PG: Actually, Ben, with all due respect, you can't see what I mean. Not at all. Your world's in Technicolor 24-7. Don't even come at me with your normative visual acuity.

BH: I'm sorry. I have shortcomings. Sometimes I say stuff without thinking. Just now, I'll admit it, I absolutely 100 percent failed to consider your color blindness.

PG: Yeah, well, that's your privilege, isn't it? And it's *color vision deficiency,* you insensitive idiot. If you're gonna use your words, use them the right way. *Color blindness.* Come on. What are you, five? Don't you even know what that means?

BH: Doesn't it mean . . . ?

PG: *glares*

BH: . . . ?

PG: Are you fucking kidding me right now? Do you mean I have to actually *explain* this to you? Do you even live in the world?

BH: *hangs head*

PG: (*SIGH*) *Color-blind* is what certain self-righteous wrong-headed assholes will say about themselves when it comes to their attitude toward other people. *I love everybody! I'm color-blind!* I mean, do those ignorant assholes even hear themselves? Do you even hear *yourself*, Benjamin?

BH: But . . . wait. What'd I say? Did I say *I* was color-blind? I would never say that. Never.

PG: *Color vision deficient.* Don't make me say it again.

BH: Right. I would never say I was color vision deficient.

PG: Psssht! Listen to you, with your big fancy words. Now you're just posturing. Now you're just appropriating, you stupid parrot.

BH: . . .

PG: Whatever. It's not my job to understand this shit

for you. Either you're kind and you're thoughtful and you use your words with some measure of fucking sensitivity, or you don't. I don't really have time for this tedious little education session, okay?

BH: Um, okay?

PG: Great. Moving on.

BH: *clears throat* Right. Let's talk triggers.

PG: I mean, where do you even want me to start? You really *don't* live in the world, do you? Ever seen a traffic light? Ever laid your precious privileged normative eyes upon any typical American high-school summer reading list?

BH: Well —

PG: *The Color Purple. The Red Badge of Courage. The Scarlet Letter. The Bluest Eye. Gravity's* Fucking *Rainbow.* I mean, are you serious? I'm expected to read all that horrible insensitive shit? Who even puts these lists together? Do they have brains in their stupid heads?

BH: So would you consider yourself . . . opposed to those books?

PG: Have you listened to one word I've said? You had one job. One! To fucking listen!

BH: I'm sorry. I'll try to do better, not just words-wise, but, you know, through my actions as well. I owe you an apology.

PG: Yeah, well. Just make sure you do it online. You think this face-to-face nonsense counts? Be real, Benjamin. Either you own your fucking transgressions or you don't.

BH: Owning them, sir. Thanks for being with us at the *Thorax* this morning. I hope the rest of your day is less taxing.

PG: My pleasure, asshole.

Comments have been closed.

GAVIN PRINCE-MILLER TELLS HIS TALE

(11:15 PM EDT)

Ima let April finish because this is #herstory, not mine, but first Ima get my own two cents in, so listen up.

We made it out of that closet. #officergoodcop came back to get us just like he said he would and Nate Salisbury escorted Gina out into the light on his arm and Valentino, he was the first one to see me coming, he ran right up to me and just about knocked me over in a Valentino-hug, feet all slung over my shoulders, sleek, cold nose pressed against my ear, his heart all beat beat beating under that shiny silver fur.

Today at our school, a kid named Pal Gakhar died. Go ahead, bitches. Ask me what I knew about him. Ask me what kind of person he was, if I ever saw any signs, blah blah blah, whatever. Listen, this thing happened hours ago and I know what can happen in an hour, how an

« « «

hour—minutes, even—can turn a person into a hero or a monster. So I'm going to try to be truthful here. To tell the truth, which is that Pal was part of our school, our class of 2013—that I loved him as much or as little as I love the rest of these bitches I share my life with every day—and now he's gone, and he took his secrets with him. And really, that's it. That's the thing here. The mystery. Who knows, who ever *really* knows, what's going on in somebody else's head, somebody else's heart? It's the mystery of all mysteries, bitches, and it's not for me to even say. Or for you to say, either, so just hold off, please—just for today, okay? this is me begging—on the hero/monster thing. On your thousands of questions, same as the ones I've got and that the next guy has, too. I don't know the answers, is what I'm saying.

I don't know. I don't know. I don't know. I don't know. I don't know.

What I do know is that we made it back to our homes, our beds, our dogs, our parents, our friends. At April's house—because what are you going to do, right? life goes on, and you might as well know what's what—we sat in front of the television and watched the fifteen-second news spot about the shootings, and then we watched in real time as the Boston Police Department hauled that bomber out of a boat in some guy's backyard. Man, that bomber looked like us. Like any guy that I would race against in a meet or that Gina would bewitch or April would crush on or that would sit behind me in History, or in the Lockdown

Closet, or wherever. In one of the pictures of the guy, his T-shirt was all yanked up so you could see the skin on his stomach, and this—this glimpse of the guy's bare stomach—is what finally made April cry. After an entire day of nightmare hell, it was this two inches of skin on this guy's belly that made April lose it, and when she finally did, she cried so hard Gina and I worried for a second that we were losing *her.*

April swears Pal wasn't trying to hurt anybody else, and I believe her. Are they going to believe her in court? You think they will? Because you know this is just the beginning of some long nightmare, that scene in the pool on repeat. That scene where she thinks she could have changed things. April, I said, sweetheart, you can't go saving everybody at once. How about just one person at a time, starting with your own magnificent self. One day you're going to have to climb on out of that pool.

Can't you just see her, though? April? Here's Pal Gakhar with a policeman's bullet all lodged in his chest, and here comes April, hauling him up out of that pool just like the mermaid in that painting—the one Gina's got on this big-ass poster in her room, the one with the mermaid saving that half-dead shipwrecked sailor wearing the red hat and the diaper or whatever that thing is? Howard Pyle, bitches. Look it on up.

Listen. In all seriousness, you've got to heed Mr. Rogers, man, and #lookforthehelpers. Sometimes they're swimming around in the ocean trying to save people and sometimes they're your mom or your best friend or your physics teacher or your therapist and sometimes they're in disguise, like you have to look close to recognize them, but they're there. They're everywhere, I promise you. You have to believe that they are. Not just believe it, but know it deep down in that place in your heart where the true stuff lives.

So what happens next? What happens is that first chance I get, I'm gonna sign on up for next year's Boston Marathon. I'll be the one flying across the finish line with a smile on my face and an American flag on my back. Home of the free, man. Long may she wave, and all of that.

But first, I'm going to prom. See you there, bitches. You'd better have your dancing shoes on.

#overandout

APRIL ON PAPER

(11:57 PM EDT)

Dear Lincoln,

Do you remember me? We used to be neighbors and friends. In the first grade you kissed me on my eyelid and I've never forgotten it. You gave me your state quarters, and one by one I gathered the rest until your collection was complete. I wanted you to know that I found all fifty of them. The quarters have been in my attic for a long time, but tonight I climbed up there and got them. I wanted to hold them in my hand, you know? Maine, Massachusetts, New Hampshire, the others. I wanted to put them in my palm and hold them there.

Anyway. Lincoln. The other night I had a dream and you were in it, and some weird part of me thinks you

« « «

might have saved — or at least forever changed — my life. So I just wanted to say thanks.

And thanks for the quarters. I'm sending Delaware back to you. You keep it. Hold it in your palm and think of me.

Love,
April Hope Donovan
Delaware, The United States of America
4/19/13

I'm in the attic.

Downstairs, everybody's asleep. I just did my rounds, just checked on them all, so I know. Monica fell asleep in her usual pose: on her right side, arms shoved under the pillow, one leg stretched long, the other jackknifed up so she looks like she's been caught mid-run. *What does your sleeping position say about you?* I fell down that online rabbit hole once, and I learned that Monica's pose is called the Yearner. *What are you running from?* I thought as I stretched out next to her in the bed. *What are you yearning for?* She had fallen asleep with her earbuds in. Really gently, so she wouldn't wake up, I took out the one not pressed to the pillow and I put it in my own ear. This heartbreak of a song, full of planes and hurricanes and ringing bells. I held on to my sleeping sister, breathed in her detergent-and-citrus smell, and let the song play itself out into both our ears. Then it started back up again, and again: Monica had it on repeat. When I couldn't listen anymore I turned off the song and pressed my ear to Monica's back and listened instead to the in-and-out music of her breath. The bedroom window was open just a little, and through it I could hear the baby owl that lives somewhere in our yellow poplar tree out back. It makes this trilling sound, like it's rolling its *R*s or revving its tiny engine—*rrrrr rrrrr rrrrr*. I've never seen it but just to know it's there gives me a thrill. The mystery of things.

My mom's sleeping position—the fetal curl—is the same as mine. It's called the Protector, which seems apt. Dad's is called Freefall. Mom was wrapped around a novel, outstretched arm marking her place. I returned the book to the bedside table and stared for a while at the shadowed form of my sleeping mother: there she was, all of her, and next to her my father, freefalling.

There's so much stuff in this attic, I can't even tell you. I found the quarters. I found a sheaf of horrible middle school–era stationery and wrote a letter to Lincoln Evans. Then I sat in the dark and played with my mom's ancient Lite-Brite for a while: the satisfaction of inserting the pegs, the pleasure of that specific glow. It felt like a relic from a million years ago, but then so did the morning of that very day—my birthday and the cupcake and the slip of paper still folded in my pocket: Dr. Angel, PhD. I stared at the numbers and thought for a second about calling him. I even did the math to figure out what time it would be on the West Coast. Still too late, of course.

Too late, too late.

Remember for me a perfect day, Gavin said to me once. I laughed then and said, *No, that's not how it works. I can't do it on demand.*

Before I even know what's going on I'm shredding the paper in my hands. No way, Dr. Angel, PhD. No way, whoever you are.

Come on, Gavin said. *Just give me a good day. When we were happy from start to finish.*

Okay. Okay, here it is. A perfect day. April 20, 2013 (*But wait,* I can just hear Gavin interrupting. *It doesn't count if you're not* remembering *it. It can't be a day that hasn't hap*—Shhh. Just shut up and listen to my perfect day. Listen to how good it is). Saturday morning, clear and cool and bright. After a night curled in the fetal position of the Protector, April Hope Donovan rises, refreshed. Coffee, bacon, toast: it smells like the weekend. It smells like home. April's got this feeling—she can't really say what it is, but it's that feeling you get when you know that something good is about to happen. Around the breakfast table are her family members: the Yearner, the Freefaller, the fellow Protector. Everybody's sleepy and mussed and nobody's really looking at anybody, but that's okay. They're all there.

What've you got going on today, kiddo? asks the Freefaller, eyes never leaving the newspaper.

April Donovan, mug of fragrant coffee in hand, closes her eyes to consider the possibilities. In her favorite scenario, she and Gina and Gavin are Gerbil-ing around upstairs on the big bed, half napping under the lazy stir of the ceiling fan. They're listening to some old record spin, that song about leaving for the coast, and weighing their thousand and one options. Gina suggests shopping for prom stuff and maybe they argue about that for a few seconds but then decide wait, yes! And afterward, you know what, we should go to the drive-in movie theater. We haven't done that in forever! Oh my God, April, do you remember that time we went there and you and Gavin hid in the trunk of my car so you could get in for free and at the ticket booth I was all Sure, dude, I come to drive-in movies by myself all the time. Do you remember that?

April Hope Donovan, stretched out on her back, comfortable in the nearness of her friends, stares up at the fan, attaching her gaze to just one of the blades, the better to concentrate on how long it really takes for the whole apparatus to go around and around and around. When you look at the whole thing together it's just this *whoosh*ing blur. But the one blade—if you choose to lock your eye to just that (Pulling, it feels like it's pulling at your eye. Come *on*, it's saying, let's go.), you can see how steady the path is, how clear.

April! Do you remember?

This perfect day, man, it is so beautiful. It is stretching

out before them like a rolling green lawn. It is lush, deep, alive. April wants to go swimming in it.

No, April says, zooming her gaze back out so that the fan is just one big *whoosh*. She's smiling so hard her face hurts.

I don't remember any of that at all.

ACKNOWLEDGMENTS

Listen: What you should know about Stephanie Berrong if you want to be friends with her is that she's always saying stealable stuff. For real and for true. What you should know about me is that I'm indebted to Stephanie, and also to the following: Elizabeth Kaplan, several million times over. Nicole Raymond, editor and kindred spirit, who knows what I want to say before I say it. Emily Quill, Maggie Deslaurier, Martha Dwyer, Hannah Mahoney, Nathan Pyritz, Matt Roeser, Angela Dombroski, Jamie Tan, and every brilliant soul at Candlewick Press. Randi Ewing, who is the real deal. The Psychologist Amys: Amy Wendell and Amy Detjen, whose expertise, empathy, and patience know no bounds. Pat Gerhard, Jennifer Mattox, and Ginger Phillips: Work half as hard as any of these women, be half as generous and kind, and you might be onto something. Kate Hattemer: *Multas multas gratias tibi ago, amice.*

My girls (all girls, everywhere, but especially *my* girls): We know what makes the world go round. The love in this book is you. Shine on, all you diamonds.

My family, all of you, and most of all Huston Combs (whose name even after all this time I can scarcely write without nearing tears, such is my gratitude, such is my astonishing luck): Everyday life with you is the brightest, most fantastic of all.

Most importantly, readers, this book is for you. You matter. I acknowledge you. If you or someone you know is thinking about suicide, please call the National Suicide Prevention Lifeline:

(800) 273-8255
HOURS: 24 hours, 7 days a week
LANGUAGES: English, Spanish
WEBSITE: www.suicidepreventionlifeline.org